WAKE
OF THE
HORNET

—

VAL DAVIS

BANTAM BOOKS
New York • Toronto • London
Sydney • Auckland

WAKE OF THE HORNET

A Bantam Book / January 2000

ISBN 0-553-57804-9

Published simultaneously in the United States and Canada

Bantam Books are published by Bantam Books, a division of Random
House, Inc. Its trademark, consisting of the words "Bantam Books" and
the portrayal of a rooster, is Registered in U.S. Patent and Trademark
Office and in other countries. Marca Registrada. Bantam Books, 1540
Broadway, New York, New York 10036.

PRINTED IN THE UNITED STATES OF AMERICA

OPM   10   9   8   7   6   5   4   3   2   1

To
Cassie Goddard

AUTHOR'S NOTE

Cargo Cults are real and have been active in Melanesia and New Guinea since the nineteenth century. "Cargo" means "foreign goods possessed by Europeans."

The cult of John Frum came into prominence in the 1940s. John Frum, or sometimes Jonfrum, is a messianic figure that is sometimes described as a man with blond hair and clad in a coat with shining buttons. He promised the natives of Tanna, an island in what was once the New Hebrides, that if they would get rid of all their money they would become as rich as Americans. He also directed them to build runways and airplanes to attract cargo.

While the cult of John Frum is real, the island of Balesin is not.

THE ISLAND OF BALESIN

Mount Nomenuk

river

Mission Highway

Balabat

N

1

His wife was cheating on him. He could tell. It wasn't so much in what she said, but he could read between the lines. The time between letters was stretching out and she no longer included those little tidbits about her girls'-night-out with the other wives. The letters were still all about how she was spending his dough, the new curtains, the washing machine on layaway and how difficult rationing was. But she'd stopped mentioning what she did with her time.

What did he expect? He'd guessed that she was a party girl, a tramp. They'd only known each other a few days before they got hitched. The war did that. It taught you to move fast and not ask too many questions. But still it rankled. He felt the anger rise up in his gut.

If he made it back home, he'd take care of things. He didn't like being made a fool of.

He folded up the letter. It was almost coming apart at the creases. It had been over a month since he'd received it and there hadn't been another since. He'd waited each time mail call had come around, holding his breath, waiting for the final insult, the "Dear John" letter giving him the brush-off. It might never come, he told himself. After all, she had a good deal going. She could spend his money and do what she liked. And if she was lucky, she'd soon be a widow.

He thrust the thought aside. He'd been trained to kill, and he'd been trained to survive.

The great aircraft carrier pitched and rolled but he'd gotten used to it. He turned over in his bunk to go to sleep. He'd need all his wits about him in the morning. If he had any sense he'd be afraid, but it wasn't fear that kept him awake. He had murder in his heart.

2

July 12, 1999
The South Pacific

Taking off, the Widgeon bounced from wave to wave for nearly a mile before one final ricochet sent it lumbering into the air. Nicolette Scott, hanging on for dear life, clutched the wobbling armrest of her seat and muttered, "Elliot, I'm going to get you for this." Although her famous father was seated right behind her in the cramped cabin she was sure that he hadn't heard. The roar of the seaplane's twin engines was too loud.

The call from her father had come less than twenty-four hours ago.

"Nick, this is your lucky day," Elliot had said without preamble.

"You sound like you're in a tunnel."

"I'm on a radio phone."

"Don't you mean cell phone?" she said.

"Where do you think I am?"

She hated it when he teased her. Her academic degrees and all her years of hard work slipped away and she was a small child again, waiting for him to come home from some impossibly faraway place.

In exasperation she said, "I'll bite, Elliot. Where are you?"

"Do you remember me telling you about Curt Buettner?"

Nick started to say no, then caught herself. Elliot and Buettner had gone to school together. Snapshots of the two of them filled several pages of Elliot's scrapbook.

"Isn't he the one you call Crazy Curt?"

"That's him. Only he isn't as crazy as I used to think."

That wasn't the way Nick remembered the stories. One in particular had fascinated her. Buettner had faked the discovery of a Zuni artifact during an archaeological field trip, earning himself a top grade. But when his sense of humor got the better of him and he'd finally owned up to what he'd done, the instructor was too embarrassed to admit he'd been bamboozled and refused to change the grade. Shortly after that, Buettner inherited money and gave up grad school altogether to sail around the world.

"Your stories made him sound crazy," Nick reminded her father.

"He's come up with a theory about the Anasazi."

"I'm listening."

"First, you ought to know that we're three thousand miles east of Hawaii at the moment, in the middle of the Pacific Ocean. Floating off an island called Balesin, to be precise."

"Elliot, I seem to remember you telling me not to call you for the next two weeks, that you were on deadline and didn't want to be disturbed because your manuscript is overdue. I think you also mentioned something about having spent the publisher's advance already."

"If you were awake in my classes, daughter, you'll remember that my Anasazi started dying out during the great drought at the end of the thirteenth century. That's the accepted wisdom, anyway."

"Has something changed?"

"What if they didn't die out? What if they migrated?"

"To where?"

"That's where Curt comes in. He's been sailing the Pacific and following the trade winds for years. Sort of a Thor Heyerdahl with a yacht instead of a raft. Anyway, he thinks it's possible that the Anasazi abandoned the Southwestern desert and worked their way to the West Coast, where they built rafts and sailed away."

Nick sighed. "Have you and Curt been drinking?"

"Curt's gone legitimate. He went back to school and took his doctorate at the University of Hawaii. He even teaches classes there on cultures of the Pacific. That's how he happened to send me photos of a gourd pot he found in the Caroline Islands. It has an elaborately painted design that's quite reminiscent of late Anasazi artwork."

"Are you telling me you flew all that way to look at a pot?"

"Nick, it could have been important to my research."

"Was it?"

"Okay, so it's not Anasazi, despite the similarity in design," Elliot said. "But Curt paid my airfare. And I needed a vacation from that damned manuscript of mine."

"Where exactly is this island?"

"West of Borneo, north of New Guinea, south of Japan. You won't find it on your standard atlas at the moment, but we can change that, Nick. Together we can make the place famous."

"Where are you really?"

"Like I said, floating offshore."

"On Curt's yacht?"

"In a seaplane."

Nick sighed. When it came to the Anasazi, her father had been obsessed as long as Nick could remember. In fact, her earliest memory was of her mother, Elaine, complaining that Elliot cared more about long-dead Indians that he did his own family.

"Elliot," she said, "how does this involve me?"

"We've visited the island, and there's more than gourd pots involved here."

"Such as?"

"Airplanes. World War Two airplanes."

Nick caught her breath. She'd been in love with World War Two airplanes as long as she could remember. They'd filled her room as a child; they'd flown above her bed, suspended on nearly invisible black thread. And they'd helped her spirit fly away when her mother's black moods became too much to bear.

"What kind of planes?" Nick asked her father.

"That's your field, daughter, not mine. But it gets better. We've found a culture that seems to worship airplanes. Curt's mounting an expedition to prove his Anasazi theory. But he's also offered to fly you out as our airplane expert. If you remember, he inherited more money than sense."

"The fall semester is coming up."

"Do you actually believe that Ben Gilbert is going to reinstate you?"

Nick had been placed on "academic leave" by her department head for becoming involved with a plane crash in the New Mexican desert. The fact that a highly placed government official wanted to avoid any publicity had prevented Gilbert from being able to fire her outright. However, the entire episode had prevented Nick from publishing any paper that year. Gilbert had leapt on that excuse to suspend her.

"Come on, Nick. The start of school is nearly two months away."

"There's a little matter of my department chairman."

"So what's Ben Gilbert going to do, fire you? That would be the best thing that ever happened."

"I was on my way to see him when you called. I'm about to add my name to one of the lawsuits pending against the university. I'm looking forward to seeing the look on his face when I tell him. Of course, he may have gotten wind of it ahead of time, since he was too damned polite on the phone when I asked for a meeting."

"Take my advice, Nick, and stick to old airplanes. Living in the past is a lot safer than lawsuits in the present."

"I'll call you after I talk to Gilbert."

"Curt says to tell you that a ticket will be waiting at the San Francisco airport. First class. I'll call you at your apartment in, say, two hours, and you can tell me what Ben had to say."

Ben Gilbert didn't say anything at first. Instead, he grabbed her hand like a long-lost uncle and pulled her into his office. But there, already waiting, was Assistant Chancellor Janet Bombard. She was seated in the one comfortable chair in Gilbert's office, leaving Nick to occupy the same kind of straight-backed metal chair she'd had in her own, smaller office. The straight-backs—known affectionately among the faculty as Spanish Inquisitors—were designed to keep student visits as brief as possible.

"Good of you to come, Nick," Gilbert said at last.

Bombard nodded. As always, she looked perfect. Her pin-striped Anne Klein suit didn't show so much as a wrinkle. Her dark hair was set to perfection, and the thigh-high slit in her skirt was revealing enough elegantly hosed leg to cause Gilbert's eyes to shimmy. Everything about her contrasted with Nick's own appearance. Having no classes to teach, she'd come to campus dressed more like a student than an assistant professor, wearing jeans and a *Cal Bears* sweatshirt screaming for a Maytag.

"On the phone I asked to meet with *you*, Ben," Nick said, keeping her eyes on Bombard.

"This is strictly informal," he replied. "The chancellor's presence is just a coincidence."

The back of Nick's neck prickled. As far as she was concerned, the assistant chancellor's actions were as premeditated as her dress.

"Think of it as an off-the-record talk between colleagues," Bombard clarified.

Sure, Nick thought, fighting the urge to strip-search them both for hidden recording devices. Instead, she grabbed the Spanish Inquisitor, spun it around, and swung a denimed leg over the seat as if mounting a horse. Her beat-up Nikes came toe-to-toe with Bombard's stylish Ferragamos.

Nick forced a smile. "Something tells me you've heard from my lawyer."

Gilbert's jaw dropped open. But Bombard concealed her surprise, if indeed she had been surprised. Or maybe she knew Nick didn't have a lawyer. Nick had butted heads with the assistant chancellor before; neither one of them had come out unscathed.

"I assume you're referring to the rumor about a class-action suit," Bombard said.

"I'm not sure rumor is the right word."

"Since nothing has reached our attorneys, I don't know what else to call it."

Nick broadened her smile. They both knew that the university had already paid out millions of dollars in public funds to female professors who'd been denied tenure unfairly. Those settlements had all contained the usual secrecy clauses forbidding the injured parties to speak out. But the payoffs had become open knowledge on campus.

"I'm not talking about reinstatement," Nick said.

"Of course," Gilbert said, "that's why we're here, to put things right."

"How can we do that if it's off the record?"

"We were hoping to reach a verbal agreement first, then put it on the record." He turned to Bombard. "Isn't that right, chancellor."

"I can't speak for the administration," Bombard replied. "Not officially anyway. But I'm sure my recommendation . . ." She smiled knowingly at Gilbert. ". . . our recommendation would be listened to if we can come to an equitable agreement here today."

"I'm listening," Nick said.

Bombard nodded. "The university is quite aware that the Scott name is synonymous with archaeology."

"I'm not my father."

"I didn't mean to imply that. You're well-known in your own right, Nick. Still, it would be unfortunate to see the Scott name on any kind of lawsuit."

"You said it was a rumor."

"Hypothetically, then."

"Are you making an offer?" Nick said.

"As I said, I'm not authorized to speak for the administration," Bombard said. "But, again hypothetically, I think tenure after reinstatement would be assured if we could report back that you are firmly committed to the university."

Nick sighed. More than ever, she felt certain that their conversation was being recorded. Otherwise, Bombard's careful choice of words made no sense. But did it matter? Nick was in the driver's seat, even if it was called the Spanish Inquisitor. All she had to do was add her name to the lawsuit if the university reneged on the promised tenure. The question was, did she really want it now that it was being offered? And could she live with herself if she made her own, separate deal?

"Are you making the offer of tenure to everyone in my situation?" Nick asked.

"What offer?" Bombard said.

"Hypothetically speaking, then."

"If I were you, Nick, I'd worry about myself."

Nick stood up. She'd let them squirm for a while. "I'm going to need some time to think this over."

"There's plenty of time to get a paper together before the next semester," Gilbert said. "Get back on the tenure track. That's the thing to do."

Nick shook her head. "I had something more immediate in mind, like joining my father on a dig tomorrow."

"I didn't know he was in the desert again this summer," Gilbert said.

"He's after the Anasazi, that's for sure," Nick answered, skirting the truth.

Bombard shifted her position, removing her Ferragamos from harm's way. "If we schedule you for the next semester, what assurances do we have that you'll cooperate?"

"I haven't reached a final decision. That's all I can say at the moment."

Bombard, her lips pressed into a tight line, turned to Gilbert. "How much time would you need to find a replacement instructor to take Nick's classes?"

"I'm sure that won't be necessary," Gilbert said.

"I'll be back in plenty of time to let you know," Nick had replied. She'd never been so wrong in her life.

3

Sam Ohmura was used to being in charge. He controlled his department and he controlled his students in many subtle ways that they weren't aware of. He was a contingency planner too. He could have been a grand master in chess if he hadn't devoted his life to anthropology and other things.

But he wasn't used to panic, so his brain felt numb as he fought his way through the crowd. The shrill chattering of the tourists beat on his ears like the sharp beaks of persistent birds determined to peck their way into his brain.

With a sigh of relief he spotted an available phone and forced his way to it with an uncharacteristic rudeness. At all times he was polite and self-effacing, except for today. He didn't like using an open phone line, but he had no choice. His plane was going to be late leaving the Guam airport and time was precious. It might be considered an error to wait, especially if something went wrong, and errors were not tolerated.

His fingers, damp with fright, fumbled on the keypad as he punched in the number he had so carefully committed to memory. As always, the call was answered after a single ring.

"This is an open line," he immediately warned his superior.

"Unwise." The single word was spoken without emotion, but to Ohmura it might just as well have been the voice of doom.

"There's been a complication," Ohmura hurriedly added, desperately feeling the need to justify his security lapse.

There was no reply, but then he hadn't expected one. He plunged ahead. "The travelers are on their way as expected." He checked his watch. "They should be arriving anytime now, but there is, as I said, a complication."

Again, there was silence.

"Someone else went before them. Someone unexpected."

"Are you saying there's an unaccounted visitor to the island?" The tone was a definite rebuke.

Ohmura, used to deference and respect, felt as if the word *fool* had been painted on his back for the entire world to see. He stared wildly about him, but no one was looking. He forced himself to reply calmly. "Yes, as far as I know."

"Who are we talking about?" The voice now took on a definite edge.

He hesitated. Hadn't he just said that this was an

open line? "We're . . . we're . . . ," he stammered, ". . . not on a safe line."

"I repeat, who?" the voice demanded.

Security was being thrown to the wind. Ohmura shuddered and wished now that he had never called. "Another anthropologist, a crackpot really. He's the student of the man I told you about, the one with the crazy theory. What can be the harm in that?"

"If there's no harm, why are you calling? You are due here in a few hours," the voice reminded.

One must be prepared for all contingencies, Ohmura thought, but didn't say so. "The unexpected visitor is Walt Duncan. His file is included with the others." He hoped his foresight would be appreciated.

All hopes were dashed as the voice said coldly, "When did he arrive?"

"Evidently, a week or so ago."

"You are a fool."

Ohmura sucked in his breath. Never before had he been spoken to like that. Again, he looked around on the off-chance that someone else might have heard.

"You are to report to me without delay," the voice continued.

"Yes, sir," Ohmura replied to an already dead line. Something in his childhood training made him bow in abject humiliation to an uncaring presence a thousand miles away. A presence whose name he dared not speak aloud in public, Kobayashi.

4

"Wake up!" Elliot shouted.

Nick gritted her teeth. "I wasn't asleep."

"You could have fooled me, daughter."

Nick realized that she felt stiff and ached all over. Perhaps she had been asleep. To think I used to enjoy flying, she thought to herself. But that was before she'd encountered the copilot's seat in the Widgeon, technically a Grumman G44, but a twin-engine relic just the same.

But nothing seemed to have fazed her father, nor his boyhood friend, Curt Buettner, both of whom were seated directly behind her. Both were gnawing on drumsticks and drinking beer. The greasy smell of Kentucky Fried Chicken filled the seaplane's small cabin.

"Couldn't you two have brought something other than the worst excesses of American culture?"

"We had no time left after we ran into Sam Ohmura."

Nick shook her head. "You spend half a day talking to a man you ordinarily see every day?"

"I don't get to see my department head that much," Buettner replied. "It was sheer luck that we ran into him. He was on his way to a conference in Tokyo."

Lee Coltrane, their pilot, was seated to her left. He hadn't shaved in days, and had that kind of gleam in his blue eyes that Nick's mother had warned her about. He glanced her way and smiled.

"You look a little green around the gills," he told her. "You should have eaten before takeoff."

"And whose fault was that?" she snapped back. "I seem to remember half the engine lying in pieces all over the dock when I arrived. I also seem to remember you pleading for someone to give you a hand. On top of that, I had to make two trips to the airport to look for my lost luggage."

"Peace, Doc. We'll be in the air two hours more at least, even if the winds are with us. If not, it will be closer to three. I'll tell you what. You can dip into my emergency rations."

With a sigh she realized that he was right. She was starting to feel sick to her stomach. She had trouble extracting the waterproof cooler without groping Coltrane's thigh. She felt certain that the bush pilot was getting a lot of fun out of her difficulties.

The plastic cooler wasn't much bigger than a lunch box. One half held ice, the other was crammed with candy bars and packets of high-energy trail mix.

Nick hoped that eating something would make her feel better. She took a small, tentative bite of one of the candy bars and realized that she was starving. Quickly, she finished the bar and unwrapped a second.

"I owe you one," she told Coltrane.

"I'll remember that, Doc," he replied with a suggestive leer.

You'd be surprised what kind of payment I had in mind, she thought, and leaned back to enjoy the view. She had worked in New Guinea two years ago, but they were traveling to a spot well north of that jungle hell. She hoped it would be cooler and drier. Especially since most of her gear had been put on a plane to Tokyo by mistake.

As if reading her mind, Coltrane took down a map clipped to the sun visor and handed it to her. "I thought you might like to see where we're going, Doc." Balesin Island was circled in Day-Glo orange. She wasn't certain of the map's scale, but the island's nearest neighbor of any size looked to be hundreds of miles away.

He tapped the glass covering the compass. "You don't really need this baby much anymore, not with the satellites tracking you. They say those birds can locate you within twelve feet."

"Where are we, then?" she asked.

Coltrane shrugged. "Out here nothing looks familiar until you hit land."

"And if you don't?"

"So far, so good, Doc. Hell, if I'd ever missed my mark you wouldn't be sitting here with me, now would you?" He chuckled.

"How many times have you flown to Balesin?"

"This makes three, or is it four, in the last week. Before your father flew in to join Mr. Buettner, I landed that guy Duncan on the island."

"So I heard."

"He was very secretive about it. He had me land him well away from the village."

"Did he say why?"

"No. He said he was a doctor, too, like you. A doctor of anthropology."

"Did you call him *Doc*?" Nick couldn't miss the opportunity to take a little jab.

Coltrane smiled. "Before that, I'd only made one trip to Balesin in four years."

"That's what's so great about Balesin," Buettner said

from behind her. "There's virtually no tourist trade. We're heading for virgin territory, Nick, or practically, anyway."

Coltrane nodded. "Balesin's off the beaten path, all right. It's small, too. If it were much bigger it would have Hyatts and Outrigger Hotels like every place else. Or maybe a Club Med." He grimaced at the thought.

Buettner leaned forward so he was closer to Nick's ear, though he still had to speak up over the engines' roar. "What Lee's saying is true. And thank God. Otherwise we'd be out of luck. Where there are tourists there's no real native culture left, only the shows they put on for the paying guests. Besides being too small to support much of a population, Balesin is out of the trade winds. As a result, the climate isn't as temperate as most of the islands."

Nick's research had been perfunctory at best. After Elliot's telephoned summons, she had barely an hour at the Bancroft Library to ferret out information on the Caroline Islands. What she'd come up with had made no reference to Balesin, with one exception. Buettner's department head, the man they'd run into at the airport, had written a book twenty years ago on Cargo Cults and one chapter was devoted to the island. She'd nearly forgotten about Cargo Cults, since the phenomenon was considered more of an oddity than a proper subject of study in graduate school. What she remembered was sketchy at best. The worship of cargo had spread throughout much of the Pacific during the nineteenth century but only came to prominence after World War Two, when GIs brought home tales of fake airfields built to lure unwary aircraft. Those aircraft, the cult believed, carried cargo from the gods.

Coltrane nudged her. "It ain't the heat, Doc, that keeps people away. It's the island's reputation."

"The Balesin islanders massacred the first sailors to land, back in the seventeenth century," Buettner explained.

"And they've been killing people ever since," Coltrane added. "Regular headhunters."

Nick rolled her eyes.

"It's the truth, Doc. One expedition up and disappeared completely."

"I've heard that story already. It happened fifty years ago, if I remember correctly."

"Eaten by cannibals. That's what I heard."

"Come on," Nick chided.

"I never believe rumors. I only repeat them."

"I'm listening."

"Like I said, Doc, I don't believe most things I hear."

Before Nick could respond, Buettner spoke up. "We shouldn't dismiss folk tales too quickly. There's usually a few kernels of truth buried in there somewhere. Things were chaotic as hell out here after the war. When that expedition went missing in early forty-seven, we were still rooting out a few Japanese soldiers who'd refused to surrender. Of course, Balesin wasn't invaded by our forces initially. The island wasn't important enough, so we bypassed it on the way to more lucrative targets. Hell, all the Japanese had on the island were a few planes, a couple of tanks, and a lighthouse they built to warn their ships about the vicious reefs that surround the place."

"Folk tales are one thing," Nick said, "old wives' quite another."

"Don't get me wrong. I'm not buying cannibalism and the like. But many an eighteenth-century explorer ended up dead on these islands. The Marshall Islanders were particularly savage, if you'll remember."

Nick glanced at her father, half-suspecting that he was behind such tall tales. But he looked innocent enough. Of course, Nick's mother liked to say that Elliot had the look of a cherub and the heart of a demon.

"The way I heard it, Doc," Coltrane went on, "that missing expedition was delicious."

From the rear seat, Elliot snorted. "How about some chicken, Nick? It's finger-lickin' good."

"No you don't," she said. "I've done *some* reading on this area of the Pacific. After the war, all these islands became American possessions. Nowadays, even the schools out here teach English."

The pilot shrugged. "Sure, they speak American. They drink Coke, too, when they can get it. But there's always a gleam in their eyes as if they're measuring you for the pot. Besides, I like my passengers to know what they're getting into. Better safe than sorry, Doc."

"I'm not a tourist."

"Hell, Doc, most tourists are too smart to come to a place like Balesin."

"I'd rather you call me Nick."

"Don't confuse me when I'm flying, Doc. I might make a mistake and get us lost."

She craned her neck to see what her father had to say for himself. But his only answer was to cup a hand to his ear and shake his head, pretending he couldn't hear the pilot's last remarks. It was just as well, she thought, since she was growing hoarse from shouting over the engine noise. Sighing, she settled back and scanned the horizon, which now looked hazy compared to the dazzling sunlight glaring off the ocean around them. She squinted. The haze took shape.

"Are those clouds ahead?"

"Probably," Coltrane said. "It rains damn near all the time out here."

"How big is our island?"

"Fifteen miles long and maybe eight across."

Nick took a deep breath and let it out slowly. She didn't relish the idea of flying through cloud cover in the middle of the Pacific Ocean, no matter how accurate Coltrane's satellite navigational system was.

"Don't worry, Doc," he said as if reading her mind, "this time of year it's mostly squalls. Later on though, you get typhoons out here. When that happens, everything's grounded."

"What was it like the last time you were here?"

"Not bad, but it was raining like hell when I dropped off Doctor Duncan. The swells were bad, too. I had a hell of a time taking off. After that, the clouds bounced me around good. I damn near upchucked myself."

Nick groaned.

"I thought you liked airplanes," Coltrane said. "At least that's what your father told me."

"As an archaeologist, I prefer them on the ground and in pieces."

"I know what you mean, Doc. Every time I work on the Widgeon here, I have pieces left over." He snorted. "One day, I figure, I'll have enough left over to build me a whole second plane."

No you don't, Nick thought. He wasn't getting her to bite on that one.

She changed the subject. "Have you been on the island yourself?"

"Nah. So far, I've only done flyovers and float around offshore."

"What about Sam Ohmura? Have you ever taken him to Balesin?"

Coltrane shook his head. "I don't know the man."

"Sam hasn't been on Balesin in years," Buettner answered. "But he did remember the local shaman, a man named Yali. Your father and I met him briefly on our first trip, so he's expecting us back."

"As a pilot," Nick said to Coltrane, "what do you think of the airplane mock-ups on Balesin?"

Instead of responding, he tilted his head to one side as if listening to the starboard engine. After a moment, he nodded, apparently satisfied with whatever had caught his attention, and said, "On a foggy day, I might be fooled. But close up?" He shook his head. "Those people are nuts if they think their decoys are good enough to fool experienced pilots."

"It's the cargo they're after, not the pilots. That's why they call it the Cargo Cult."

"I don't see how you can get one without the other, Doc. If me and the Widgeon go down, it'll be on water, not one of their fake airfields." Coltrane jerked a thumb over his shoulder. "You see that yellow case just behind me?"

Nick swiveled her head. Lashed to the bulkhead was a case the size of a footlocker. It was made of heavy-duty plastic and had floats attached to its sides.

"That's my survival kit," Coltrane went. "It's Navy issue, the same kind of gear they drop to downed pilots at sea. It's tough enough to make it through damn near anything, even a crash."

There were two more similar cases farther back in the cargo area, she noticed. Both were the same bright yellow and both had parachutes and rigging attached.

"And the other two?" she asked.

"Out here, Doc, everything has to be protected against the climate. What the dampness doesn't rot, the bugs get. That's why I check my survival kit more often than I do my engines. If you want to last out here, you don't fly anywhere without your kit. I've got MREs in it, water, a life raft, a radio, and a rifle. That's the minimum you need for survival. I also carry a .45." He tapped the bottom of his seat. "So if anybody tries luring me and my cargo, Doc, they're in for trouble."

"Don't listen to him," Buettner said. "We aren't going to need guns to survive on Balesin."

"That guy Duncan said the same thing," Coltrane said.

"He was right."

"Maybe," Coltrane conceded. "But he was smart enough to land on the far side of the island, well away from the village."

Sighing, Nick closed her eyes and feigned sleep.

"You ain't fooling me, Doc. And don't say I didn't warn you about this part of the Pacific."

5

In Tokyo, Akiro Kobayashi sat back and stared at the Tang Dynasty figure gracing the teak credenza that faced his desk. The light softly caressed the finely crackled glaze of rich amber brown. Only one pottery piece in ten of this period was glazed and, of those, few were so rich a color. Usually the sight of the saddled Sancai horse calmed him, reminding him of family and continuity. The figure had been a trophy of war brought home by his grandfather following the great Nanking victory in 1937. A figure much like it had brought forty thousand dollars at Sotheby's only last year, but he would never sell it. The serene beauty of the piece had been a part of his life for as long as he could remember. The eyes of the horse were flecked with a deeper brown that held depths of knowledge that Kobayashi could only dream of. It had survived for over a thousand years and reminded him that even fragile things sometimes withstood the on-slaught of time. At the moment, though, the Sancai was a reminder that old sins cast long shadows. His grandfa-ther had bequeathed something else to Kobayashi be-sides the horse.

To some, Kobayashi, a small-boned, slender man, looked too young to be a vice president at Tokyo's presti-gious Nomoto Bank. He was thirty-two and a brilliant economist with advanced degrees from both Tokyo Uni-versity and Harvard, the latter earned when he was only twenty-one years of age. It was rumored that he would be president of the bank before his thirty-third birthday.

If the rumor came true, it would have nothing to do with his financial expertise, but rather his position in military intelligence, a branch that no longer existed, at least on paper, and hadn't since the Second World War. It had been outlawed by General MacArthur, only to be reinstated secretly—with full funding—by the CIA.

"Old sins," Kobayashi murmured, staring at the phone which linked him, via scrambled satellite trans-mission, to his counterpart at CIA headquarters in Lang-ley. If he picked it up, Ohmura's failure, which more than likely would have amounted to nothing in the end, would now take on a life of its own. But if Kobayashi didn't pick up the phone, and the old sins came out of the shadows without warning, his thirty-third birthday would find him out of work, or worse.

Outside his tenth-story window, the light changed. The sun had disappeared behind a cloud; its diffused light cast no shadows.

Kobayashi took it as a sign and picked up the phone.

Reed Farrington, his counterpart at Langley, answered quickly.

Ten minutes later, they both agreed that Walt Duncan was probably harmless, but worth watching just the same.

As Kobayashi hung up the sun reappeared, causing a soft glow in the knowing eyes of the ancient Tang horse.

6

Henry Yali stood at the base of Mount Nomenuk, staring up at the sacred mountain with the same sense of awe he'd felt as a child. Since the day Yali had met his God, he'd made a daily pilgrimage to the mountain to renew himself. Here was where John Frum had left his people; here was where he would return. When that time came he would lead his chosen people, Yali's people, to salvation and riches.

But today Yali felt uneasy. He'd been feeling that way since the day last week when the two scientists had come poking around. Oh, their promises had sounded sincere enough. We want only to study your ways, they'd told him. We want to record Balesin's lifestyle before it changes forever.

Yali shook his head at the thought. Only John Frum had the power to change Balesin. He would do that when the time was right, and then Balesin would be as rich and powerful as America. In the meantime, Frum must be honored, his secrets protected, his shrine cared for. That was Yali's job as Frum's priest.

He knelt in prayer, hoping to shake off his uneasiness. But his mind kept wandering. Finally, Yali shook his head in frustration and rose to his feet. He'd pray at John Frum's shrine.

Nodding to himself, he strode along the path that wound its way up Mount Nomenuk. The path had been worn smooth over the years by Yali's pilgrimages. Once a month, all of Balesin made the trip, though that would have to stop once the scientists arrived. Secrecy demanded it.

Always before, Yali had felt himself growing closer to John Frum with each step. But today, there was no comfort in the climb. Today, the jungle seemed to close in ominously on both sides of the trail, and he felt as if he wasn't alone.

He paused, tilting his head to listen, but heard nothing but the jungle's hum.

"Relax, old man," he murmured softly. Everyone on the island knew this was his time with John Frum. They wouldn't dare intrude.

By the time he reached the halfway point, his breath was coming in ragged gasps. Sweat poured from him, though the day was no hotter than always. He paused to rest. Only last week, his resting point had been a good hundred yards farther up the mountain. Old age was upon him, no doubt about it. Soon he would have to train an acolyte to take his place.

He started climbing again, more slowly than before as the path grew steeper. When finally it leveled out, he sighed with relief. John Frum's tabernacle was near at hand.

He paused one last time, preparing himself, and that's when he heard the nasty clicking sound. He recognized it immediately, coconut crabs at work. But on what? he wondered. This part of the mountain had been cleared of coconut palms and leveled by hand. Here, there was nothing for the crabs to eat.

He shuddered. Here, the clicking could mean only one thing. Something had died to bring out the scavenger crabs, something large judging by the intensity of sound. And the only animal on Balesin large enough to provide such a feast was man.

"Sacrilege," Yali muttered angrily and hurried forward to find out who had dared such a thing.

Beside the shrine, in the deep shade cast by the trees left in place as shelter, he saw the body. No wonder the usually nocturnal crabs were out in force.

Yali moved to get a closer look. The feet told him enough. The dead man was an outsider who had angered John Frum and paid the price.

Yali backed away, fearing Frum's further vengeance. In that moment, he heard the airplane. John Frum had come in a plane and would so again. Perhaps now was the time. Yali hurried down the mountain to meet him.

Farrington cradled the phone, swung his feet up on the desk, and smiled at the picture of the president hanging on the wall. It was nice to know the Japanese were on the job, albeit a little late.

Farrington had known about the extra outsider on Balesin for the past twenty-four hours. Of course, there was always the chance that Kobayashi wasn't late at all, but merely late reporting the situation. Which would be typical of the man. God, how the Japanese loved thinking of themselves as inscrutable.

Jesus. What a can of worms this was turning out to be. Farrington turned to his computer and called up the Balesin file and reread the biographies of those involved. Under normal circumstances, the presence of scientists wouldn't have caused more than a ripple. Except for a few esoteric journals, no one paid any attention to anthropologists and archaeologists. But an expert on airplanes, that was another matter.

Groaning, Farrington studied the electronic image of Nicolette Scott. She didn't look like anyone to worry about. With a little bit of makeup and a decent hairdo she'd be a knockout, and in Farrington's experience good-looking women were good for only one thing.

But the data in her file said otherwise. One word popped out that made Farrington clench his teeth. Tenacious. *The subject appears extraordinarily tenacious regarding airplanes.* The report went on to discuss an incident in New Mexico that was well documented and a less well documented affair in Arizona that had sent ripples through a shadowy intelligence organization known to Farrington for its effective and ruthless competition.

Farrington clenched his teeth. Tenacity could get a lot of people killed.

On top of everything else, her father had an international reputation. And his daughter's reputation as a historical archaeologist wasn't far behind. Christ! He hadn't known what a historical archaeologist was until he looked it up. An expert in the near past, that was her.

And Balesin had one hell of a recent past. He ground his teeth. Complications like that had to be taken into account should contingency plans become necessary. If a nobody went missing on a remote Pacific island, who'd care? But the Scotts?

Farrington took a deep breath and let it out like a man blowing smoke rings. Maybe the cover would hold. After all, they were under constant observation, their every move being carefully guided. If nothing went wrong, they'd see only what they were supposed to. And that ought to satisfy any scientist.

The trouble was, the man Duncan had been moving around unobserved. Well, thank God he was a nobody.

7

Nick jerked awake. She realized that she had fallen asleep again.

"There she is, Doc," Coltrane said. "Straight ahead. Balesin Island."

From two thousand feet up and a mile away, the island looked as unreal as one of those lush tropical paradises pictured on the front of travel brochures. The beaches were white and dazzling, fringed by a dark green that was probably coconut palms. Beyond the palms, there appeared to be cultivated areas that Nick guessed to be breadfruit trees. After the breadfruit came a vibrant green canopy of exotic plants, jungle-thick and formidable. At the island's center rose a two-thousand-foot peak. Since all land in the area was volcanic in origin, she hoped this particular mountain was dormant.

As for the surrounding ocean, it was emerald blue and clear enough to see the coral reefs lurking not far below the surface.

"Deceptive, isn't it?" Coltrane said.

"It's beautiful whatever you say."

"Women are beautiful too, Doc, but a man's got to be leery of them." He tapped the fuel gauge, then spoke over his shoulder. "Should we give her the grand tour?"

"Absolutely," Elliot said. "While you do that, we'll get the cargo ready."

Nick scrunched around to see Buettner and her father positioning the two yellow plastic cases near the door at the rear of the fuselage.

"Offerings to the gods," Elliot shouted at her.

"Cargo," Buettner added.

"Bribes," Coltrane clarified.

She must have looked skeptical because her father grinned and said, "Now, Nick. It's not like we're trading beads for Manhattan."

"What, then?"

"Flashlights, canned food and goodies, things like that, and all we get in return is knowledge and cooperation."

"Out here you've got to keep everything dry," Coltrane said. "Otherwise, flashlights and batteries don't last long. Hell, nothing does."

"How much rain does Balesin get?" Nick said.

"Two hundred inches a year, minimum. Of course it was less during El Niño."

At the moment, they were flying in bright sunlight, though they were surrounded by distant clouds.

"It looks like we're in the eye of a storm," Nick said.

Coltrane snorted. "This isn't a real storm. If we were in a real eye out here, we'd be looking the devil in the face."

Wherever Nick looked there were squall lines.

"This is what we call a sucker hole," Coltrane said. "They're benign enough in this kind of weather."

As he spoke, he banked east to fly parallel to the coast. The turn allowed Nick to look directly down at the island. At its eastern tip, she noticed a second, smaller island. It couldn't have been more than a half mile across and reminded her of an exclamation point. It was separated from the main body of land by a narrow channel that couldn't have been more than a few hundred yards wide. She pointed at it.

"That's Balabat," Coltrane said, "though if you ask me it should all be counted as one island."

Nick checked the map. The exclamation point was indeed named Balabat. As far as she could see, the smaller land mass was nothing but solid jungle.

The pilot turned inland and immediately began gaining altitude as he headed toward the mountain at the island's center. The map identified the peak as Mount Nomenuk. A few stunted trees were sprouting in the crater at the top.

"Is that mountain active?" Nick said.

"Don't ask me, Doc. You're the scientist."

"The answer to that is *no*," Buettner said from right behind her. "At least, there's no recorded history of eruptions. Of course, we don't have any real data prior to the eighteenth century."

"It's not the crater we want you to see," Elliot said. "It's what's on the other side of the island."

A moment later, the Widgeon swept over the top of the peak, throttled back, and half-glided down the far slope, following the meandering path of a narrow river on its way to the sea.

Then suddenly she saw it, the village at the mouth of the river, where it ran into the sea. She was surprised by its location on the wet side of the island. But the village was near a river, which gave it drinking water and immediate access to the sea.

Coltrane throttled up, and banked to the southwest. Half a minute later they passed over a clearing that ran as straight as a runway. She blinked. By God, it was a runway. Cut into the jungle the way it was, it looked stark and unreal, like some freak of nature.

Fifty yards from the runway, swallowed by the jungle and invisible except from the air, stood a crumbling watchtower. Near its base was the burnt-out hulk of a World War Two tank, probably one of the lightweight models the Japanese brought ashore on landing craft.

"Can you get us any lower?" she said.

"I thought you might say that, Doc." Coltrane pushed the yoke forward. The Widgeon dropped like a rock.

Nick swallowed to keep her stomach in check, but never once took her eyes from the runway.

"Don't circle," Elliot said. "Don't make it obvious that we're snooping."

Her father was right, of course. Until they knew the local customs, and the local taboos, it paid to be both respectful and careful.

"Slower," Nick said.

"Anything you say, Doc. Flaps coming down."

Then she saw the planes, two of them at the head of the runway, as if poised for takeoff. They looked very real.

"Twin-engine jobs," Coltrane pointed out.

Nick nodded. "The Japanese had bombers about that size and shape."

"So did we."

"True, but the Japanese had an airfield here during the war, so they're the most likely models."

"Whatever you say, Doc." Coltrane increased power and adjusted the flaps. "We were getting close to stall speed there for a moment, and I wouldn't want to try setting you folks down on that runway."

"It looks perfectly usable enough, though, doesn't it?" she said.

"That's the strange part when you think about it, Doc. Why go to so much trouble building a runway to scale when they don't have any real airplanes?"

"If you want the gods to send real planes, you have to prepare the way. How else can you fool the gods?" She studied her map again. "Besides, that is the old Japanese airstrip."

Coltrane shrugged. "They're nothing but Sirens, if you ask me. But I'm just a simple pilot for hire. What do I know?"

Sure, she thought. But it wasn't a bad comparison, the more she thought about it.

More accurately though, the worshipers of the Cargo Cult built planes and runways for their messiah, John Frum, who one day would send them cargo from the skies. When that day came, they would be as strong as America. At least that is what the Baleseans believed, according to Sam Ohmura. For the moment, however, she decided to forgo making any assumptions. It was better to wait until she'd had the chance to study the Baleseans for herself. "Never trust conventional wisdom," her father had drummed into his students. "Too often it's anything but wise."

"Why the name John Frum?" Nick wondered out loud.

"From where?" Coltrane asked.

"It's pronounced *from* but spelled F-R-U-M. He's the Cargo Cult's messiah."

"Oh, him."

"Are you familiar with the concept?"

"Just what I've read in the *National Geographic*," Coltrane replied.

She squinted at him suspiciously, doubtful that he was just the simple bush pilot he pretended to be.

"Remind me not to take things for granted," she told him. "Or judge by appearances."

Grinning, Coltrane spoke over his shoulder. "Get ready with your cargo."

The Widgeon banked full circle until it was following the river again, toward the village.

From the air she could see that the village was laid out surrounding a central square. Radiating out from that square were thatched-roof huts spread over an area the size of what she judged to be four city blocks. The huts numbered fifty at least, maybe seventy-five. To the south, on the inland side of the village, a narrow dirt road ran for about a mile before ending at a clearing that held what looked to be a large shed and a couple of ancillary buildings.

As the distance closed, Nick realized that her initial impression was wrong. Huts was the wrong word for the dwellings. They were far too sturdy for that. True enough, primitive thatched roofs dominated, but the underlying timber structure was obvious. That timbering was even more apparent in the four larger buildings that immediately surrounded the square. Most likely, they were communal meeting places, possibly of religious significance, though Nick reserved judgment for the moment. Whatever they were, they too had thatched roofs. Their walls appeared to be made of mismatched, rusty metal siding.

An American flag flew from a pole in the middle of the square, which was quickly filling with people, all of them staring up at the Widgeon.

Before she could point out the landmark, Coltrane banked sharply and shouted, "Bombs away!"

Out went the two cargo cases. Bright red parachutes blossomed immediately.

As soon as the chutes landed in the village square, Coltrane headed out to sea. After a mile or so, he turned back to line up his landing with the inlet at the mouth of the river.

"Tighten your seat belts," he said, "and we'll see if I can set this thing down without hitting a coral reef."

Nick felt her stomach lurch again.

8

Watching the descending plane, the Reverend George Innis felt a growing sense of frustration. Arriving planes made his life harder. Each time was the same. Word would go out that John Frum's promised flight had finally arrived. The villagers would gather, and Henry Yali, prophet and soothsayer to the Cargo Cult, would declare a miracle.

And this time was even worse. There were

parachutes to go with the plane. That would really cause a furor. And worse luck was the color of those parachutes, red. Red was John Frum's color.

The reverend clenched his teeth in frustration and lowered his binoculars. He could hear Henry Yali now. "It's a sign!" Yali would shout. "John Frum is at hand."

Yali, prognosticator, high priest, and old friend, would make the reverend's life a misery for the next few days. Church attendance would fall off. Little work would get done. And all because John Frum, the Cargo Cult's long-awaited messiah, was due on the next plane.

Yali had made such predictions before, of course, but it never seemed to matter to his followers that Frum never came, or that the planes carried no cargo for the villagers, only supplies for the island's single store. Somehow, no blame ever fell Yali's way. Instead, the Reverend Innis took the brunt. His flock, so carefully nurtured over the years, would grow restless.

Yali's prediction wasn't a failure, they'd say, but a precursor. John Frum's coming was just around the corner.

Only after weeks had passed, or months depending on the strength of the sign seen by Yali, would worshipers begin straggling back to the True Church. And each time they did, he saw his own failure mirrored in their eyes. Their lack of faith mocked him, and forced him to realize that all his years of work on this godforsaken island took a back seat to John Frum. Probably it always would.

The Reverend Innis wiped sweat from the eyepieces and went back to watching the seaplane. At least there were no more parachutes floating down. Still, he had to admire the newcomers' ingenuity. If he had it all to do over again, he'd do the same thing. He'd announce his arrival by dropping gifts from heaven.

He refocused his binoculars. This plane looked like the same one that had visited Balesin last week.

Innis gritted his teeth. God knew what this third flight, coming soon after the first two, would do to his attendance. Last Sunday's service had been a disaster, with only a single pew filled with diehards. Henry had been among them, smiling up at Innis, a Cheshire smile, like a cat stalking a bird.

Innis nodded to himself, knowing that the Lord would have to be content with an empty house this coming Sunday. It wouldn't be the first.

But today was a first, in his tenure anyway. The first time scientists had come to Balesin in force.

Usually, the island's only visitors were misguided tourists, who quickly left when confronted with the island's inhospitable climate. Once or twice, the Hawaiian professor had come, but his impact had been minimal as far as the reverend's services were concerned. And even the Hawaiian had been glad to get away before the rainy season.

"You have to be born here to feel at peace with Balesin," Yali liked to say.

"I was raised here," Innis would point out.

"But you left for a while."

The reverend smiled grimly. He was an old-timer now, in years anyway. He'd learned to cope with the heat, though at the moment he had to shift his sandaled feet to keep from blistering them on the metal roof underfoot. He was standing in the bell tower, or rather what passed for one, though there never had been a bell. In reality, the tower was nothing but a makeshift platform bolted to the corrugated roof of his one-story church and could be reached only by a ladder. During rainstorms, the bolt holes caused slow leaks on the pews below. One of these days he'd get around to caulking the holes, but not now. Not in this heat.

He focused on the plane one more time. It was land-ing all right.

Maybe, as a Christian, he should make the near-mile trek to the village to greet the newcomers. Surely even scientists would welcome a friendly, civilized face.

No, he told himself. An educated face was the best he could offer, because the reverend was anything but civilized. Otherwise, why would he be standing here, praying for disaster to strike.

"And why not?" he thought out loud. "It would be better for everyone if that plane hit a reef right now and sank. That way, there'd be no more trouble. No more risking the wrath of John Frum."

Hearing himself, denying everything he believed, he banged a fist against his bare thigh. When that didn't help, he pinched his flesh as hard as he could. Thoughts like that had no place in a preacher's mind. Surely what had happened in the past had nothing to do with John Frum, despite what Yali and his acolytes claimed. Most likely the expedition had disappeared because of some natural disaster. Better yet, maybe it never happened. Maybe it was just another old wives' tale to scare off outsiders. Maybe no one had disappeared. Maybe no one had died.

Innis shook his head. He knew better. From personal experience, or so he'd been told, though memory failed him on that point.

He twitched. A sudden chill made him shiver. And in heat like this. That's what he got for thinking about a man like Henry Yali. Still, it might be best to talk over the situation with the man. That way, Innis's conscience would be clear no matter what happened.

The reverend nodded at the wisdom of such a decision. The last thing he needed was something else haunting him at night.

Sighing, he took one last look through his binoculars. It was worse than he thought. This time the cargo was for the villagers. They were flocking to the beach, where the red parachutes were already being waved like banners of welcome.

"It's best you stay here," his wife called from the foot of the ladder. "You'd just be in the way if you went into town. We both would."

"You saw the parachutes?"

"Yes. Sunday services are going to suffer."

Innis smiled down at his wife, hoping to cheer her up. Leading the choir was the highlight of Ruth's week.

"Why don't you come down off that roof before you get sunstroke," she said. "I'll hold the ladder for you."

As soon as he was safely down, she took his hand and said, "Poor Ichabod."

It had been her pet name for him since the first time they had met. Back then, he'd been thin and gangling and had reminded her of Ichabod Crane, the character from "The Legend of Sleepy Hollow."

"It's a pastor's duty to welcome newcomers," he said without enthusiasm.

"To quote one of your own sermons, Ichabod, never try to compete with the locals. Show them a different road and pray that they will travel it."

He smiled. She made him sound like a great dispenser of wisdom, though that was far from the truth. To his ear, his Sunday rambles sounded confusing more often than not.

"I understand one of the scientists is a woman," his wife said. "Why don't we wait till they settle in and then we'll invite her to tea."

"A woman? I hadn't heard that."

She patted his hand. "You were the one who told me, dear."

Innis sighed. Sometimes he didn't know whose memory was slipping, hers or his.

"What kind of scientist is she?" he asked.

"An archaeologist," his wife replied. "Just like those people who disappeared fifty years ago."

"They were anthropologists," he said. "There's a difference." He shivered again. John Frum hated all those who pried, or so said Henry Yali.

How did Frum feel about ministers? Innis wondered, then shook himself. What the hell was he thinking about? Frum was nothing but a superstition.

Ruth gripped his hand. "You feel cold, dear. We'd better get you out of the sun. You don't want to make yourself sick."

Innis allowed himself to be led inside the church. There, lying down with his eyes closed, he kept seeing fiery flashes, like the after-burn from staring at the sun.

You're a fool, he told himself. John Frum is a legend, a way of coping with life on Balesin. He doesn't exist.

Innis sighed. The trouble was, Henry Yali said the same thing about Jesus. And Henry claimed to have met Frum once, in another incarnation. "Can you say the same about your God?" Henry liked to taunt.

Henry Yali knew better than to expect John Frum as soon as he saw the plane up close. It was the same one that had come before carrying scientists.

Yali, exhausted from his headlong rush down the

mountain, plunged into the surf. The water renewed him, cleansed him, washed him of sin, he hoped.

But what if the scientists were part of a test, John Frum's way of assessing Yali's faith.

Yali shook his head as he waded through the rippling water. There was no need of a test. He had already passed with flying colors. What counted was Yali's willingness to serve John Frum by protecting his holy place. Frum would understand that; Frum would condone it.

After all, hadn't Yali met John Frum personally? Hadn't John Frum reached out to him, to Henry Yali, asking for help? Didn't that make Yali the chosen one?

Lily had been close by, too. She was his witness. She was . . . His mind veered away. He tried to erase all painful memories from his thoughts, but one would not go.

Yali staggered, startling those around him. To allay the sudden concern he saw in their faces, he smiled and said, "Such planes come from God whether they know it or not. They must all be greeted accordingly. We must never doubt John Frum's promise. One day *He* will make Balesin great."

But Yali had secret doubts, not of Frum but of the other man—the outsider—who claimed to act in His best interests. *Keep an eye on these new interlopers*, he'd told Henry. *They are unbelievers. If they are not watched, they will sow false seeds among your followers.* But how strong was the outsider's faith? Was he merely paying lip service? Yali smiled. He would pay more than that. And that pay, Yali felt certain, had to be part of John Frum's plan. Perhaps, in some way yet to be revealed, the trespasser on the mountain was part of that plan.

Besides, the new ones had supplied Yali with cargo,

with the promise of more to come. And didn't all cargo come from John Frum, no matter who delivered it? Weren't the delivery men His messengers, unwitting or not? Yali nodded. John Frum's will be done.

But the outsiders wanted something in exchange, while John Frum attached no such conditions.

Yali left the water to pace along the beach. He couldn't shake the thought that he was being tested. Yet if that were the case, there would be no harm in going along with the outsiders. The cargo would benefit his people no matter what the intention of those who gave it. Yali smiled to himself. He'd outsmart them all, with John Frum's help.

As he squinted at the sea, the airplane settled onto the water. Its engines roared, then throttled back as it headed for the shore.

Yali waved. His heart soared. Maybe, despite everything, it would be John Frum at the controls.

Those around him cheered. He joined in, shouting for all he was worth. John Frum would expect such a welcome. But would Yali recognize Him again after so many years?

He closed his eyes, trying to summon up his memory of that long-ago meeting. But the image was shadowy. He rubbed his eyes, but to no avail. *Please*, he prayed, *let me not fail Him now.*

Then it hit him. Enlightenment. John Frum wouldn't change, not if He didn't want to. Such was His power. Which meant he could look like anyone if that, too, was His desire.

Yali sighed. He would have to be very careful. After all, the power of life and death was in his hands. And he hoped, prayed, that John Frum would not demand the spilling of any more blood, not like before, all those years ago.

Yali retreated into the trees, to await the correct moment to make his official entrance.

9

Nick admired Coltrane's technique as he cut the engines and allowed the Widgeon's momentum to carry it toward shore, where the island's only freshwater river emptied into the sea. Already, the beach was lined with villagers.

Along the water's edge, a line of young men ran back and forth, carrying the parachutes from Curt's cargo drop. They waved the red silk over their collective heads, reminding Nick of the dragons that snaked through San Francisco's Chinatown during parades.

As the Widgeon drifted closer to the beach, Nick was struck by the beauty of the people. Their skins glowed with a richness sunbathers only dream about. Their hair was dark, as were their eyes. Their clothes were scant, mostly Western in origin, with some scattering of "missionary" cloth garments hinting at a nineteenth-century corruption of traditions. None of the women were bare-breasted. There were no penis pouches, such as she had encountered in New Guinea. Not such virgin territory after all, she thought.

"We were right about dropping the cargo," Elliot said. "It seems to have been a big hit."

Buettner nodded. "Guests should always arrive bearing gifts."

The Widgeon's hull bumped bottom while still a good ten yards from shore. Buettner opened the door.

Nick left her seat to join him in the doorway, hoping for a cool breeze. What she got was a face full of hot, clammy air. The intensity of it stunned her. It was beyond anything she'd ever experienced in New Guinea. Even in the scorching deserts of the Southwest where she and Elliot so often dug for Anasazi relics paled by comparison. This heat felt as if someone had thrown a sopping, hot blanket over her head.

She gasped. Only yesterday, she'd been coping with one of Berkeley's frigid summers and longing for tropical sunshine.

"I'll stay with the plane," Coltrane said, "until I'm sure the natives are friendly."

"Will you drop the tourist crap?" Nick snapped at him as she pulled on her Cubs cap to keep the sweat out of her eyes. As usual, the heat didn't seem to affect her father, who continued to look crisp and cool, while she felt on the verge of a meltdown.

"Come on, Nick," he said, "let's get to work. We've got a lot of supplies to unload before Lee can fly home." Elliot pushed past her and plunged into the surf, followed closely by Buettner.

As Coltrane and Nick began handing out the gear to them, the islanders waded toward the plane to help. They formed a line so that supplies could be passed ashore hand to hand. Sleeping bags, tents, cameras, recorders, video gear, the portable generator, and food enough for a week made it ashore without putting their watertight containers to the test.

When the last container had been unloaded, Nick

sagged against the Widgeon's door frame and mopped her face.

"Sorry to kick you out, Doc," Coltrane said into her ear, "but I've got to be on my way if I'm going to make Guam before dark."

She stared at him in amazement. He, like Elliot, seemed oblivious to the heat. To her, the thought of taking off again and flying back to Guam alone, across the featureless ocean, was appalling. For one thing, she'd never be able to stay awake that long, not without company.

"Why don't you fly back in the morning after you've had some rest?" she said.

He shook his head. "I spent the night here the last trip, Doc. You haven't."

He pushed her out the door, gently to be sure, but a push nevertheless. She hit the water expecting some kind of cooling relief. Instead, she felt as if she'd landed in hot Jell-O.

By the time she'd waded the few feet to shore, her legs were rubbery. On dry land, her waterlogged desert boots sank into the sand. Each step became a struggle.

Halfway to the neatly stacked supplies where Buettner and her father were eagerly shaking hands with the islanders, her knees buckled. She would have fallen on her face if it hadn't been for the iron grasp of a small, frail-looking woman, who looked old enough to be Nick's grandmother.

"Don't worry, dear," the woman whispered into her ear. "It happens to every *h'alie* who comes visiting." Her English was unaccented and very American. "You'll be fine in a few minutes."

Nick nodded gratefully.

Despite the woman's wrinkles, there was something

ageless about her. She could have been sixty or eighty. She moved easily across the sand, her broad-soled rubber sandals acting like snowshoes. As far as Nick could see, all the islanders were wearing the same kind of no-nonsense footwear. The sandals looked as if they'd been cut from tire treads.

"I was standing on the beach when your father and his friend landed last week," the woman said. "They were as weak as babies by the time they waded ashore."

Nick managed a smile.

"My name's Lily," the woman said, her voice rising against the shouts and laughter coming from the islanders gathered around Elliot and Buettner. "And this is Josephine, my granddaughter." She pushed forward a young girl who Nick guessed to be about eight or nine and who presented Nick with a small palm frond shaped like a fan.

"Thank you, Josephine," Nick said, accepting the gift. The girl giggled shyly and hid behind her grandmother. "I'm Nicolette, but everybody calls me Nick."

"Nick," Lily repeated as if testing the sound of it. "Yes, I like that."

On impulse, Nick reached into her pocket and found an unopened, though limp candy bar from Coltrane's emergency rations and presented it to Josephine. The little girl clapped her hands to her face and then looked up at her grandmother as if seeking permission. The older woman nodded and Josephine snatched the bar from Nick and ran off.

"You are a wise woman." Lily winked. "For a *h'alie*."

Nick would have bet that *h'alie* was the native word for outsiders, probably Caucasian outsiders.

"Does everyone speak English as well as you, Lily?"

"We all speak American. Our island is part of America. It has been, since the war."

"Since World War Two?" Nick asked.

"The only war there has been," Lily replied.

For a moment Nick was stunned and then realized that for these islanders it was the only war that they had known. It had probably shaped their lives and defined their history in ways that Nick couldn't begin to imagine.

"And before that?" Nick said.

Lily held a finger to her lips. The commotion around Elliot and Buettner subsided as two men, walking in a ceremonial fashion, approached the beach. The man in the lead, white-haired and mummy-thin, looked ancient, though his posture was as stiff-necked as a soldier's. The other man was merely a younger version, who still had some fat left on his bones. One day, age would mummify him also, Nick suspected, and turn his skin to shrink-wrap too.

"Come," Lily said, tugging at Nick. "That is Henry Yali. You must pay your respects."

The moment Nick was introduced, Yali took her hand and held on insistently, staring intently into her eyes. Finally, he nodded and said, "Yes, I have been expecting you, Dr. Scott. For a long time."

Yali, she remembered, was the island's shaman. And a shaman's reputation, not to mention his living, depended upon magic, mystical remarks, and predictions that were always vague enough to be interpreted as supporting both sides of any issue.

She said, "I, too, have looked forward to this meeting." Privately, she was disappointed that he was dressed in faded jeans and an open-neck short-sleeve shirt.

Yali's eyes narrowed, and for a moment Nick wondered if her remark had sounded like a challenge, as if she were claiming psychic insight.

"What I mean is . . ."

Lily laid her hand on Yali's. "What she means, Henry, is that your reputation has reached even as far as America."

A broad smile lit up his face. "Is that true?"

"Only yesterday I was in America," Nick said. "In California. I flew all the way here to meet you and see the wonders of your island."

Still beaming, he released Nick's hand into Lily's keeping. "One day," he said, "we will be like America, rich enough to buy any cargo." He turned to watch the Widgeon, which was now drifting away from the shore-line.

"Our pilot will be returning with more of our friends," Nick said. "And with more cargo to help with our work."

Yali looked mesmerized. "It must be wonderful to fly like the gods."

Nick was tempted to offer him a test flight when Coltrane returned. But that might cause trouble if there were others who demanded similar treatment. Besides, she wasn't certain how Coltrane would react to joyriding sightseers.

"There will be time for talk of airplanes later, Henry," Lily intervened. "But first Nick must meet our chief, Jim Jeban." With that, the woman led Nick to the man who'd been walking in Yali's footsteps.

Nick blinked in surprise. She'd assumed the man to be Yali's disciple, not the chief. *Never make assumptions.* Her father's dictum, drummed into her since she was old enough to accompany him on her first dig, echoed in her mind.

So where did the real power lay? she wondered. By following in Yali's footsteps did the chief take a back seat? Or were there subtleties involved? Perhaps by leading the way, Yali announced Chief Jeban's coming?

Nick sighed. The answers would take a while, though there was no guarantee that the nuances of Balesin's culture would ever be completely understood by outsiders. But she had to keep an open mind, that was for sure.

She glanced at her father, who answered with a raised eyebrow as if he, too, had been taken by surprise. Well, she'd let Elliot and Buettner worry about island ritual while she stuck to airplanes.

The chief, unlike Yali, looked Nick up and down in open appraisal before focusing on her Cubs cap.

"Do you know about baseball?" she asked, taking off her cap.

Both Jeban and Yali laughed as if she had made a joke. Behind him, Buettner arched his eyebrow suggestively and shook his finger at her. His other hand held a small two-way radio. Probably it didn't have much range, though over water that might be amplified somewhat. Their gear, she knew, contained a radio capable of reaching just about anywhere via satellite. Cell-phone technology hadn't caught up with the remote islands of the Pacific.

"We will take you to our village," Jeban said. At his signal, villagers began loading the expedition's supplies onto their shoulders. They were about to start for the village when one of the Widgeon's engines coughed to life. The roar stopped everyone in their tracks. As one, they stood and watched as the second engine started up. They clapped as the seaplane began its takeoff run. At liftoff a loud cheer went up.

Only then did Lily lead the way off the beach. Strangely enough, Yali and Jeban fell in behind Lily and Nick. Once under cover of the palm trees, the deep sand gave way to a hard-packed path that meandered alongside the river. On solid ground, Nick's legs stopped wobbling and her strength returned.

Within a hundred yards, the palms gave way to a heavier, jungle-like growth. The air came alive, humming with insects. To keep from breathing them in, Nick pressed her lips tightly together, all the time squinting against their swarming attacks.

Beside her, Lily seemed oblivious to the onslaught.

"You see," Lily said, holding onto Nick's arm as they moved along the well-trodden track. "Now it's an old woman's turn to lean on you."

But as far as Nick could see, Lily was only being kind. She needed no help. In fact, the pace she set had Nick bathed in sweat by the time they reached the outskirts of the village. There, they crossed the river on a hand-hewn timber bridge. Another quarter of a mile brought them to the village square, which was ringed by the large buildings that Nick had seen from the air. Up close, they looked rough-hewn and very solid.

By now Nick was exhausted again, and Buettner and her father didn't look much better. All of them were constantly swatting at insects, though with no apparent effect.

"We would like to set up camp here." Buettner indicated an open spot in the square.

Lily pressed her lips together, then replied, "As you wish." Immediately, their gear was stacked on the spot.

Through the dense cloud cover they suddenly heard the roar of an airplane. Lily and the others moved to the center of the square, where they stood staring up at the grey sky.

Buettner used his handheld radio. "Coltrane, this is base. Do you read us? We don't have our long-range set unpacked yet."

"Loud and clear. I decided to circle a while to make sure they didn't eat you."

Off-mike, Buettner said, "He's only kidding. I asked him to stick around until we got settled."

"Don't tell me you believe his cannibal stories," Nick whispered, then looked around to make sure none of the natives had heard her.

Buettner snorted. "Not quite. Besides, Sam Ohmura was here before us, though not long enough, thank God, to fully study the island culture. Otherwise, there'd be nothing left for us to do. Anyway, there was always the chance we might lose some equipment in the water. Had that happened, Coltrane would fly in replacements tomorrow."

"How about a prefab house?" Nick suggested.

"We don't have a big enough payload for that," Buettner told her before going back to his radio. "Lee, the weather has closed in down here."

"That's no surprise this time of day," Coltrane answered.

"When we set up the main radio, we'll be able to contact you on Guam tomorrow morning at dawn."

"Roger that. By the way, I spotted what looks like another airfield at the base of the mountain. I couldn't get much of a look at it because the cloud cover was closing in there, too."

Nick beckoned for the transmitter, which Buettner handed over. She hit the transmit button and said, "Lee, did you see any planes on the strip?"

"I caught a glimpse of something, but the light was bad."

"Anything else?"

"At the edge of the trees, I thought I spotted something that looked man-made. But it was starting to rain by then and I couldn't get a close enough look to verify that. Hell, maybe I was seeing things anyway."

Nick doubted that. "Can you give me a precise location of the airstrip?"

"It's on the far side of the mountain, out of sight of the village. We didn't see it on our approach because of the heavy overgrowth in that area. Chances are it's an abandoned strip. If you'd like, I could make a low-level approach on my next trip, assuming the weather's better."

"You might want to keep an eye out for Walt Duncan too," Nick said.

"Sorry, Doc, the visibility's not good enough."

Elliot tapped Nick on the shoulder to warn her that Henry Yali was heading their way again and already in earshot. Lily was close behind him.

"Stand by," Nick said.

"Sorry, Doc. I can't hang around any longer. I have to head for home and I'll be out of range damn fast."

"Understood."

"Just take care of yourself, Doc." Static punctuated the remark.

Yali came to a stop in front of Nick, his face only inches away. His stare was so intense that the skin around his eyes quivered. "John Frum has many places on Balesin," he said. "Some are known only to His people."

Nick understood the implication, that some areas of the island were off-limits to outsiders.

"Lee," she transmitted, "no more low-level surveillance until we contact you. Is that understood."

Yali walked way.

"You're breaking up, Doc."

Nick repeated herself.

"Okay, Doc. I get the picture. Over."

"Out," Nick said and handed the transmitter back to Buettner. She felt suddenly cut off from the outside world. The sooner they got the tents up and assembled the radio gear, the better.

10

At Nick's urging, the three of them went to work on the tents. The villagers lent a hand, surprisingly under Lily's supervision. Yali and Chief Jeban stood aloof, alternating between approving nods and negative head shakes.

The work progressed quickly and soon their three individual tents, each a bright yellow for easy spotting from the air, were up and pegged into place. After that, work began on a fourth, larger tent, also yellow, that would serve as their radio shack and mess tent. The last to go up was their communal shower tent, which included a self-composting commode, said to be state-of-the-art.

Once everything was in place, Jeban walked slowly around the perimeter, his expression clearly radiating condemnation. Finally, he stopped beside the radio tent, fingered its material, and said, "You would be better off staying on the beach, or in your airplane if it had remained behind."

"Trekking back and forth would waste too much time," Buettner told him.

"The chief is right," Yali said.

"It's better we stay here," Buettner insisted.

"Absolutely," Elliot agreed.

Nick felt uneasy. If they set up the camp somewhere else, their observations of village life would be limited. To be out of the mainstream of activity would be a fundamental error in scientific procedure. But she was bothered by the insistence of the village leaders.

"An associate of ours came here a few days ago," she said to Yali. "Walt Duncan. Where is he camping?"

"You are the only outsiders on Balesin," the shaman said.

"He flew in just as we did," she insisted. "You must have seen his airplane."

Yali shook his head.

Buettner started to say something, then bit his lip.

Yali said, "Moving back to the beach would be for your own good."

Nick, scratching the worst of her insect bites, muttered to her father in pig Latin, an old childhood code, "Ixnay, adday. Etslay evelay."

Yali and the chief exchanged looks but said nothing. Instead, all eyes turned toward Lily, who began circling the tents. When she'd completed her tour, she smiled benevolently. "Our guests don't have the advantage of our experience and knowledge. They must do what they think is best."

Yali slapped his thigh and laughed. Soon all the villagers joined in. Once the laughter subsided, Lily said goodbye and led the exodus away from the campsite.

Most disappeared from sight, but Yali, Jeban, and Lily lingered on the porch of one of the communal buildings at the edge of the square. There, they looked to be in animated conversation, though they were too far away to be heard.

"What was that all about?" Elliot turned to Nick. "Why do you want to leave?"

"I think we're in trouble."

"How do you mean?"

She sighed. "The tents."

"They're guaranteed," Buettner said. "The best money can buy. They've been used on Everest. They'll stand up under anything."

"It's colder on Everest," Elliot pointed out.

"They don't want the tents here," Nick persisted.

"Why ever not?" Buettner replied blandly. "Lily said it was okay."

Elliot nodded his agreement. "She may be the real power here, at least in temporal matters."

Nick eyed the four long houses that surrounded the square. All were built on pylons and raised well off the ground, no doubt for good reason. Probably the square flooded during heavy rains. She was about to suggest that they negotiate for more permanent quarters when she noticed Lily and Jeban returning.

"There will be a feast tonight in your honor," Lily announced. "I will come to fetch you when it's time." With that, she and Jeban walked away.

"What do you make of that, Nick?" Elliot asked.

"I've got better things to worry about." Frantically, she began swatting at the ever-increasing mosquitoes.

"Did you see the way the chief was looking at you?" Elliot wiggled an eyebrow. "My guess is, he's looking for another wife."

"Forget me. What about Walt Duncan?"

"Knowing Walt," Buettner assured her, "he'll keep out of the way until he's ready to spring some discovery on us."

Elliot shook his head. "Maybe. I just hope he didn't get himself lost somewhere."

"Will you two shut up for a minute," Nick said, squirming, "and help me find some bug spray."

11

Lee Coltrane leveled off at five-thousand feet, verified his position with the satellite tracking system, and set the autopilot. Once satisfied with the Widgeon's feel, he settled back and tried to relax. But Nick kept getting in the way. Usually women like her turned him off. He found their self-sufficiency and intelligence intimidating. She had a Ph.D., for Christ's sake. So what would she want with a bum like him?

And he was a bum, no getting around it. He'd knocked about all over the world and never managed to settle down. Now he made a pretty good living, but there wasn't much between him and destitution if something went wrong with the Widgeon that he couldn't fix himself. What was he thinking? He had nothing to offer her. Besides, all she was interested in was the Widgeon. He'd have a better chance with her if he grew wings and a propeller.

Coltrane shook his head. To think that he'd meet a

woman like her in a godforsaken place like Balesin. All
it had to offer was heat, bugs, and those damn crabs.
And now Nick Scott.

Most women would run screaming from such a
place, at least the ones he knew. But Nick was another
species altogether. If any woman could cope, she'd be the
one. Probably she was tougher than he was. Still,
wouldn't it be nice if she needed rescuing, so he could
come flying over the waves like an airborne knight. He
laughed at himself. The best he could probably do was
find her lost luggage.

He allowed himself a small daydream. Developers
had been sniffing around Balesin so said the bush pilots'
telegraph. In his mind's eye a thirty-story Hyatt rose up
on the Island's beach. The tourist trade was good for the
charter business and in his daydream he was rich.
Balesin's awful weather was magically transformed into
balmy trade winds. And amidst the tourist throngs there
was Nick dressed in some kind of sarong thing draped
around her body, welcoming him home after a hard day's
flight.

He laughed so hard he nearly disengaged the autopilot. He caught his reflection in the Plexiglas side window.

"Look at you." He winked to himself. "Stick to flying and don't get your underwear in an uproar." But he
couldn't help wondering if things could have been different. All those choices he'd made over the years. He'd
never been sorry until now.

Grimacing, he verified his position and course once
again, then switched radio frequencies to check the
weather. A major storm was building to the northwest,
but still a long way off. The drizzle shrouding Balesin was
localized to the small land mass and normal for this time

of year. Guam was overcast though, which might make a night landing touchy. He searched the horizon, looking for any sign of the incoming storm. Ahead of him there was nothing but blue sky and a bluer ocean. No doubt the weather forecast was wrong as usual. At the moment a cloud would be welcome, anything to break the monotony.

Come on, he told himself, relax and stop feeling sorry for yourself.

Usually, he didn't mind flying alone, especially when the fuel was already bought and paid for by someone else. But today he felt lonely. That was the trouble with female company. Give a man a taste and he wanted more, particularly when it came to a good-looking redhead like Nick.

Coltrane checked his watch. Guam was still a long way off. To pass the time, he fiddled with the radio, searching for an active frequency. Even commercial airliner traffic would be better than nothing. As a last resort, he could always tune to one of Guam's radio stations, though the strongest signal over this part of the ocean was country and western, not his favorite.

A burst of static crackled in his earphones. He adjusted the dial, fine-tuning.

"Another scientist," someone said. "Over." The voice sounded distorted and grating like the screech of chalk on a blackboard.

"Understood. Over."

"What additional action do you want taken?" the voice croaked. "Over."

Coltrane tensed. The only scientists he knew were the ones he'd flown into Balesin, though that was no proof that this transmission had anything to do with them. But the signal was strong. Either it was coming from somewhere as close as Balesin, or atmospherics were playing tricks.

"Take no action. Watch only. Over."

"Understood. Over."

"There will be no further discussion on an open channel. Out."

Coltrane didn't like the sound of that. He switched to the frequency that he and Buettner had agreed upon. "Balesin, this is Coltrane. Over."

There was no response.

"Come in Balesin. This is Coltrane. Over."

Maybe they'd hadn't set up their long-range radio yet. And even if they had, they certainly wouldn't be monitoring it on a full-time basis. Buettner had promised to make contact tomorrow morning.

Coltrane took a deep breath and advanced the throttle, pushing the Widgeon. Probably he was being an old lady. Probably the transmission had nothing to do with Nick and her father, or Buettner either for that matter. But he'd sure as hell feel better when he could talk to them. Or see them.

"Listen to yourself. You're thinking like a lovestruck teenager."

But knowing that didn't help any.

12

A downpour had driven Nick into her tent, where she lay huddled with a towel over her head to fend off the mosquitoes. Their hum, thank God, was drowned out by the rain drumming on the fabric roof. But their blood-thirsty persistence was downright Transylvanian. This was worse than anything she'd experienced in New Guinea.

"We're going to try the radio," Elliot announced from just outside her zippered flap.

"I have nothing to say," she shouted back. What she needed was sleep and a pizza. And maybe a flamethrower to use against the bugs.

"The rain's slowing up."

"Call me when it's dry."

"You might as well come out, Nick. The sun's going down and we're expected for dinner in a few minutes."

"We're probably the main course," she said, going along with Coltrane's litany. The real truth was, the bugs had half-eaten her already. But her stomach was beyond caring. It wanted to be fed, or put out of its misery.

"You win." She emerged with the towel still wrapped around her head, with only a peephole.

One look at her father and she said, "My God, your face is swollen."

"You think that's bad. Look at my hands." He displayed fingers that reminded her of link sausage.

"What about me?" She whipped open her towel.

Elliot whistled. "A regular Graf Zeppelin."

Nick was about to cover up again when she realized that the outside air, suddenly rain-free, was relatively clear of insects for the moment. At least, what bugs there were seemed lethargic. One thing was for sure, the heat was worse than before, and so was the humidity. But a steam bath was better than being bled dry by vampire mosquitoes. Or maybe they were resting long enough to digest their earlier transfusions.

"Come on," Elliot said. "You're the airplane expert. Curt's having trouble contacting Guam."

"He told Coltrane he'd contact him tomorrow."

"That doesn't mean he won't be listening."

Rather than argue with her father's faulty logic, she followed him to the radio tent. Its dry, lofty interior was providing hangar facilities for squadrons of flying insects. "You see. I told you these tents were waterproof," Buettner said. His face, too, showed a welter of inflamed bites. "Not a wet bug in the place."

He pumped up a Coleman lantern, then lit it. The fuel hissed under pressure as the filament grew bright. Bugs flocked to the light.

"I'm sorry about the insect spray," Buettner said. "It's useless. I don't know what the hell we're going to do."

Elliot coughed politely. It was a sound Nick knew well. He'd been using it on his students for years, a personal fanfare to let them know he was about to dispense a pearl of wisdom.

"All right, Elliot," Nick said. "You have our full attention."

"Am I missing something?" Buettner said.

"Only that the great man is about to enlighten us," Nick replied.

"While you two have been hiding in your tents or fooling with radios," Elliot said, "I've been working in the field like any respectable archaeologist would do." He wiggled an eyebrow. "My initial research has proved successful. The Baleseans have solved their insect problem."

"What the hell are they using?" Buettner asked.

Elliot pressed his lips together, looking sly.

"Mother hated it when you did that," Nick told him.

"Your mother was good at hating."

Nick sighed. "Just spit it out, Elliot. Cut the dramatics and astound us. Otherwise, I'm going to scratch myself to death."

"If you insist, daughter. What's this long . . ." He held his forefingers about six inches apart. ". . . has large eyes, belongs to the family Gekkonidae, and can eat its weight in insects?"

"Geckos," Nick answered, annoyed with herself for not having thought of it before.

Buettner banged his forehead. "What a dummy. I should have thought of lizards in the rafters. Nature's own pest control."

"We're still in trouble," Nick pointed out. "I don't think geckos like clinging to the sides of nylon tents."

"So we negotiate for a house," Elliot said. "Like we should have done in the first place."

"I seem to remember suggesting something along those lines earlier," she answered, with a sly grin she hoped was as annoying as her father's.

Buettner snapped his fingers. "We offer them more cargo."

"Such as?" Nick asked.

Buettner produced a crafty look every bit the equal of her father's. "I filled one of our cases with goodies. I thought we might want to indulge ourselves after the flight, but escaping these bugs is more important."

"What kind of goodies?" Elliot asked.

"Candy bars and ice cream packed in dry ice."

"How about a sample?" Nick said. "I'm starving."

"You know the rules," Elliot said, handing her a bottle of Pepto-Bismol.

"That's not what I had in mind," she said, but downed a couple of mouthfuls just the same. A stomach coating was always a good idea when in the field and about to partake of the local diet. She'd repeat the dosage before going to bed.

"Before you two get drunk on that," Buettner said, "I want some help with this damned radio. I'd like to order a different brand of pesticide."

"I don't know anything about radios," Nick said.

"Airplanes have radios, don't they?" Buettner responded. "And they're your field, Nick."

She sighed. "Give me the checklist."

Buettner handed it over. As far as Nick could see, Buettner had assembled it correctly. There were no loose connections, and the frequency setting matched the one Coltrane had written on the tab next to the dial.

Nick toggled the on-off switch. Nothing happened.

"Maybe it got wet coming ashore," she said.

"It was sealed in a watertight container," Buettner reminded her.

"You heard what Coltrane said. This climate is death on batteries."

"I've just changed them to be on the safe side," Buettner answered.

"Maybe someone dropped the radio on the way from the beach," Elliot said.

"No way. I had this baby in my sights the whole time."

"Did you test it before we came?" Nick asked.

"Give me some credit, Nick. I have been in the field before."

"We could try military tactics on it." She grinned. "Immediate action, they call it."

"Go ahead."

Nick banged her fist on the top of the radio's metal casing. The speaker hissed in response. "There must be a loose connection."

"Don't jiggle it, then," Buettner said and immediately tried contacting Coltrane, but without success.

"What happens if he doesn't hear from us?" Nick asked.

"No big deal, really," Buettner said. "He's scheduled to fly in my grad students and their supplies whether we contact him or not. We'll try again in the morning when he's expecting us to call."

He switched frequencies and contacted the airport at Guam. Despite a weak signal, he was able to leave a message for Coltrane as a precaution in case the connection came loose again.

The moment he signed off, Buettner said, "We'll fire up the generator tomorrow and run this baby on direct current. That ought to boost the signal."

"I think I'd rather have a refrigerator than a radio," Nick said.

Elliot chuckled. "Curt and I considered bringing one along, but we ruled it out because the generator would have to be kept running night and day. That would take a lot of fuel and the noise wouldn't make us any too welcome around here either."

"There's a store on the island," Buettner said. "They have a refrigerator. It's the only place on Balesin you can get a cold beer, though they charge an arm and a leg."

"You shouldn't be saying things like that," a voice said from the darkness outside the tent. "It could be misleading."

Buettner twitched. Elliot caught his breath. And Nick said, "Is that you, Lily?"

Without answering, Lily stepped out of the darkness and into the lantern's circle of light. She was wearing a flowered muumuu that could have come from the pages of a travel brochure. She looked cool, totally at ease, and immune to the ever-swarming insects.

"It was only a figure of speech," Nick explained.

"Stories from the old days cling to us like chains," Lily said. "First the English explorers came, then the Spanish and the Portuguese. They all stole from us. They took what they wanted, even women and children. When we fought back, they made up lies to justify killing us. We were savages, they said. We were cannibals."

Nick reached out, but stopped herself short of contact for fear of breaching etiquette. "I'm sorry, Lily. We're here to study your people. We will take nothing away with us but knowledge."

"I understand your intentions, but there are others who won't."

She took Nick's hand. "There was a time when Henry Yali claimed descent from Captain Henry Wilson, the English explorer who came to these islands in 1783. Henry was named for him, or so he was told as a boy. But then John Frum came, and Henry no longer spoke of such things."

"Are you saying that John Frum actually came here to Balesin in person?" Elliot asked.

"It's a tale Henry loves telling."

"What do *you* say, Lily?" Nick probed gently.

The woman smiled. "The food is waiting and I've been sent to show you the way."

"I'll just get the cargo, then." Buettner grabbed one of the sealed containers stacked inside the tent.

Lily looked dubious.

"We're bringing dessert," Nick explained.

"And the others?" Lily indicated the half-dozen cases stacked inside the tent. "This isn't a safe place to keep food."

"Everything's sealed," Buettner said. "And damn near indestructible." He kicked one of the plastic chests to prove his point.

"Have you ever tried to open a coconut?"

Buettner shook his head.

"We have coconut crabs who find it no trouble at all. I think they'll make quick work of your containers."

"What do you suggest, then?" Nick asked.

"Leave your lantern lit at night. Crabs usually stick to the shadows."

"How big are they?" Nick said.

Lily spread her arms to their limit.

"Swell," Elliot said. "That's all we need, creepy crawlers in the night."

Nick laughed, though she didn't like the thought of encountering anything that big in the dark, or broad daylight either, for that matter. If the local crustaceans could crack open coconuts, her desert boots would offer no resistance at all.

Nick glanced at Lily's feet. The woman might as well have been barefoot for all the protection her rubber sandals afforded.

Lily smiled as if reading Nick's thoughts. "Don't worry, child. Our crabs don't eat people, not as long as they're still moving anyway. Now come. We mustn't keep Henry Yali waiting."

They took Lily's advice and left a blazing lantern behind in the tent. Outside, the village was dark except for torches burning in front of one of the communal houses. Homing on the torchlight was easy enough, though the dancing shadows cast by the flames had Nick seeing scuttling crabs everywhere.

13

The last rays of the setting sun embraced the Tang horse and threw its subtle modeling into high relief. Kobayashi wished he could lose himself in the deep amber glaze that glowed so warmly on the pottery figure's surface. He shook himself and sighed with regret. It was now dark and the horse stood in shadow. He could barely see it.

Kobayashi lifted his hand to turn on the light and then stopped. This kind of thing was best done in the dark. Besides, he didn't need to see to activate the radio, so he waited in the dark for the agent to report. No doubt Farrington had already made similar contact.

He already regretted letting Farrington choose the man. Still, if anything should go wrong, it might be better if an American were involved. Favors were owed on both sides and debts ensured silence.

At the prearranged time, Kobayashi received the signal.

"Are you in place?" he asked.

He got an affirmative reply.

"Have you made contact with my agent in place?"

"No."

Kobayashi waited.

"The beacon was in place and activated," the voice continued. "I had no trouble finding it, but no one showed."

"That is not possible," Kobayashi said in spite of himself, regretting immediately that he had allowed himself to be caught off guard. Of course it was possible. His own sleeper had been put in place many years ago and it was known that a small percentage of sleeper agents simply integrated into their new lives and were never heard from again.

"Keep to your mission," Kobyashi warned. "Observe and report."

"It's my ass on the line and it's your man that didn't show."

Kobyashi frowned in displeasure. That was the trouble with Americans, they were crude. "You must be patient. The beacon was activated. Perhaps he was called away."

"Fuck that," came the harsh reply. "I'm not going to hang around here any longer. I can do this job on my own, but if I ever run into this asshole, his ass is grass. You understand?"

"I understand very well," Kobyashi replied smoothly. "I believe that the agreement was that I would provide extraction, was it not? However, it is a small matter. No doubt Mr. Farrington will make the extraction effort and not mind."

"The guy better have a good excuse," came the muted reply. The tone was still aggressive, but Kobyashi knew that his point had been taken.

He broke the connection without a further word. Let the man worry. It was important to show Americans who was in control. It was part of their culture.

14

Nick and Lily led the way. At Lily's insistence, they stopped in front of the communal house and waited for Henry Yali and Chief Jeban to come down the steps to greet them. Both men bowed formally. Nick answered in kind, as did Buettner and her father. But Lily stood aloof, as if watching over the ceremony like a chief of protocol. Around them insects swarmed and hummed. Occasionally, one sizzled when it got too close to the flaming torches.

"We have special treats all the way from America," Buettner announced, holding out the plastic chest at arm's length.

Which wasn't quite true, Nick thought, since America implied the mainland, not just Guam, or even Hawaii.

Yali and Jeban bowed again, but neither made a move to accept the gift or show the party inside. Only when Lily nodded her approval did Yali say, "We are in your debt."

"Iced dessert," Buettner clarified as he opened the lid, displaying an extensive array of Popsicles, Snickers, Milky Ways, and Hershey bars. Nick's mouth watered even as the last piece of dry ice melted into vapor as the hot air hit it.

Yali caught his breath, obviously in awe. Jeban's jaw dropped open.

Yali's hand reached into the vapor. "There is a store on the far side of our island." He pointed inland. "They have ice but nothing like this. There is no other full-time refrigeration on Balesin."

"They have a generator," Jeban explained.

"We brought one, too," Buettner told him. "It's very small, though, and good only for our radio."

Jeban nodded. "The church has such a one, but for lights only."

"Your church?" Nick asked.

"The Reverend Innis's church. It's on the other side of the island next to the store," Yali answered. "Not John Frum's church."

Buettner changed the subject. "I hope we've enough dessert for everyone."

"How can we repay such a debt?" Yali said.

Buettner started to reply but Lily spoke first. "Now is not the time for business, Henry. Our guests are hungry. Later we can talk."

"Of course," the priest said immediately.

He and Jeban stood to one side so that Lily could lead the way up the steps, through mosquito netting, and inside the communal hall. At first glance, Nick thought there was only a single large meeting room. But when her eyes adjusted to the flickering lantern light, she realized that one end of the room was divided off by a curtain of hanging bamboo that had been cut into sections and strung together like wind chimes. The area beyond served as a kitchen and was populated by women and children.

The main room was filled with tables from one end to the other, like a mess hall. Only the head table remained empty; the others were already crammed with adult villagers, both men and women.

Nick blinked against the sweat flooding into her stinging eyes. As hot as it was outside, inside was worse. The steamy aroma from the kitchen area was both mouth-watering and sauna-like. But, she realized suddenly, there were no insects inside the hall.

Nick glanced at her father. For once even Elliot seemed overwhelmed by the heat. His hair lay plastered against his scalp; his shirt stuck to him.

It's mind over matter, she mouthed at him silently, reminding him of his own advice whenever she complained on one of their digs. *Think cool.*

He held up a finger to indicate she'd scored a point. His crooked smile said the next would be his.

It would be, too, because basically his advice was sound enough. Heat didn't matter, or cold either when it came down to it. Because no matter what, field trips were an archaeologist's lifeblood. Without them, without the breakthroughs and scientific discoveries they provided, archaeology would be nothing but classroom theory.

So do your job, Nick reminded herself. Observe, learn, and next time bring a sweatband. And remember, even a steam bath like this is better than being eaten alive by bloodsucking bugs.

She wiped her eyes with a tissue and began by studying the interior architecture. The vaulted ceiling caught her attention. The thatch, held in place by rafters made of unmilled tree limbs, had been blackened over the years, probably from torches when lanterns hadn't been available.

Squinting at the thatch, she looked for movement, for any sign of geckos. But maybe they couldn't cope with the soot, or the heat either, for that matter. Scratch that, she thought. Most likely, the geckos' survival was strictly a matter of insects. If the mosquito netting was effective, the geckos would find someplace else to live. Or else there were bigger bugs to keep them busy in the thatch.

Nick sighed, her mind again dwelling on the stifling atmosphere. If she were a gecko, she'd sure as hell find someplace else to call home.

She was still looking for signs of thatch life when Lily grasped her elbow and guided her across the hand-hewn plank flooring to the head table. There, after another bow from Yali, the plastic cooler changed hands and was placed in the center of the table.

Longing for comfortable clothing like Lily's, Nick rolled up her sweat-sodden shirtsleeves. A cold drink would have been a godsend, something with ice, anything with ice. But even the dry ice was gone from the cooler, vaporized by the consuming heat. Soon the candy bars would melt into goo. At the moment, Nick felt as if she, too, was about to dissolve into a shapeless puddle.

Risking a breach in protocol, she whispered in Lily's ear. "I think the dessert should be served before it melts."

Lily passed on the whispered advice to Yali, who immediately signaled the kitchen. Children came running through the bamboo curtains, ringing them like chimes, and began passing out the dessert to everyone in the meeting hall.

While that was being done, Lily seated everyone along a pew-like bench. Nick found herself sandwiched between Lily and Yali, while her father and Curt Buettner sat on either side of Jim Jeban.

By now, Nick felt totally spent. It was all she could do to sit upright and not collapse headfirst onto the table. When she closed her eyes, visions of frosty drinks overwhelmed her. By force of will, she shook off the mirage and raised her eyelids in time to see Lily's granddaughter placing a Snickers bar on the table in front of her. Lily had a Snickers, too, as did everyone else at the table.

"Thank you, Josephine," Lily said to the girl, who immediately hung her head shyly. "You remember Nick, don't you? Say hello."

"Hello," the girl whispered without looking up.

"Her mother says Josephine takes after me," Lily said.

"I can see the resemblance," Nick replied.

The girl risked a peek at Nick, then scampered off into the kitchen.

"I think Josephine was trying to tell you something," Lily said. "I agree with her. I know the look. You'll feel better once you've eaten."

Nick eyed the Snickers bar. She needed something, that was certain. Her last decent meal had been in Berkeley. But the thought of a sticky, limp candy bar didn't appeal to her. She nudged it gingerly and made a face.

Lily laughed, tore open the wrapper on her own Snickers bar, and took a bite as if setting an example. As she chewed, her head nodded constantly. Finally, Lily swallowed and said, "You and your friends made a big hit tonight with your gift. We don't often get such treats. When we do, we can't afford to let them spoil."

Nick got the hint. To let the Snickers lie there would be a breach of manners. On the other hand, maybe Lily might welcome a second helping. But offering it to her, instead of Nick eating it herself, might also be impolite. It could also be misconstrued. And the last thing Nick wanted was to imply that the candy wasn't safe to eat.

She took a bite. She'd never been a Snickers fan. But this time the taste astonished her. It was pure ambrosia. Or maybe it was hunger that made the candy taste so good. Whatever the case, she didn't care; she just chewed.

By the time the bar was gone, pitchers brimming with native beer arrived. When everyone had been served, Henry Yali stood and proposed a toast. "To our new friends. Thank you for the gifts you've bestowed upon us." He paused. "And to John Frum who sent them, as He sends us all things."

Lily leaned close. "You don't have to worry about Henry. He's a good Christian too."

Nick nodded and took a sip. The taste was familiar but unlike any beer she'd tried before.

"It's called *Tuba*," Lily said. "It's made from coconut sap and very cooling."

Nick emptied her cup and felt immediately refreshed.

"Don't be fooled by the taste. It's got quite a kick." Grinning, Lily refilled Nick's cup.

"There's a price to be paid," Yali told Nick abruptly.

"I'll be careful," she said, thinking he'd been referring to the *Tuba*.

He dismissed her comment with a wave of his hand. "Gifts come with obligations. I understand that, but some of John Frum's subjects may not be so enlightened as I am."

Nick glanced at Lily, hoping for a word or even a look that might guide her response. But Lily only smiled.

"There are no strings attached to our gift," Nick said finally. "We want only to learn your ways."

Yali shook his head. "There's always a price. You may see it as nothing, but to us the cost might be more than we dare pay. For all we know, you may have come here to steal away our beliefs."

Buettner spoke up. "We know there have been visitors here before. Have they stolen from you?"

"Tourists, you mean?" Yali pursed his lips. "To them, we aren't real. They think we are only actors. So we oblige them and create the kind of life they wish to see. That way, whatever they steal is unimportant to us."

Smiling, Yali spread his hands, a gesture of innocence. But the shrewd look in his eyes started alarm bells clanging in Nick's head. Many an anthropologist had been suckered by so-called primitive peoples who told sophisticated lies rather than reveal their real way of life. One anthropologist had actually been convinced that an entire Pacific Island culture was based on the acquisition of yams. So it was quite possible that Henry Yali and his followers would spin similar yarns to protect their most sacred beliefs.

Elliot caught Nick's eye. She sensed immediately that the same doubts were going through his mind. He raised an eyebrow, cueing her that he intended to put his doubts to the test.

But Buettner spoke first. "Would you be happier if a price were set here and now? That we pay you for your honest help?"

"We are in your debt now and that must be honored first."

Ask for a house, Nick thought. A house filled with geckos.

"I've heard stories," Buettner began, "that your people originally came here from across the sea, that the currents swept them all the way across the Pacific from America."

Oh, no, not his Anasazi theory again, not now, not with the prospect of going back to those damned tents.

Yali's eyes went wide with amazement.

"Modern men have ridden those currents," Buettner persisted. "They've proved that such a journey can be made across the sea."

"Such men haven't come here," Yali answered.

"What about red-feather money, then," Buettner went on. "Early Americans used woodpecker scalps. That's a bird with red feathers."

"We use American money now," Yali replied.

"All I want is to learn how your people found their way to Balesin," Buettner said.

"Memory doesn't go back that far."

"But legends do."

"And that is the payment you want?"

Buettner nodded.

Nick gnashed her teeth and murmured, "A house."

Yali stared at her for a moment, then tilted his head to one side as if mulling things over. Finally, he stood, smiled broadly, and signaled the kitchen. "We offer you our native food in exchange for your American delicacies."

By the time he sat down again, platters of food were on their way. To Nick, the food looked vaguely Chinese. She recognized fish on a bed of rice, a noodle and fish casserole spiced with onions and shredded coconut, and what she guessed to be baked taro root. There were also side dishes of fried breadfruit and bananas, plus a number of items she couldn't identify at all. Like all small island cultures, the main staple would be fish, or anything else that could be harvested from the sea.

Nick thanked God for Pepto-Bismol, threw caution to the wind, and heaped her plate with everything in sight. As she dug in, Elliot turned to Yali and said, "If you treat us like tourists, our work here will be useless. Tourists seek their own enjoyment. We want to know you and your people. We want to record your ways so they will last forever."

"If I came to your country, would I see the truth?" Yali replied. "Would I understand your beliefs?"

"Not if you came as a tourist. But if you lived among us, you might."

Yali laughed. "I understand now. You want to live in one of our houses." He nodded at Nick. "Just as the young lady said."

Nick, who'd just bitten into a piece of meat from one of the rice dishes, stopped chewing.

"Didn't I predict it?" Yali said, his voice rising so that everyone in the room could hear. "Didn't I say that they wouldn't be able to cope on their own?"

Around the room, heads nodded.

"We will pay for the privilege, of course," Buettner said, snubbing the shaman by turning to the chief.

"With what?" Jeban asked.

Nick held her breath. It wasn't her money, but she

sure as hell hoped Buettner wanted out of the tents as badly as she did.

"We could fly in more cargo," Buettner said.

The chief's eyes lit up.

Lily interrupted sharply. "Now is not the time or the place. We do not discuss such things at dinner. A meeting must be called first."

The chief bowed his head and Yali glowered but said nothing.

Judging by the men's deference, that right belonged to Lily. Or maybe to all the women, though Nick suspected that Lily held the true power as the island's matriarch. Just where the dividing line was between Yali's domain and Lily's remained to be seen.

Nick speared another chunk of meat, which she'd yet to identify, and chewed thoughtfully. If only Lily's meeting could be held tonight, then the tents could be abandoned without delay. But Nick knew better than to push the matter. That wouldn't be polite, and the last thing she wanted to do was anger Lily.

Sighing deeply, she popped another piece of mystery meat into her mouth.

"Is the food to your liking?" Lily asked.

"Delicious," Nick assured her. "What is it?"

"We serve it only on special occasions. It's Spam. You must know it. It comes all the way from your country."

Nick forced a swallow. It was either that or gag. Spam brought back memories of her mother's infrequent forays into the kitchen, several of which had ended in food poisoning. True enough, the Balesin version didn't taste like Spam, not the way Elaine had served it, straight and unadorned from the can. But the thought of it was enough to turn Nick's stomach.

"Spam, you say," Elliot said, coming to Nick's rescue. "One of my absolute favorites. Hand over that plate, daughter, so I can finish your share."

Gratefully, Nick exchanged plates with her father.

Watching the transfer, Lily smiled at Nick. "You didn't have to eat it, you know. We wouldn't have been insulted."

"You see everything, don't you?" Nick said.

"I can see that you're different from the others who've come here."

"Have many tourists come to Balesin?"

"Not many," Lily conceded. "Not yet anyway, but someday it may be different. There has been talk of building a hotel on our island."

Nick blinked in surprise.

"It's one of Henry's ideas. One of his dreams. If it comes to pass, he says, it will be John Frum's way of making us rich like Americans."

At the mention of his name, Yali leaned closer, but that didn't stop Lily from talking about him. "Henry says we can turn Balesin into . . ." She paused and looked shyly at Yali. ". . . a 'getaway from winter.' I think he read that in a magazine somewhere. Bringing Americans to Balesin has always been his plan."

"If we're rich enough, we can buy all the cargo we need," Yali interjected. "Then John Frum will come from America and stay forever."

"Will he come in an airplane?" Nick asked.

"Of course, just like before." He seemed surprised at her evident stupidity.

Nick took a deep breath. She wanted to pursue the subject of airplanes, but hesitated. If housing was taboo during meals, what else might be off-limits? And just how far did Lily's veto power extend?

"Airplanes are my love," Nick said. "I built models when I was a child."

Yali's eyes narrowed. "To fly in?"

Nick had wanted to fly away in them, to escape her mother's dark moods. Time and again, she had soared in her imagination.

"No, I only built small models," she said, indicating the wingspan with her hands.

Yali nodded. "They weren't real, then?"

"No, not as real as yours."

"What do you know of our planes?" Yali's tone alerted Nick to go slowly.

"Books have been written about such planes," she told him. "They are seen throughout the Pacific."

Yali nodded. "There are those who try to delude John Frum. But He will not be fooled."

"I'd like to see your airplanes," Nick ventured.

Yali stood up. "They are not mine. They are John Frum's." Abruptly, he left the table and disappeared through the bamboo curtain.

Nick turned to Lily. "Did I say something wrong?"

"No one understands Henry all the time, but I think he went to get some airplanes for you."

Nick rubbed her eyes, causing them to sting all the more.

"Take my advice, dear, and have another cup of *Tuba* and wait and see." Lily laid a hand on Nick's arm. "Everything's been arranged."

As if on cue, conversation began to ebb until the hall fell silent. Around the room people started stamping their feet in a steady, regular cadence. At a nod from Lily, Nick joined in, remembering how as a child she'd stomped her feet at the movies, waiting for the feature to begin.

Behind them the bamboo curtain rattled. Nick swung around to see children parading into the meeting room, led by Josephine. They moved in unison, boys and girls alike, in step to the beat of the stomping feet. It was half march, half dance, and almost certainly ritualistic.

As one, the children thrust their right arms into the air. Their upraised hands held model airplanes. The models were crude, carved of wood with no painted features. But they all had two engines like the mock-ups on the landing strips that Nick had seen from the air. The placement of the wings, high on the fuselage, reminded Nick of the Widgeon. But there was no sign of pontoons. Then again, there weren't any wheels either.

Nick clenched her teeth in frustration. They should have brought video cameras to record the ceremony. She leaned around Lily, tapped her father's shoulder, and mimed the act of taking pictures.

He shook his head at her, a reminder that using a camera was always a risk. Its presence could inhibit one person while bringing out the show-off in another. Or it could cause sacred ritual to be edited on the spot. Or worse yet, there was always the chance of violating some key taboo.

As if on cue, the children spread throughout the room, though Josephine remained near the head table. At her lead, the dancers stopped where they were and began turning in slow circles.

Suddenly, the beat stopped. Left-handed, the children tossed small bundles into the air, all the way to the rafters. There, the bundles blossomed into small parachutes, which floated down carrying cargo. Josephine's bundle landed on the table near Nick. The cargo was a small reed container, no more than an inch square.

Were the children recreating today's cargo drop

from the Widgeon? she wondered. Or was this a longer-standing ritual? If so, how far back did it go? World War Two seemed the most likely answer, though to know for sure, Nick would have to identify the type of airplane being used.

Applause broke out. At the sound of it, the children scurried to retrieve their parachuted cargo and then retreated behind the bamboo. Only Josephine left hers where it was, in front of Nick.

"It's her gift to you," Lily explained.

The reed container rattled.

"Open it," Lily said.

Nick looked inside the tiny box. She wasn't certain what she was looking at. For a moment she thought the box held nothing but a small, round green stone, then realized the stone was actually corroded metal, about a quarter of an inch wide with fragments of material adhering to it. The material was brittle and slightly curled, possibly leather. If so, the green metal could be an eyelet of some kind.

She turned and looked at Lily, who seemed surprised. "My grandchild has given you her most prized possession," Lily said. "She believes you are the forerunner. Perhaps she is right."

She closed Nick's hand over the box. "You must guard it with your life. It has great power."

Nick caught Yali staring at her. The look on his face startled her. It seemed both sly and covetous at the same time. What was so important about the tiny piece of metal? Certainly metal was hard to come by in the islands. Perhaps that was why Yali so obviously prized it.

Next to her, Lily laughed.

15

He knew it was time. He could feel the aircraft carrier pitch as she turned into the wind. He felt sorry for the poor bastards in the sixteen B-25 bombers cramming the flight deck. Eight hundred miles in weather like this and not enough fuel to make it back, even if the *Hornet* could stick around. He shook his head. At the same time he envied them. They were going to show the Japanese Empire that it was as vulnerable as the United States had been at Pearl Harbor.

The loudspeakers came to life. "Air crews, man your planes."

The colonel was already at the fuselage door of the last plane in line when he arrived. The colonel was talking to an angry-looking pilot.

"This is Captain Robert Johns, your new navigator," the colonel said, introducing him to the pilot.

He offered his hand.

"What happened to Lawrence?" the pilot snapped.

"Bob, this is Captain Watson," the colonel continued smoothly, ignoring the question.

Watson gave Johns an appraising look, then shook his hand. "What happened to Lawrence?" he repeated. Johns liked the pilot's persistence. It showed that he cared about his crew.

"Don't waste time asking questions." The colonel

held out his credentials: U.S. Army Counterintelligence Corps. "Captain Johns will brief you once you're on your way." He handed Watson an envelope. "Here are your orders. From this moment on, you are to take your instructions from Captain Johns. Is that clear?"

Johns could see that the pilot wasn't happy and he regretted that the colonel had been so officious. It was important that the crew work smoothly together. He would now have to overcome their resentment.

At the head of the flight deck, one of the B-25s started its engines.

The colonel shouted over the howl of the Wright Cyclone engines. "You're out of time."

With a look of pure frustration the pilot turned and lifted himself into the plane. Johns followed him to the cockpit.

Watson gave him a questioning glance before scanning the orders. Johns knew that they had been signed by Colonel Jimmy Doolittle himself.

"What's going on?" the copilot asked.

"I'm Johns, the new navigator."

"Lou Pappas." The pilot motioned to the copilot. "Read this," he said and gave Pappas the papers.

"Holy cow!" Pappas whistled. "So that's why we're carrying extra gasoline instead of bombs."

While Pappas continued to read, Watson slid open the Plexiglas window by his side. The damp, cold air from the forty-knot gale howling outside the cockpit sent a chill through Johns.

"It's bad luck to break up a crew," the pilot said. "Don't tell me this storm isn't bad luck."

"I think we make our own luck," Johns replied.

Pappas started to say something, but Watson silenced him. "You'd better get into position," he told Johns. "It's time to go."

Johns climbed back into the navigator's seat and waited.

When their turn came, the B-25 lifted off easily. They had chosen a good pilot for him, Johns thought. According to specs, a fully loaded B-25 needed a long runway. They had had to make do with a little more than five hundred feet. Johns had felt no loss of altitude as they had cleared the deck, though he'd seen some of the planes dipping close to the sea before managing to climb away.

As soon as the B-25 was trimmed, he grabbed the intercom mike. What he had to say was going to make the skipper even more unhappy. "Permission to come forward," he said, and didn't wait for a reply.

16

By morning Nick felt mildewed, and she was afraid she smelled worse. Everything inside her tent was damp. The humidity had puckered her skin, especially her fingers, which looked as if they'd been washing dishes nonstop for days. Her face and neck itched from bug bites, and the rest of her didn't feel much better.

To make matters worse, she heard sloshing footsteps approaching the outside of her tent. From the sound of them, the mud had to be six inches deep.

"Good morning," Buettner announced.

She groaned. How could the man be so damned cheerful so early?

"Come on, Nick," he shouted. "Get up. The sun's out. It's a beautiful day, and it's time for sunrise services."

Unzipping her tent, she peered outside. The night rain had turned their campsite into a quagmire. Mud was steaming in the sunlight. But that was only secondary to the sight in front of her. Just as Buettner had said, services were being held in the village square. A platoon of village men, carrying sticks of bamboo-like rifles, were marching in military precision. They were led by Chief Jeban, who brought them to a stop in front of the flagpole that Nick had seen from the air. Each man in the ranks had the letters USA painted on their chests in red.

"Present arms," Jeban ordered, sounding like a drill sergeant.

The bamboo rifles snapped into position.

"Flag orderlies step forward," Jeban barked.

Two men broke ranks, one of them carrying what looked like a folded flag, and quick-timed to the flagpole.

"What do you think?" Buettner asked quietly. "They had to copy that from the military, if I'm any judge."

Nick nodded her agreement. "Just like their planes."

Jeban, who wasn't carrying a rifle, saluted as the orderlies raised the American flag.

"The question is," Nick said, "whose military did they copy originally, ours or the Japanese? The 'USA' on their chests could be grafted onto an earlier tradition."

Buettner snorted. "My guess is, they were raising the rising sun during the occupation."

"Possibly," Nick replied, "but they probably weren't getting much cargo from the Japanese."

Once the flag was tied into position, the platoon

marched away, disappearing behind one of the communal buildings. Such ceremonies weren't unique to Balesin, Nick knew from scanning Sam Ohmura's book.

With a groan, she struggled out of her sleeping bag and pulled on her jeans. But when she tried to slip into her suede desert boots, it was a painful tug-of-war. Her feet had swollen during the night. Making matters worse, the suede was still damp and smelled like wet animal fur.

"My feet are like balloons. I need some sandals like the villagers wear," she announced, though God knew what the mosquitoes would do to her naked toes.

"Tell me about it," Buettner shot back. "They don't need human cannibals here. It's the bugs that eat you alive."

Once Nick had her boots on, she crawled outside, getting muddy in the process. On top of everything else, the sun was blinding, and so were the attacking mosquitoes.

"You should have warned me about the place," she said, longing for Berkeley's fog.

"It was dry the first time your father and I landed here." Buettner ducked his head. "But you're right. I seem to have miscalculated our needs."

Nick pointed a condemning finger at the communal meeting houses across the square. "Don't you notice something, Curt. Those houses are built on stilts. Why would that be, do you think? Maybe because this whole area is a swamp, except around the flagpole."

"Maybe it won't rain again."

Nick shook her head. "That's wishful thinking and you know it. We've got to get off the ground. To do that, we need a house of our own."

"You heard what Lily said last night. They have to

hold a town meeting first before committing to something like that."

"Are you listening to me, Curt? I say we buy ourselves a house if we have to. Otherwise, we're going to be too miserable to get any decent work done."

"Nick, I—" He broke off to scratch his scalp.

She dug out her soggy Cubs cap, pulled it on, and adjusted the brim to get the sun out of her eyes. For the first time that morning she got a good look at Buettner. Lines etched his swollen face. Gray stubble covered his chin and cheeks. Yesterday his eyes had burned with youthful enthusiasm; today he reminded Nick of an old dog with cataracts.

"Don't listen to me," she said, relenting. "I'm always grumpy first thing in the morning."

"What you both need is a bath," Elliot said as he came up behind them unnoticed.

Nick blinked in disbelief. Somehow her father looked as cool and refreshed as always. His khaki shorts had a crease and his open sandals looked new. He appeared to be totally unconcerned about the swarming mosquitoes. With him was Chief Jim Jeban, who was also wearing the ubiquitous sandals of Balesin. When Elliot saw Nick admiring his sandals, he winked, wiggled his toes, and sighed contentedly.

Nick glared.

Buettner said, "Where the hell have you been, Elliot?"

Instead of answering, Elliot resorted to one of his enigmatic smiles, which momentarily infuriated Nick. Then she caught herself. Fury would have been her mother's reaction.

Taking a deep breath, she smiled coyly and said,

"You know the rules, Elliot. The first one up in the morning makes the coffee."

He returned her smile with a wink. "It's already done."

Another deep breath revealed the subtle aroma of coffee. Only then did she see the propane stove set up outside their supply tent.

"And the bath?" she asked, since they'd yet to fill the canvas holding tanks in their shower tent.

"I've had mine, thanks," Elliot said.

"In the river, I suppose."

Jeban held up a restraining hand. "We wash in the sea, not the Malakal River."

"Sorry." Nick should have known better. Unlike modern man, primitive peoples usually knew better than to pollute their source of drinking water.

"How was the water?" Buettner asked.

"Not a shark in sight," Elliot said.

"It is wise to watch for them," Jeban said, nodding his head. "Usually, they don't come near the mouth of the river. But there are other places . . ." He turned to gaze toward the eastern side of the island. ". . . that are very dangerous and not to be attempted."

"Where exactly?" Nick asked.

Jeban shrugged. "Who's to say with certainty. Sharks swim where they want, but I have seen them often in the channel that separates our island from Balabat. There, men have died. There, the water has run red with blood. It is one of John Frum's forbidden places."

"We'll remember that," Nick said, turning away from the chief to stare daggers at her father. "Now, Elliot, if you don't mind, tell us where you got those sandals."

"They're imported, I'm told, and can be purchased at the store on the other side of the island."

"Are you telling us that you've been there and back already?"

"The chief had an extra pair which he loaned me. In return, I've invited him to join us for coffee."

Once they'd settled around the stove, Elliot had a hard time keeping a straight face. Finally, one of his annoying smiles broke free.

No, strike that, Nick thought. It wasn't a smile exactly, but more of a smirk. It was the kind of look he got when astounding students with his expertise. It was also the kind of look that would have sent Elaine into one of her moods.

Elliot improved on the smirk by adding one of his annoying eyebrow wiggles.

"You're up to something," Nick said.

"Me?" he replied innocently.

She fumed and pretended to concentrate on her coffee. As usual, it was laced with canned milk and sugar, and delicious. It had been a staple of her father's field expeditions for as long as she could remember, and was a treat Nick had come to enjoy. At the moment, though, she wanted to throttle him. No, she thought, throttling would have to wait until she'd had a bath, sharks or no sharks. In the water at least, the mosquitoes wouldn't be able to get at her more tender parts.

"Well, daughter?" Elliot said, breaking the silence. "I haven't lost my touch, have I? Wouldn't you say this coffee is pure ambrosia?"

"All right, Elliot. You win. I surrender. What is it you're dying to tell us?"

"Me?" He poked himself in the chest. "Daughter,

you misjudge me. It's Chief Jeban who has an announce-ment. We're to have a house."

"Thank God," Nick said. "When?"

"It will have to be built," Jeban said. "Of course, a site must be selected, and other such matters taken into careful consideration."

How long would that take? she wondered. A few more nights in that steaming tent and she'd turn into a prune. Or be bled dry by ravenous mosquitoes.

"Naturally, there are rituals to be observed," Elliot said, glancing at the chief. "Suffice it to say, daughter, while you and Curt have been sleeping I've been negoti-ating. Now let's get on the radio. I've promised more cargo in exchange for some quick work on our future abode."

As soon as Buettner entered the tent and began throwing switches, Nick crossed her fingers. Static crack-led from the speaker as her mind raced, calculating the number of things that could go wrong even with a strong radio signal. She'd reached four—sunspots, storms, satel-lite failure, and Coltrane asleep at his end—when Col-trane answered. "I read you five-by-five," he said. "Over."

Nick sagged with relief.

"We need more supplies," Buettner told him.

"Already?" Coltrane answered. "Are you all right?"

"We will be when you get here."

"Has there been trouble?"

"Why do you ask?"

"I picked up a transmission on my flight back yester-day," Coltrane replied. "There was talk about scientists and open channels. I thought it might have come from Balesin."

Buettner looked around. Nick shrugged and so did her father. Jeban didn't react at all.

"There's nothing wrong here," Buettner transmitted, "except we need more cargo. How soon can you load up?"

"I'm airborne already. When I didn't hear from you at first light, I decided to take off."

"And my students, Tracy and Axelrad?"

"They're with me."

Buettner looked at Nick and shook his head. "You're going to have to make another quick trip, then. We're exchanging cargo for some better living quarters."

"What is it you need exactly?" Coltrane asked.

"Hold on a minute." Buettner turned to Jeban for guidance.

"Cargo is always in John Frum's hands," the chief said. "It is He who decides our fate. But Lily has long wished for a generator to light up the night. Her eyes aren't getting any younger, you know, and she finds it difficult to work by lantern light these days." His weak smile said his eyes could use the help too. "And fuel to run the generator would be appreciated also."

Buettner relayed the request.

"That's okay by me," Coltrane replied. "As soon as I drop off your students, I'll return to Guam and see what I can do."

"Frank Axelrad has the credit card we use to refuel the yacht. You can charge whatever you need on it."

"Maybe we should turn around and send him back now," Nick said. Anything was better than spending more time in the tents.

"Have you reached the halfway point?" Buettner asked.

"Absolutely," Coltrane answered. "I've got my throttles wide open."

Nodding, Buettner turned his most imploring smile on Jeban. "What about it, Chief? Shall I send him all the way back to Guam or keep him coming with my students?"

Jeban fingered his lower lip. "John Frum has been waiting a long time for a light to see his way. Lily, too, for that matter. For both their sakes a light is very important. But for your sake . . ." He bowed at Nick. ". . . we will begin construction today and trust you to secure our sacred cargo soon after."

Nick felt like hugging him but held back for fear of breaking some sexual taboo. Instead, she settled for a handshake.

"Thank you, Chief," she said. "We're in your debt."

"Talk to me," Coltrane said over the radio. "Am I coming or going?"

"Keep coming," Buettner told him. "You can pick up the generator on your next trip."

"Roger. Out."

Nick smiled at Jeban. "Chief, how soon will we be in our new home?"

Jeban thought for a moment, pulling at his lip again. "I will ask everyone in the village to help. That way you should be able to move in before dark."

"It sounds like an old-fashioned barn raising," Elliot said.

"We're going to need geckos too," Nick said, thinking an army of them would be needed to cope with the bugs that had invaded her tent last night. But a new house, with the freshly thatched roof, probably wouldn't come equipped with bug-eating wildlife.

"You will have what you need," the chief said.

With a satisfied sigh, Nick removed her cap and ran her fingers through her sweat-matted hair.

A look of disappointment sagged the corners of Jeban's mouth.

"I think he was expecting your curls," Elliot said.

Jeban rolled his eyes but didn't contradict him.

"They'll be back soon enough," she said. "Right now, though, I feel like shaving my head."

The chief's jaw dropped open. He looked truly appalled.

"Don't pay any attention to her," Elliot said. "She'll feel better when she's had a bath."

"What I need is a cold shower," Nick said.

Elliot wrinkled his nose. "I don't think it can wait that long. Besides, we haven't stocked the shower's holding tank yet."

Nick laughed. He was right, of course. She smelled like an old gym sock. "Why is it, Elliot, that you look so damned chipper?"

"That's easy, daughter. I saw Lily this morning. She gave me something to give you for the bugs. Since I didn't want to take any chances with your delicate skin without testing it, I tried some of the stuff on me first. It seems to work."

"How does it smell?"

"Better than you two do, that's for sure."

"I'll get the soap," Buettner said.

By the time they reached the beach, half the village was there ahead of them.

"This has to be the chief's doing," Nick said. "Nobody else knew we were coming."

"I don't see him," Buettner said.

"Look again," Elliot replied, pointing beyond the line of villagers. "Here he comes with Henry Yali."

The pair of them, walking side by side, were emerging from the trees. They quickly passed through an opening in the ranks of villagers and headed straight for Nick. But they stopped twenty-five yards short. The moment they did, the rest of the villagers took up positions right behind them. Then, almost as one, they sat cross-legged on the white sand, and leaned forward expectantly, reminding Nick of the gallery at a tennis match.

"I was hoping for some privacy," she announced loudly.

"Since red appears to be John Frum's color," Elliot told her, "I think they want to make sure your hair color is real, if you take my meaning."

Buettner grinned. "Frum be praised."

"They're going to be disappointed, then," Nick said. "I'm keeping my underwear on."

"I'd advise against it," Elliot said.

"Me too," Buettner added, ogling her for effect.

"Some uncle you turned out to be," she said.

Elliot intervened. "I think what Curt's trying to say is that your red hair is not only a rarity on Balesin, it has religious implications. So chances are Yali and his followers are going to be hounding you until they're satisfied."

"Besides," Buettner added, "if the chief likes what he sees, he might make an offer for you. With any luck, he'll swap us a house that's already built."

Elliot nodded toward the crowd. "Judging by the look on Yali's face, he might pay more than that."

"So I'm to be a peep show in the name of John Frum, is that it?"

"Think of it as your duty as an anthropologist," Buettner said, smiling.

"I'm an archaeologist," Nick responded, trying to

look angry. But unfortunately Elliot and Buettner were right. When working in the field, both archaeologists and anthropologists were expected to blend in with primitive cultures, if that's what it took to fully understand the mores and customs. If that meant eating bugs or going naked, so be it. The trouble was, the English-speaking Baleseans weren't Nick's idea of a truly primitive culture. And archaeologists usually dealt with long-dead cultures. This time, however, the airplanes and airstrips she was after belonged to the living.

"What the hell," she said, "at least there aren't many mosquitoes on the beach." She began unbuttoning her shirt.

"Hold it," Buettner said, looking panicked. "I'll bathe further down the beach."

He hurried away, with Elliot right behind him.

So much for Uncle Curt's ogling, she thought with a sigh of relief. She quickly removed all of her clothes and carefully folded them so they would be as sand-free as possible. Then she closed her eyes and pirouetted slowly, giving the gallery an eyeful. Even twenty-five yards away, the "ahs" of satisfaction coming from the villagers could be heard over the incoming waves.

That's enough, she thought, and plunged into the surf. Her fist dip in Balesin Bay had reminded her of hot Jell-O. But today, the water felt cool and refreshing. The itching on her arms and face quickly subsided. She submerged completely, swimming underwater long enough to spot several colorful fish. When she surfaced, the water was breast deep and her feet were treading on sharp coral. She retreated until she was about twenty yards out from the shore, where she floated on her back for a while. Finally, she came out of the water to fetch her soap.

By then, the gallery had thinned to a few diehards, Yali and the chief among them.

"Show's over," she called out, and started shampooing her hair. The last of the onlookers seemed to lose interest and began straggling into the trees on the path that led to the village.

Thank God for some privacy, Nick thought as she submerged again to rinse off the suds. When that was done, she headed for shore.

Halfway there she heard the airplane. She should have known better than to stay put and look up. But she did, and just in time to see the Widgeon flash overhead. It couldn't have been more than a hundred feet off the ground. It banked immediately, circling. Coltrane's face—close enough for Nick to see his eager grin—was pressed against the Plexiglas. His passengers were getting an eyeful, too.

"Swell," Nick murmured as she grabbed her clothes.

Coltrane didn't stop circling until she was fully dressed. By then Elliot and Buettner had rejoined her.

Nick pointed a finger at Buettner. "Your pilot is a dead man. What does he think I am, some kind of tourist attraction?"

"I'd say he appreciates a good-looking woman when he sees one," Elliot said, trying to repress a smile but failing badly.

"Join the club," Buettner said.

Nick flushed. "Give me some of that bug lotion Lily provided. Maybe it repels pilots as well as mosquitoes."

17

As the Widgeon taxied toward shore, the villagers reappeared and began lining the approach. By now, the eighty-degree early morning air had given way to a steamy ninety degrees, maybe more. As the heat intensified, the mosquitoes became more frenzied in their swarming. But so far, Lily's lotion was keeping them at bay. And even the lotion's noxious smell had subsided somewhat. Or maybe Nick's nose just didn't care anymore.

She left her father and Buettner behind and headed for Lily, hoping the woman might provide insight into the islanders' attitude toward airplanes, and the Widgeon in particular. The last time the seaplane had arrived, Nick had been a passenger and too exhausted to think clearly enough to observe the islanders' reactions.

Lily greeted her with a smile and a comment that was lost in the deafening roar of the Widgeon's twin turboprops. But the noise didn't stop Henry Yali from gesturing excitedly as the plane maneuvered. Surrounded by his admiring followers, Yali reminded Nick of a fighter pilot using his hands to describe a dogfight. Judging by the look in his eyes, he loved airplanes as much as she did. Only in his case, there were religious overtones.

Or maybe she was misreading Yali. Certainly the traditional Cargo Cult was more interested in what airplanes carried than in the aircraft themselves.

But what would happen if one of the passengers had red hair, particularly if that passenger turned out to be male? Would his arrival be seen as an omen? Would he be viewed as an emissary or even as John Frum himself, the returning messiah? Would he have to strip himself naked just as Nick had done? For that matter, what had the fact that Nick was a real redhead proved? Maybe Lily would tell her.

Don't start making guesses, Nick reminded herself. Just ask questions, listen, and observe.

As Coltrane cut the engines, Yali raised a triumphant fist in the air. The gesture drew a cheer. No doubt it was meant to show off Yali's priestly power. Probably he was taking credit for luring the Widgeon back to Balesin.

Stop, Nick told herself. Stop making assumptions.

A high tide allowed the seaplane to drift right up to the beach before bumping against a sandbar. An instant later the fuselage door opened and Coltrane appeared. He paused on the threshold to wave, then jumped into the knee-high surf, carrying a rope with which to anchor the Widgeon. Right behind him came two people who Nick assumed were Buettner's students. Both were very young and very tanned. They waded ashore holding hands like lovers, oblivious to the heat that had staggered Nick the first time she'd set foot on Balesin. Both had dark brown hair, with not so much as a hint of red.

It seemed to Nick that Yali looked disappointed, while Lily looked relieved. Or was that another assumption? No, Nick decided, it was a valid observation until proved otherwise.

She turned to Lily and asked, "Have you ever flown in an airplane?"

"That's Henry's province, not mine."

"Has Henry flown, then?"

Lily paused for a moment before answering. "He says he flies every night in his dreams. John Frum is with him there, he says. Of course, as John Frum's priest that is expected. It is also his right."

"Maybe we could arrange a real flight for you?"

"I'm tempted, child. But Henry would never forgive me if I went first."

"I meant for both of you," Nick said.

Lily smiled. "I know, but I would still be tempted to go first."

"Should I ask Henry to go first?"

Lily gazed at Yali, whose group now included Elliot and Buettner, then shook her head. "A priest's dreams are very important. They can be God's way of communicating with him, and to all of us. To actually fly might hinder that."

"Is that what Henry says?" Nick probed gently.

"Everyone knows that revelations come in many forms. Even the Reverend Innis says that the Christian God sometimes reveals Himself in dreams. The reverend is from America, you know, and has his church on the other side of our island. Ever since the war, we have heard about America. We want to be like Americans. You are a powerful people. We wish to be the same. That is why we attend the reverend's church, to become Christians and be like Americans."

"Even Henry?" Nick asked.

"He is often to be seen among the reverend's flock."

That didn't answer the question exactly, Nick realized, but decided not to push the matter. Many primitive cultures welcomed missionaries with open arms, converting to a new faith while continuing to cling to their old beliefs. To them, two faiths were better than one.

"Nice perfume," Coltrane said into her ear.

Nick jumped. "Don't sneak up on me like that."

"I saw him coming," Lily said.

"Then you should have warned me."

Lily eyed Coltrane. "A woman my age knows better than to interfere with young people when they're courting."

Nick started to protest, then caught herself. She had a better idea, one that would be helpful in her work.

"Lily," she said, slipping her hand into Coltrane's, "Lee and I would like to go flying together." Nick squeezed his hand, hoping he'd have sense enough to keep quiet. He got the message all right, and took advantage of it to kiss her cheek.

Lily smiled like a matchmaker sensing victory.

"We need your blessing," Nick continued, "because we'd like to go sight-seeing over the island and wouldn't want to upset anyone or infringe on any of your customs."

"You are right to ask ahead of time," Lily said. "Henry can be very touchy about such things. I will speak to him for you. But you must understand that certain places belong to John Frum and must not be violated. Even Henry doesn't have the power to set aside such restrictions. Those who have ignored them have lived to regret it."

"Maybe you'd better tell her what you had in mind, Doc," Coltrane interrupted. "You know, the surprise."

"You go ahead," Nick said, since she had no idea what he was talking about.

"You haven't forgotten about our special cargo, have you, Doc?"

Nick managed a smile.

"You don't have to worry," Nick said. "When we

drop our cargo, we'll be so high the ground will be nothing but a blur to us."

"How high will you fly?" Lily asked.

"We'll be no more than specks in the sky," Coltrane assured her.

Lily craned her neck, staring up into the bright blue sky as if assessing altitude.

"You might not even be able see us from the ground," Coltrane added.

Lily bowed her head. "You mustn't get too close to Mount Nomenuk. That is John Frum's high place and the entrance into His world."

"We promise, don't we, Doc?" He squeezed Nick's hand.

"We'll be careful," she responded without committing herself.

"Wait here," Lily said, and hurried away to speak with Henry Yali.

As soon as she was out of earshot, Nick whispered, "I hope the hell you have some cargo we can drop."

"You haven't been listening, have you, Doc? Like I said, I'm a pro. A pro is ready for any contingency. If you get forced down somewhere, you have to be able to survive. One way to do that is to come equipped with trading material to pay for your keep if the natives take you in."

"What kind of materials?"

"Fireworks for one thing, and an extra flare gun. Loud noises and pretty colors are always popular. But what I'm thinking about is my stash of canned food, which includes plenty of the local favorite, Spam."

Nick was impressed. "What about your fuel supply?"

"We can probably run the engines on that perfume of yours."

"You know damn well I'm not wearing perfume. It's insect repellent. The islanders make it."

He grinned. "Kiss me and you might learn something."

"Keep your mind on flying."

"Kiss me and you can have some cargo too."

"All I want is another aerial view of the island."

"You don't know what you're missing."

"You conceited—"

Coltrane burst out laughing. As she glared at him, it suddenly dawned on her that he was putting her on.

Without warning he leaned close and said, "Is your nose out of order?"

She was about to kick him where it would hurt the most when she realized he smelled as badly as she did. "You're wearing repellent, too, dammit. How long have you known about it?"

"If you fly these islands like I do, you learn the ins and outs. If you don't, you'd better go into another line of business. I get my bug juice from an old-timer on Guam."

"You could have told us about it," she protested.

"You didn't ask."

"Bastard."

He kissed her, a peck on the cheek, and jumped back out of the way before she could retaliate.

"I should have kicked you when I had the chance."

She was sizing up his shins when she realized he was also wearing another item of indispensable island uniform, rubber sandals. "Where the hell did you get those?" she demanded.

"Like I said, Doc, I'm a professional. Out here you've got to keep your feet as dry as possible. Otherwise, you get jungle rot."

"I know."

"Now maybe you'll be interested in some of my other cargo. I tracked down your luggage. How about another kiss?"

"I'll write you a check for your trouble. Now tell me about your fuel supply."

"You're all heart, aren't you, Doc?"

Nick sensed that she'd hurt the pilot's feelings, but she didn't like to be teased. "Let's stick to business," she said.

"Suit yourself. I've got enough extra fuel for a short flight, maybe fifteen minutes. Will that do it?"

"I'd like to get a look at the airstrip you told us about on the radio yesterday."

He shrugged. "I hope I can find it again, Doc. Maybe another kiss will refresh my memory."

She groaned inwardly. Did he really think she'd fall for that airborne-soldier-of-fortune act of his? All he needed was a flying helmet and goggles. Except for the sandals, of course. They spoiled the image of the rugged aviator.

She was about to point that out when Lily returned.

"I had to vouch for you two," Lily reported. "Even so, Henry isn't happy about it, but he won't stop you from delivering cargo. That would be against the wishes of John Frum. But you must stay away from the mountain. That is in Henry's keeping."

"Thank you, Lily." Nick leaned over and kissed the older woman on the cheek.

Lily smiled. "In his dreams, Henry has flown higher than the birds. What he sees from there is John Frum's will. It would not be revealed to outsiders. So you and your airplane are safe on that count."

Her expression changed as she continued. "Be careful. A storm is coming. You can smell it in the air."

Nick smelled only dampness and the pervasive hint of rotting vegetation that continually hung in the air.

"When the storm comes," Lily went on, "John Frum will unleash His thunderbolts."

18

Once the Widgeon was airborne, Nick outlined what she had in mind, a low-level look at the landing strip on Mount Nomenuk, a definite breach of John Frum protocol.

"What happens if they see us?" Coltrane asked.

"I'm not certain, but you should have seen the look on Henry Yali's face when he overheard me talking to you about it on the radio. But the airstrip is key to my work if I'm ever going to discover what type of plane John Frum prefers."

"You act like he's a real person."

"To the islanders he is."

He shrugged. "The way I figure it, we've got to make it look good if we're going to get away with our spy flight."

"On the radio you said the strip you saw was on the far side of Mount Nomenuk, didn't you? On the side away from the village?"

"We'll be out of sight of the village, if that's what you're asking."

"So can you do it or not?" Nick asked, her tone deliberately challenging.

"How does this sound? I'll come back onto course and head directly for the village in a shallow dive. That way, we should be hauling ass when we make our cargo drop. Our speed will insure that the chutes drift a long way. When your priest and his friends start chasing them, we make our move. Your move, actually, since I'm just the chauffeur."

"We don't want to make it look too obvious."

He nudged her in the ribs. "Just stand by the door and wait for my signal to dump the cargo, Doc. The chutes will blossom over the village, then drift like hell. All the way across the river if we time it right. While they're trying to catch up with them, we go for it. What do you say?"

Nick thought it over. Lily and Henry were too old to go running after cargo, no matter how tempting. Even so, chances were they'd supervise the recovery. With luck, every eye would be diverted from the Widgeon.

"What about the engines?" Nick asked. "They may not be able to see us, but hearing's another matter."

"I'm way ahead of you. I'll cut them back and glide over the target."

"Does this thing glide?"

"Like a stone, Doc. Trust me."

Nick sighed. "One more thing. It would be nice if the cargo didn't actually land in the river."

"If you shove it out the door when I give the word, we'll be fine. Unless, of course, we crash. In that case, they'll have to settle for hamburger instead of a nice leg of redhead."

"These people are much more sophisticated than you think," she shot back.

"You can tell me about it on the headset while I get the cargo ready." He set the autopilot.

Nick peered through the windshield. "What do I do if I see something coming?"

"Disengage the autopilot and take evasive action."

"That sounds easy enough," she said sarcastically.

He blew her a kiss and left his seat. Nick heard some thumping behind her and then Coltrane's voice over the intercom. "Okay, Doc, enlighten me while I work."

She clicked the transmit button. "Can you hear me?"

"Loud and clear, Doc."

"What do you want to know?"

"You're the professor. Tell me about the Cargo Cult."

Nick scanned the sky once more, saw nothing but blue and a line of dark clouds building along the horizon, then settled back. Last night, unable to sleep, she'd glanced through Sam Ohmura's book on the Cargo Cult again and come up with some fascinating lore. Those points that had interested her, however, might bore a bush pilot to death. Still, Coltrane could tune out if he didn't like it.

"As far as is known, there was no Cargo Cult before the Europeans arrived," she began. "When they did, a new world opened up for the Pacific Islanders. Technology seems to have changed their outlook on life forever. It began first with the arrival of the great sailing ships. The islanders had never seen vessels that big before and they began building fake docks and warehouses. They fully expected those docks to lure in ships that would be filled with cargo, cargo that would make them rich like the Europeans.

"When World War Two came, and with it airplanes,

the island people traded up, so to speak. They immediately abandoned the old technology for the new, trading dock building for airstrips and mock-ups of airplanes they had seen.

"The cult is strongest in the New Guinea area, though there are interesting offshoots scattered as far as Samoa and Fiji, not to mention this immediate area of the Pacific. Some groups have even built fake radio masts and telephone poles with which they hope to contact the spirits. In some areas, the islanders have been known to paint red crosses on their chests, hoping to catch the eye of Red Cross relief planes."

Coltrane whistled. "Don't they ever get tired of waiting for cargo that never comes?"

"The Cargo Cult is like all religions. It's a matter of faith. To these people, God is the cargo giver. It's just a matter of making the correct preparations and incantations to satisfy Him. Only then will His gifts arrive."

"Since we're dropping cargo, why aren't we gods?"

"They see us strictly as helpers doing God's work."

"It sounds complicated."

"Not really. Cargo is power to them. That's why they admire America so much, because it's the most powerful country in the world. One of the Cargo Cult groups actually tried to buy President Johnson back in the sixties. To them, he symbolized power and even magic. As they saw it, his power would have been transferred to them."

"How much did they offer?" Coltrane asked.

"All they had."

"They're as nuts as the rest of the world, Doc. Nuttier even."

Nick couldn't help smiling. Coltrane's reaction was

the same as many early scholars, who considered the Cargo Cult as a kind of collective madness.

"Anthropologists now believe that John Frum is more of a Christ figure than first thought," she told him. "His promise to return one day with planeloads of cargo is symbolic of both resurrection and salvation. Salvation and resurrection are common to most religions."

"All right, Doc, cut the crap and come back here and man your post while I do the flying."

After dropping the cargo, Nick watched in fascination as the parachutes landed on the far side of the river just as Coltrane had predicted. By then she was strapped in the copilot's seat again and using her binoculars to watch the scramble for cargo. The entire population of the village looked to be lined along the riverbank, where two canoes were being launched to retrieve the gifts.

Coltrane banked steeply away from the village and started climbing at full power, heading downriver toward the ocean and well away from Mount Nomenuk. The roar from the turboprops was deafening. The Widgeon felt as if it were shaking itself to pieces.

Nick clenched her teeth and held on, wondering how much stress a World-War-Two-era airplane could take. Coltrane didn't look worried though. Judging by his grin, he was having the time of his life.

As soon as they crossed the coast, Coltrane throttled back and came around. They were now at twenty-five hundred feet, some five hundred feet above Mount Nomenuk. He veered east until the mountain was directly between them and the village. Only then did he head straight for the mountain in a shallow dive.

"Get ready," he said. "The strip's going to be on your side of the plane."

Nick slid open the side window for an unobstructed view. The wind howled along with the engines.

By now, the mountain looked as if it were rushing at them. It filled the windshield. Nick had to force herself to ignore what looked like impending disaster and concentrate on the ground below.

Suddenly, the Widgeon tilted and began sideslipping, following the contours of the mountain. The trees looked close enough to touch.

"You'll see it in just a few seconds," he said.

Without warning, he chopped the engines to idle and lowered the flaps. The Widgeon shimmied. So did Nick's stomach. The plane felt on the verge of stalling.

Nick started to say something, but the words died on her lips when she saw the airstrip. It had been hewn from a forest of breadfruit trees and looked as precisely tended as a garden. Even the grass on the runway looked closely cropped.

Two airplanes stood at the head of the runway as if poised for takeoff. They didn't look authentic exactly, since they didn't appear to have wheels or a real undercarriage, but they were a far cry from the crude replicas pictured in Sam Ohmura's book. These looked like World War Two bombers. At a guess, they'd been modeled after the Japanese Betty, a twin-engine job manufactured by Mitsubishi. Confirmation of their exact type would have to wait for a ground inspection, if ever that became possible.

Then she saw the hangar. Placed the way it was, among the trees, it would have been virtually impossible to spot from the air at a normal altitude. But the Widgeon was no more than a hundred feet off the ground at the moment, and sinking.

Part of her knew Coltrane was taking a terrible risk.

Another part of her couldn't care less and stayed focused on the hangar. Its metal walls showed no gaps; its corrugated roof looked watertight. The hangar also appeared life-size to her, more than large enough to accommodate the planes at the head of the runway, or real airplanes for that matter. Such attention to detail stunned her. The planes weren't going anywhere. But evidently that hadn't daunted the builders. To them, carving this airfield out of the wilderness must have been an act of faith. Considering the difficult locale and tools at hand, it must have taken a massive effort on the part of the islanders.

Nick jerked back from the open window, realizing suddenly that the treetops were about to brush their wingtip. She was opening her mouth to yell a warning when Coltrane hit the throttles. The sudden surge of power threw Nick back against her seat.

The Widgeon banked one way, then the other, to avoid a cluster of larger trees. Nick held her breath. Then there were even taller trees dead ahead. She clenched her teeth, expecting impact.

"Hot damn!" Coltrane whooped. "I should have been a fighter pilot."

He pulled back on the yoke and the Widgeon climbed away.

Nick caught her breath. "Let's try it again so I can take some photos."

Coltrane tapped the gas gauge on the instrument panel. "Pilots have only so much luck, you know. I've spent a lot of mine already and I don't like to make too much of the trip in the dark. Guam's not so big that I couldn't miss it. Don't forget, Amelia Putnam missed her island not all that far from here."

"You mean Amelia Earhart?"

"She was a married woman. She should have been proud to use her husband's name."

"Amelia Earhart didn't have the use of a Global Positioning System," Nick retorted, pointedly using the aviatrix's maiden name. "I'll tell you what. If you anchor here and stay overnight, I'll fix you dinner even if you are a Neanderthal." Hope you like Spam, she added to herself.

He eyed her skeptically for a moment, then shook his head as he brought the Widgeon on course for a landing at the mouth of the river. "Got a short hop scheduled in the morning," he replied.

She felt disappointed that he hadn't accepted her offer, although she wasn't certain why.

19

"Spying on people is a sin!" The shout startled the Reverend George Innis so badly he jumped half a foot and nearly fell off the church's corrugated roof. If his binoculars hadn't been strung around his neck, they'd have gone flying over the edge.

Regaining his balance, the reverend shook his head at Todd Parker, who was standing at the foot of the ladder, one of his grubby sandals already perched on the first rung, a mocking smile fixed on his unshaven face.

"Look out below," Innis called out. "I'm coming down." The last thing he wanted was to share the cramped bell tower with Parker. The man had no sense of space. He used his belly like an insect probing with its antennae. Once contact was made, Parker would stick to you like glue. Making matters worse, he reeked of the native beer. It seeped from his pores like a natural insecticide, or so he claimed.

If it hadn't been for the smell, and the beachcomber outfits—baggy white trousers and shirts, plus a tattered straw hat—he'd have been a good-looking man. The reverend's wife, Ruth, claimed it was all a pose, a kind of statement that allowed him to shun all responsibility.

Parker was younger than Innis by at least ten years, maybe even fifteen, and six inches taller than the churchman. That extra height made his tendency to invade another's space all the more intolerable, because speaking to him toe-to-toe put a kink in Innis's neck.

"Instead of spying on the newcomers," Parker shouted even louder, "you ought to pray for them."

Halfway down the ladder, Innis paused. "I was keeping an eye on things, that's all," he said, reluctant to come any closer.

"A clergyman shouldn't tell lies. You never know when God might be listening."

Damn the man, Innis thought. His doubting tone rankled.

"Can't a man admire an airplane in peace?" he said, annoyed at himself for feeling compelled to explain his actions to the likes of Parker. Worse yet, it wasn't the airplane that had been occupying his thoughts.

Parker broadened his smile as if mind reading. "You're beginning to sound like Henry Yali. If you're not careful, you'll be painting a red cross on your church and waiting around for John Frum like the rest of us." Parker grabbed hold of the ladder as if he were about to climb up to make contact.

"Watch it," Innis warned and hurried the rest of the way down.

"Well?" Parker demanded as soon as the reverend had his feet on the ground. "Don't just stand there, sky pilot. Tell me what you saw through those spy-glasses of yours. What's that airplane up to and is that lady archaeologist worth eyeballing or not?"

Innis held his breath, but it was only a matter of time before he'd have to inhale the inevitable alcoholic fumes.

"They were circling Mount Nomenuk," the reverend blurted out.

"Are you sure?" Parker demanded.

Nodding, Innis drew a quick breath and blinked in disbelief. The man smelled of mint, not beer.

"It's a long way off to be sure," Innis said. "But that's the way it looked to me"

"Mount Nomenuk, you say." Parker shook his head. "Somebody should have talked to them when they first arrived. Somebody should have explained the rules."

Innis thought that over. From the church roof, he'd had a different perspective than anyone in the village. There was a good chance the flight path had been invisible to anyone but himself.

Parker closed in. "Maybe I should volunteer to set those people straight. What do you think, Padre? Is the lady scientist worth my while?"

Innis smiled. That explained the minty mouthwash. "Be my guest."

Parker winked. "On second thought, I say to hell with it. Why waste shoe rubber when I own the only store? Sooner or later everybody has to come to me."

Behind Innis, the screen door banged. With a start,

the reverend lurched around to see his wife framed in the chapel's doorway.

"I thought you'd gone to the village," Innis said to her.

She glared at him. "George, have you been up on the roof again in this heat? You should know better than to climb up there alone. What if you'd fallen off? Who'd have been here to take care of you?"

"I heard the airplane," he said guiltily.

"You men and your planes."

Parker backed off. "I'm a boat man, myself."

"Someone had to keep an eye on the newcomers," Innis went on. "They were flying over Mount Nomenuk."

"Then it's time we paid them a visit, don't you think, dear? In this place, good, god-fearing people have to stick together." She glared at the store owner, who'd begun to edge away. "Don't you agree, Mr. Parker?"

He started to say something, then settled for a shrug.

"If that's a yes, Mr. Parker, why don't you accompany us to the village? That way we can present a united front when we introduce ourselves to the newcomers."

"I wouldn't want to close my store during business hours." Parker turned on his heels and hurried away.

"I hope we'll see you at Sunday services," Innis called after him.

Parker raised an acknowledging hand but kept walking. He'd never yet attended one of Innis' services.

"That man's impossible," Ruth said. "It's a wonder you waste your time on him. He's a born sinner who's on his way to hell."

Innis smiled. He knew Ruth didn't mean it. She was only upset because he'd gone up on the roof without someone to hold the ladder.

"I'm sorry, dear," he said. "I'll keep my feet on the ground from now on."

She kissed him on the cheek. "You go wash up and we'll be on our way to the village before it gets any hotter."

20

Nick was relieved to see the beach deserted as the Widgeon taxied toward shore. The absence of irate villagers meant that their flight over the airstrip had gone unobserved. At least Nick hoped that was the case, though the absence of a single soul was surprising, considering the value Baleseans placed on airplanes.

Coltrane cut the engines to idle and allowed the bobbing Widgeon to drift in with one of the breakers. When the seaplane bumped bottom, he turned to Nick and shook his head apologetically. "Sorry to leave you like this, Doc, but business calls."

He caught hold of her hand as she was leaving the copilot's seat. "Take care of yourself, Nick. I'll see you on the next trip."

She realized that was the first time he had used her name. "Are you getting sentimental on me?"

"Get out of here, Doc, before I forget I'm a businessman."

He pushed her toward the door before she could decide whether she was pleased or furious.

As soon as she waded ashore, the Widgeon's engines

revved once, a kind of farewell salute. Then the plane swung around and headed out to sea, bouncing from wave to wave for what seemed like a mile before one last lurch bounced it airborne.

"Macho bastard," she called after him. Her mother had warned her about good-looking men like Coltrane. But considering Elaine's record, her warnings had to be as suspect as her cooking.

Nick shook off the memory of one of Elaine's forays into food poisoning and started for the village. The vision awaiting her in the square was startling. It seemed like half the population of the island was working on the new house Nick had been promised.

Already the framing was in place and the thatch roof nearing completion. Men and women were working together, while children ran errands and played games.

"Over here!" Elliot called from the porch of the communal building where they'd dined the night before. He was perched on a long trestle table. Beside him stood Buettner and Lily.

At Nick's approach, her father shouted, "Good news. Our new quarters will be ready by nightfall. We have Henry's word on it."

The work, she noticed for the first time, was being closely supervised by Henry Yali and Chief Jeban.

"It looks like rain," she said, eyeing the clouds building overhead.

"Henry says they'll have the roof finished before the first drops fall," Buettner answered.

"Men like to make promises," Lily said, joining Nick at the foot of the stairs. "Should it rain ahead of Henry's schedule, which it often does, he'll simply declare the downpour to be mist and not rain at all. But don't worry. You will be in your house, safe and snug, by nightfall.

That's my promise, because Henry or no Henry, the rain won't stop the work. Besides, once the roof is complete, everyone will move inside to work on the walls."

Rain began to fall.

"The mist is early," Lily announced loudly, no doubt for Yali's benefit, then retreated back onto the porch, with Nick right behind her. With the rain came staggering humidity of sauna-like proportions. Nick found herself sweat-soaked and gasping as she settled into one of the half-dozen wicker chairs that were grouped around the long rough-hewn table. Her father and Buettner looked half-drowned.

Lily seemed unaffected as she said, "I think it's time for me to see to some afternoon tea for our visitors, the reverend and his wife."

Nick glanced around, found no such couple, and looked to her father and Buettner for an explanation. They both answered with shrugs that denied knowledge of any such visitation.

"At a time like this," Lily continued, looking pleased with the confusion she'd caused, "Henry would claim psychic powers. Maybe I should do the same. But the plain fact is, the reverend and his wife are almost as predictable as Henry is."

Lily pointed to an opening in the trees on the far side of the square. "That's the Mission Highway, or so the reverend calls it. It cuts straight across the island to the church and to Mr. Parker's store. My guess is the reverend and his wife will be coming along any moment."

"In this weather?" Nick asked.

"It's God's weather, the reverend would say."

"I probably should stay behind with my students," Buettner said.

"We can set places for everybody at the table, if you'd like, but I don't think we should count on your young people wanting to come. Lovers their age set their own rules." Lily smiled and Nick wondered if the woman saw lovers everywhere.

"I can assure you," Buettner snapped, "that I expect professional conduct from my students. They're on my time now."

"My wife used to say the same thing," Elliot said "It was her time I was stealing for my digs." He shook his head slowly. " 'If you loved me,' she'd say, 'you wouldn't leave me and Nick alone so much.' "

Love had been Elaine's weapon, Nick remembered, one she had wielded to perfection.

"If you loved me, you wouldn't hide from me in your room," she'd complain whenever Nick stayed too long with her model airplanes. It was her refrain, repeated over and over again, the memory of it painful even after all these years.

Nick closed her eyes and was back in her room, adding the finishing touches of paint to her newest acquisition, a Curtis P-40. Only the teeth and eyes were needed to complete the fighter's pugnacious, Flying Tiger nose.

"We'll shoot down our enemies," she whispered to the plane, "and fly away together."

"Am I the enemy?" Elaine asked.

Startled, Nick swung around so quickly she narrowly missed crashing the model plane into her mother. Elaine had opened the door without knocking.

"You're . . . you're not an enemy fighter," Nick managed to say.

"You don't fool me," Elaine said.

"This is the model Elliot gave me for my birthday."

"That was more than a month ago. You're going on thirteen now, too old for that kind of thing."

"I've been working on it in my spare time."

"If you loved me, you would be helping me around the house," Elaine countered.

"Do you want me to help now?"

Elaine's hands, pressed against her body, clenched into fists so hard that veins stood out on her forearms like taut wires. "Your father isn't here. He's never here, and now you want to fly away and leave me alone too."

Nick bit her lip. When Elaine was in one of her moods, talk was useless. Nick backed away, but Elaine followed until Nick was trapped against the wall.

"If you love your mother," Elaine said, "give me that plane."

"Elliot's looking forward to seeing it," Nick said, as much of a threat as she dared utter, hoping Elaine would come to her senses.

"You don't love me," Elaine spat as she grabbed the plane and snapped it in two.

The next day she had replaced the airplane with a boxed Barbie doll. As far as Nick knew, that box was still on the closet shelf in her old room. The box was untouched, its cellophane wrapper intact.

Nick opened her eyes, dispelling the memory as a man and woman emerged from the trees and came hurrying toward the communal house, their shared umbrella useless against the wind-driven downpour.

"The Reverend Innis is on time," Lily said matter-of-factly. "All these years and the man never has learned to read the weather. His wife, Ruth, knows better, but she keeps it to herself, I think."

And what do you keep to yourself? Nick wondered, observing Lily out of the corner of her eye. If the reverend's appearance on schedule was anything to go by, Lily read people as well as the weather.

The reverend arrived out of breath, puffing and wiping his brow. He was a portly man, wearing a wide-brimmed planter's hat to protect his pale complexion. His trousers were tan, his shirt black with an affixed white dog-collar. His age, Nick guessed, was somewhere in his fifties. His wife, dressed in an ankle-length skirt and hemp-colored blouse, looked much younger, certainly no more than her early forties. She showed no signs of breathlessness from the dash across the square. They both wore the all-pervasive rubber sandals.

Lily made the introductions, then disappeared inside to see about tea.

"We hope you'll join us for services on Sunday," Innis said as soon as everyone was seated around the table, with Nick and Mrs. Innis together on one side, facing the men.

"Now, George," his wife chided, "give them time to settle in. Can't you see that their house isn't even ready yet?"

He ducked his head, giving way with poor grace. "Of course. I'm too hasty."

His wife smiled, then turned to Nick. "If there's anything we can do to make your stay more comfortable, we'd be happy to help."

"I think we're past the worst," Nick replied. "We've learned about the insect repellent." She batted at the swarming mosquitoes, who stayed just out of range, their whine sounding like an angry protest against the repellent's force field. "Next, comes the rubber sandals, as soon as I can buy myself a pair."

"You'll find them at the island store. Mr. Parker always keeps them in stock. They're his best-seller, next to cold beer. He charges an arm and a leg for both."

"The man's no better than a bandit," Innis muttered.

"Now, George. You know the Baleseans need Mr. Parker and his store."

"You're right, dear. I'm sorry. That was a very unChristian thing to say."

"You'll have to forgive my husband," Ruth said. "He's not at his best right now. Every time an airplane arrives attendance at services falls off." She slowly shook her head. "John Frum and his airplanes. They raise absolute havoc with our congregation."

"That man Coltrane ought to be banned from the skies," the reverend said. "He's a rogue and a menace. An aerial pirate, if you ask me."

"Now, George."

"That plane of his brings back bad memories, I can tell you."

"What memories?" Nick asked.

The reverend sighed deeply before responding. "We'd be better off if no airplane had ever come to this island. One way or another, they've all caused trouble. They arrive and I'm out of a flock. And always the cry goes up that this plane is the promised one, sent by John Frum himself. No matter who sends them, they always cut into church attendance."

The reverend shook his head from side to side as if trying to shake free of his memories. "The stories I could tell you would curl your hair."

"I'd like to hear them," Nick told him.

"Your hair's already curly," Elliot pointed out.

"It's no joking matter," the reverend shot back. "Airplanes have been the ruination of this island."

"What can you tell us about John Frum's airfields?" Nick asked. "Have you ever visited them?"

The reverend stared at her for a moment, as if pondering her question. "The things I've seen don't bear talking about."

Before Nick could press the point, the reverend's wife intervened. "Don't pay any attention to my husband. He'll be out of sorts for the next few days. After that, the airplane will be forgotten and our congregation, such as it is, will be back in their pews where they belong."

"Tea," Lily announced, appearing in the doorway. Behind her came two young girls. The older girl was carrying a tray with Western-style teapot and cups, while the younger one, Josephine, had a platter of cookies and fruit. Both girls glanced at Nick shyly before depositing their loads and scampering back inside.

"It's your hair," Lily explained, as she arranged the table service and poured the tea, which was pale green.

As Lily turned to leave, Nick said, "Please, Lily, won't you join us?"

"Another time, dear. Some of the younger children are waiting for me, and I promised to tell them a story. If you need me, I'll be in the kitchen." With that, she left the porch.

"That's typical Lily for you," the reverend said. "She thinks she's doing me a favor, giving me first crack at potential converts before Henry Yali gets his hands on them."

His wife smiled indulgently. "If only it were that easy."

Innis raised an eyebrow, started to say something, then appeared to think better of it and popped a cookie into his mouth.

The cookies reminded Nick of English tea biscuits, but when she bit into one, it had the consistency of sponge cake and tasted like a stale vanilla wafer.

"Once you get used to Balesin," Ruth went on, "it's a beautiful place to live, though my husband won't admit it sometimes, especially when his work is going badly."

"Which is all the time," Innis said. "I remember singing 'Onward Christian soldiers marching as to war' in seminary, and thinking I was joining the army of the Lord and going out to fight the good war. But out here I'm on the losing side."

"Henry, you say that every time an airplane arrives."

"It's just truer, then. The rest of the time I'm kidding myself. I don't have converts. All I have is an audience."

"George, you're giving our new friends the wrong impression. You're a respected man. You have a large congregation. Even Henry Yali comes to our church on occasion."

"They respect Americans," the reverend answered. "That's all. It has nothing to do with me personally."

Elliot said, "From what I understand, the followers of John Frum want to be more like Americans than anything else."

"You're right there. They come to my services to learn about America, not God. Ruth and I teach the children to read and write English, but we never call it that. We call it American to keep everybody happy. Of course, they equate America and Americans with wealth."

Ruth said, "I hope we're not boring you with our problems."

"Not at all," Nick responded, "anything you can tell us will be of help."

"You've seen our volcano, haven't you?" Ruth nodded in the direction of the mountain that dominated the center of the island. "They say it's extinct now because John Frum uses it to travel to and from America."

Ruth busied herself refilling the teacups, giving way to her husband.

"During the war, the Japanese imprisoned all political dissenters here on Balesin," Innis said. "When America won the war, it was Americans who freed the followers of John Frum, thus the love of America."

"I'm told that Henry claims to have actually met John Frum," Nick said.

"Who told you that?" the reverend demanded sharply.

"I can't remember," Nick lied, surprised by the intensity of his reaction.

The reverend sighed. "With Henry Yali, who's to say what's true and what he dreams? Now if someone like Lily had claimed to have met John Frum that would be a different matter. In any case, John Frum is very real to these people, a living messiah."

Buettner spoke up. "I've sailed all over the Pacific, and one thing seems clear. There was probably a real model for John Frum. Many scholars think he may have been an early missionary, or even an explorer, who said he'd return one day. Most travelers say such things when they've visited a place of beauty. And for the Pacific Islanders that promise came to symbolize resurrection and redemption."

"That's a long reach," Elliot said. "Almost as bad as you and your woodpecker scalps."

"I don't understand," Innis said.

"Curt believes that the custom of using feathers for

money migrated here from America, where the Indians used woodpecker scalps as currency."

"That's appalling," Innis said. "Killing God's creatures just to create money. Whenever I find red-feather money, I burn it."

Elliot closed his eyes and Nick saw Buettner tense up. To head off an outburst, she asked, "Have you seen much of it?"

The preacher shook his head. "Not in a long time. It was a barbarous custom."

"My husband is a bird-watcher," Ruth Innis interjected. "He's cataloguing all the species on the island."

Innis raised his hands as if to belittle himself. "I have to do something to pass the time when my congregation goes missing."

"It's the crabs I watch out for," his wife added. "The big ones are three feet across. Henry says they have been known to strip a man to the bone."

"Nonsense," Innis said. "They scuttle away when they see people. You'd have to fall down unconscious before they'd come anywhere near you."

"Exactly my point," his wife said triumphantly, turning her gaze on Nick. "Have you ever tried to open a coconut?"

Nick shook her head. "Lily asked me the same question."

"Well, take it from me, it's darn near impossible unless you're a coconut crab. You should see those claws of theirs at work. It's unbelievable. That's why you have to be careful with your garbage. We had tin cans for a while, but they ripped them open as easily as coconuts."

"So how do you protect your garbage?" Nick asked.

"You don't. You keep it well away from your house

and let them have it. They're as good as a garbage disposal. That's if George and I don't eat them."

Elliot raised an eyebrow at Nick. "And to think, daughter, it was the Spam you were worried about at dinner last night."

"Spam is a favorite here," the reverend said. "It has to be imported and is therefore considered a great delicacy. Our good-hearted store owner charges top dollar for it."

Since Nick had seen no sign that the Baleseans had much money to spend, she wondered at the aptness of the reverend's assessment. Perhaps the storekeeper confined his high prices to outsiders. Most likely, he had some sort of barter arrangement with the islanders.

"How long have you lived here on Balesin?" Nick asked.

"My George has lived here for ages," Ruth answered. "Most of his life really, but I'm a newcomer. We met when I came here as a visitor a few years ago. It was George who took me in hand and showed me around the island. I thought I was coming to live in paradise."

She smiled at her husband, her expression unreadable, though Nick would have bet that with the passage of time paradise had tarnished around the edges.

"Maybe you and your husband could show me the island," Nick suggested.

"Once you get away from the beach, it's heavy jungle and rough going," Innis said. "There are only a few well-worn paths, and you have to stick to them if you don't want to get lost."

"I think Nick has something more particular in mind than following beaten paths," Ruth said.

Nick nodded. "My father and Curt are here to study

the people and their culture. But my area of expertise is airplanes."

Innis jerked upright, a look of alarm on his face. "I thought you were an archaeologist."

"I'm a historical archaeologist. We deal in more modern artifacts."

"Since when have airplanes been considered artifacts?"

"I've worked with the government on several occasions. In one case I tracked down a plane that had been lost over New Guinea during World War Two. By excavating the site, we were able to identify airmen who'd been listed as missing in action for fifty years."

The reverend pursed his lips. "There was a Japanese air base here on Balesin during the war, but I've never heard of any missing planes or aircrews."

"It's the Cargo Cult's mock-ups that I want to see. From what I've observed from the air, they're very unique."

Innis shook his head. "You're mistaken. Such constructions are spread over much of the Pacific. Ruth and I have researched the subject. These here are no different from anywhere else."

"Have you visited the airfields on this island yourself?" Nick asked.

The reverend nodded. "Only the one and then I—"

His wife interrupted. "You shouldn't put my husband in the middle. Henry Yali has set boundaries. Were we to violate them, my husband's position here would be very difficult. He might even be recalled if word of such an indiscretion ever reached his bishop."

"I saw another airfield when Lee Coltrane and I were dropping cargo," Nick persisted. "Do you know it? It was on the southeast slope of Mount Nomenuk."

"Haven't you been listening?" Innis said. "You must stay away from there. That's John Frum's mountain."

"You must avoid all of John Frum's places," his wife added quickly.

"But how are we to know where they are?" Elliot asked.

"Ah," the reverend said, pulling at his lower lip. "That's one of the problems we confront here on Balesin. Only Henry Yali knows for sure what's acceptable and what isn't. I've known the man a long time, and he's always been inconsistent when it comes to dogma. Sometimes I think he changes the rules just to confuse me, because I'm his competition." The reverend rocked back and forth, staring into space. "Since none of John Frum's dogma is written, you can't pin it down. You can't fight it."

"George," his wife said sharply, "you're not in church now. You're not wrestling with the devil or dogma. Nick needs practical advice. She has to know that it's against the rules for outsiders to set foot on Mount Nomenuk. It could even be dangerous."

"Dangerous?" her husband echoed. "Yes, that's possible, if Henry hasn't changed the rules."

"What about the other airfield?" Nick asked. "The one that's not far from where we're sitting."

"Some areas are more sacred than others, that much is clear. So my advice is to wait for Henry, or for Chief Jeban, to invite you on a tour."

"What about Lily?" Nick asked.

"An invitation from Lily would be even better. She's the matriarch around here. Even Jim Jeban bends a knee in her presence. Henry, too, at times."

"Do you think another parachute drop would pave the way for Nick?" Buettner asked.

"Cargo causes trouble," Innis replied. "I suggest you go slow."

"What my husband means," his wife added, "is that parts of this island are dangerous. Terrible things have happened to outsiders who wandered too close to the forbidden places. Imagine, a complete expedition of archaeologists was completely swallowed by the jungle once."

The reverend held up a restraining hand. "We shouldn't be spreading rumors."

She glared at her husband. "I've heard the stories, dear, and so have you."

"What kind of stories?" Nick asked, knowing that myths and legends, no matter how outlandish, often contained kernels of truth. All you had to do was look for them hard enough.

Innis looked as if his wife had inadvertently exposed their family skeleton. "We've heard tales of avenging spirits roaming the slopes of Mount Nomenuk. But if you ask me, they're just stories made up to keep unruly children in line."

"I think it's time we told them about the small island," Mrs. Innis said. "Balabat. That's the place I'm afraid of."

"Now, Ruth," the reverend soothed.

"My husband doesn't like to admit that heathen superstitions continue to exist in the face of Christianity. He takes it as a personal insult."

The reverend sighed. "I've been here a long time and have very little to show for it. I haven't done a proper job for the Lord."

"There are times when I love these people," his wife added, "especially the children. Other times, I don't understand them at all."

That made two of them, Nick thought, observing the reverend's continuing nod.

His wife said, "Even their church is a mockery. Its cross is painted red for John Frum." She hugged herself. "Sometimes I think it's red for blood."

She stood up, beckoning to her husband. "I want to be home before dark."

"It's only mid-afternoon," Nick pointed out.

Mrs. Innis's only response was to shake her head stubbornly.

Her husband stood up, taking her hand. "We'd like all of you to come to Sunday services," he said. "Who knows? If you come, Henry Yali might come too. Just follow the Mission Highway. Well, it's not really a highway, just a trail, but it leads right to our church. We like to think of the highway as a mile-long test of faith."

"A mile walk to the store to buy beer is more like it," his wife said.

"That's no way to speak of the devil," a voice said out of the rain. A moment later, a man stepped through the downpour sluicing from the roof. His face was hidden beneath a beach umbrella that was at least five feet across.

"Mr. Parker," Mrs. Innis said, her tone turning his name into an accusation, "have you been spying on us?"

"A man like me doesn't have the energy for such things. You know that. Besides, there are no secrets on Balesin."

"This is Todd Parker," the reverend said.

Parker collapsed his umbrella, then greeted the newcomers one by one, with a handshake and a formal bow. All the while Nick fought to keep a straight face. The man was like a character out of an old Hollywood beachcomber movie. His white baggy shorts were held up by a tie, old-school English by the looks of it; his loose white shirt was a mass of wrinkles worthy of a dieting elephant. And his chin was covered by several days' growth of beard. A grimy cloth bag that looked more like a pillow slip than anything else was slung over his shoulder.

"To what do we owe the honor?" Mrs. Innis asked, her sarcasm heavy-handed.

"I've come on a duty call," Parker said, bowing before her. "No, I take that back. I've come as a Good Samaritan. I've brought gifts." He unslung the bag from his shoulder. "Sandals."

The reverend laughed, which drew a sour look from his wife.

"It's true," Parker went on, pointing at Nick's feet. "If the young lady isn't careful, she's going to come down with a bad case of jungle rot. In this climate, your feet have to breathe."

"I'm afraid Mr. Parker has a vested interest," the reverend said. "He's our only source of supplies."

"I make the sandals myself," Parker said proudly.

"Come, dear," Mrs. Innis said. "I'm sure Mr. Parker is just waiting for us to leave." She looked at Nick. "Poor George tends to preach when Mr. Parker is around."

Parker snorted. "Who needs hell and brimstone when you live in a place like this?"

There was no heat to his comment, and judging by the reverend's lack of reaction, it had been said many times before. Even so, his wife took hold of her husband and led the way into the rain, refusing Parker's offer of his umbrella.

Parker immediately turned his attention to Nick, openly admiring her figure. "Now what's it going to be, Miss Scott, Michelin or Goodyear? Personally, I find the Goodyear tread better in the rain."

"Whatever you say," she said, anxious to be rid of her soggy desert boots.

He fished a pair of sandals from his bag. "I cut these out myself not an hour ago. They're not retreads either, but low-mileage tires with a lot of wear left on them."

Nick was unable to tell whether he was joking or not, but that didn't stop her from pulling off her desert boots and socks. Her toes were white and puckered.

"I'd say we caught you just in time," Parker said, going down on one knee like a shoe salesman. The rubber straps, she noticed, were adjustable.

"I've seen sandals like these in Berkeley," Nick pointed out.

"Probably imported," he said, "crap from the Orient produced by cheap labor. Mine are a work of love. Of course, I also have the exclusive franchise here on Balesin." He grinned, displaying remarkably white teeth, a flaw in his disreputable beachcomber persona. "Come to think of it, I have an exclusive on just about everything of use on this island."

"What we could use," Nick said, "is some information about the Cargo Cult's airplanes."

"There's no profit in that," he said, his fingertips straying along Nick's ankle. "Besides, franchise or no franchise, I wouldn't last long on this island if I started poking around in John Frum's business."

"You're not going to last another ten seconds if you don't keep your hands to yourself."

Parker pulled back as if scalded. "Sorry. I'll add you to my list of taboos. Just don't forget, tell everyone in your party to steer clear of John Frum."

"We're all here but my students," Buettner said.

Parker nodded. "Yeah, I saw them on the way here."

"And?"

Parker wiggled an eyebrow and leered. "You're lucky. Most of the sexual taboos here on Balesin belong to the reverend."

21

Kobayashi linked with the CIA in Virginia, setting up a three-way conference call via satellite. The transmission, fully encrypted by Fuji mainframe computers in both Tokyo and Langley, was crystal clear.

"Targets marked," the agent reported.

"What about airplanes?" Farrington asked from Virginia. His question had Kobayashi grinning. What did the CIA man expect, miracles?

"Are you talking about the seaplane?" the agent asked. "Or the crap the natives build?"

"Just tell me what you've seen."

As the agent continued, Kobayashi appreciated how Farrington kept the man in line.

"The seaplane arrived, took off again with the lady archaeologist, circled for a while, then landed again to drop her off, and then left, heading toward Guam."

"Circling where?" Farrington asked, beating Kobayashi to the question by a split second.

"From where I was located, it looked like a reconnaissance of the old volcano. But it's only a guess, since they were out of my line of sight most of the time."

Kobayashi banged himself on the forehead. Satellite photos showed the planes on Mount Nomenuk to look much like the bomber that had started all this. But only if you knew what you were looking for, he consoled himself. An outsider, even an expert like the Scott woman, wouldn't know where to start.

"Have you seen the native airplanes?" Kobayashi asked.

"Yes. I'm not a hundred yards from the ones nearest the village."

"And?" Kobayashi asked, knowing full well what they looked like, since he was looking at a blowup of the airfield even as they spoke.

"If you ask me, they look like the models kids build. They're pretty good but wouldn't fool anybody."

"Are you satisfied that you're ready for all contingencies?" Kobayashi asked.

"Roger that," the agent answered.

Kobayashi thought all Americans were overconfident. "Very well. I don't have any more questions for the moment."

"I'm agreed," Farrington said from Langley.

"Stand by at the extraction point until we contact you," Kobayashi said and broke the link to the island. To Farrington he said, "Maybe we're worrying for nothing. We've both been over the photos. What is there to see after so many years? Nothing new, certainly."

"If there's nothing to worry about, why didn't your in-place agent show?"

"Perhaps he couldn't get away."

"We have a saying here," Farrington answered. "Sometimes the mouse may go where the tiger cannot."

Kobayashi glared at the microphone. What the hell did that mean? Was the man trying to be funny, or was his comment meant as some kind of insult?

"Go on," Kobayashi probed.

"It all depends on who's the mouse."

"Who do you have in mind?"

"Nick Scott is on the ground. We're not. There may be more to see there than what our satellites show."

"We've had people on the ground for years," Kobayashi pointed out. "And nothing has shown up."

"Are you telling me, you don't see any risk?"

"It's minimal," Kobayashi answered.

"Then you haven't done your homework on Nick Scott." Farrington laughed and broke the connection.

Kobayashi felt the beginnings of a pain in his chest and willed himself to relax. He turned his gaze toward the Tang horse as he often did in moments of stress and admired the delicate molding of the saddle. The statue had endured for centuries. He too could endure.

22

Nick joined Lily in the communal kitchen as soon as she could get away from Parker. The woman was perched on a stool with half a dozen children gathered around her, sitting cross-legged on the floor. They were staring up at her in awe, while she read from a Superman comic book.

At Nick's approach, Lily closed the book and nodded at the children, who immediately scampered out the door and into the sunset, visible now that the rain had stopped.

"I need your help," Nick said, having decided on a straightforward approach.

"I know. You want to see the airplanes. Sooner or later, everyone who comes here does."

"I'm no tourist, Lily. Airplanes are part of my work. I've written articles about the lost planes I've found."

"Not Henry's kind of planes, surely."

"Not until now, I admit."

"What kind of planes have you found?"

"World War Two planes, mostly. B-17s, B-24s, and a B-26."

"I was a young girl during the war. We had your kind of planes here then." Her eyes closed as if she were reliving the memory. "When they first came, we thought it wonderful, but the Japanese were very brutal. Many of our men were imprisoned or killed. We were not sorry to see them take their planes and leave."

"Did Henry model his planes after the Japanese planes he saw?"

"I can't speak for Henry."

"Then I'll have to ask him," Nick said in frustration.

Lily smiled. "Don't worry. I'll speak with Henry tonight. I'm sure he'll agree to a tour. Meet us in the square first thing tomorrow morning. The two of us will escort you to the old Japanese landing strip, which is now John Frum's."

Before Nick could thank her, a metallic clang sounded in the distance.

"Henry has kept his promise," Lily said as she took Nick by the hand and led her out the kitchen door and across the square to the newly constructed house. Elliot and Buettner had already inspected the place, she was told, and were even now fetching gear from the radio tent, with Tracy and Axelrad.

The house was a mixture of traditional building materials and what looked like salvage from World War

Two. The roof was thatched and steeply pitched, the walls an interlacing of bamboo and closely woven reeds. Inside, the floor was constructed of overlapping sheets of corrugated metal siding, scavenged from old Quonset huts, Nick guessed. Walking on it would have been precarious if it hadn't been for her new Goodyear footwear.

A series of rolled rattan mats hung from the crossbeams, held in place by sash cords. Like blinds, the mats could be lowered to partition the single room into private cubicles.

There were no furnishings at all.

"I apologize for the state of this place," Lily said. "With a big storm coming we had to cut corners to get the work done quickly. Otherwise, you would have been washed away."

Nick blinked in surprise and turned to peer back the way they'd come. Through the open doorway she could see the red sky.

"Don't be fooled," Lily said. "That wasn't the real storm. It was just a squall running before it. When John Frum sends a great storm, everything runs before it."

"But this isn't the cyclone season."

Lily smiled, as if to say John Frum's storms paid no attention to seasons.

"How soon will the storm be here?" Nick asked, thinking that once it arrived, she'd be unable to trek into the jungle. Coltrane would be grounded too.

"Henry says two days, no more."

"And you, Lily? What do you say?"

"It will be here with or without Henry's approval, but there will be enough time tomorrow for what you want."

As if emphasizing Lily's comment, the light changed

abruptly, the muted twilight giving way to darkness without transition.

"It's time," Lily said, grasping Nick's hand.

As Nick and Lily stepped onto the porch, torches flared to life, a semicircle of them surrounding the front of the house. In the flickering light, Nick saw that the villagers had gathered together outside without making so much as a sound. They stood in ranks, facing the house like an audience, and for a moment Nick felt as if the porch had become a stage and she an actor expected to perform.

She looked at Lily, who reassured her with a smile and a whisper. "Sit and watch while John Frum blesses your house."

Setting the example, Lily sat on the top step, beckoning Nick down beside her. Even as Nick was settling onto the step, Buettner and her father arrived, escorted by Henry Yali and the chief. Axelrad and Tracy trailed behind. With precise ceremony, all were seated, Buettner and Elliot one step below Nick and Lily, and the students at the bottom.

The ranking reinforced Nick's initial impression that Lily held the true power on Balesin. Yet it was Yali who raised a hand, a signal for a rhythmic clapping to begin. It was only then that Nick saw an American flag painted on the shaman's bare chest.

As one the crowd parted, forming an aisle down which ran half a dozen young boys. Cardboard wings had been attached to their arms, which they held out as they pretended to be airplanes. The wings were painted with five-pointed stars, the insignia of the American Air Force.

Nick groaned silently, thinking of the monumental

task ahead of her, sorting one cultural influence from
another.

As the boys drew closer, she saw that white circles
had been painted around their eyes, probably represent-
ing goggles. Their torsos were painted in a mottled camouflage design, similar to that used on airplanes during
World War Two.

The boys held spinning pinwheels in each hand as
they wheeled and maneuvered into a V-shaped formation directly in front of the porch. One by one they
came to a stop, their propellers still, and dropped their
arms to their sides.

Out of the corner of her eye, Nick saw Yali nod his
head. The boys responded immediately, raising their
hands to their hearts like soldiers pledging allegiance.

At a second signal from Yali, the boys extended
their arms toward Nick in a precise salute, or maybe the
salute was directed at the house, she couldn't be certain.
Whatever the intention, Nick felt confident that it was a
gesture of welcome.

She longed to whip out her camera but was afraid of
giving offense. There was nothing like a photograph to
lend credibility to a theory, no matter how crackpot.
Though as yet, she reminded herself, she had no right to
any kind of theory. So far, the only Cargo Cult planes
she'd seen had been glimpsed from the air, and at a
considerable distance.

The boys swept their hands away from their hearts
to point at the sky, then repeated the gesture, heart to
sky and back again.

It was a supplication to the gods, Nick felt certain.
Probably they were asking John Frum to bless the new
house. Or maybe they were beckoning to his spirit to
descend, to come in for a landing and join them. She

clenched her teeth in frustration. She wished she were more of an anthropologist instead of an archaeologist, but her expertise lay in objects rather than people.

As if reading her mind, Elliot leaned back to whisper, "Propellers in each hand. What do you make of that?"

Nick glanced at Lily, checking her response to Elliot's whisper. Lily nodded as if encouraging Nick to arrive at an answer that was probably an open secret among the islanders. Nick was feeling particularly dense. She replied, "Twin-engine planes like all the rest."

"Like the Widgeon, you mean?"

Nick sighed. Her father had put his finger on the problem. Which came first, the Widgeon or the egg? Logic said the twin-engine phenomena dated from the war. The most likely model was the medium-range Japanese bomber known as the Betty. But the markings on the young boys' "wings" had been American. Had the American symbol of power been superimposed on the Japanese plane or was the Widgeon the original model? It, too, had twin engines and offered a perfectly good template for the mock-ups Nick had seen. Certainly, she couldn't ignore the Widgeon as a possible corrupting influence if she eventually published anything on Balesin's Cargo Cult.

At Yali's command, the boys ran off, pretending to be airplanes once again. Yali followed in their wake. His departure triggered an exodus of villagers. The torchbearers remained.

Nick turned to Lily, hoping for help.

Lily said, "Mr. Parker at the store ordered the pinwheels for us, though Henry is working on his own version, with bigger propeller blades. He says we must be inventive like Americans." She smiled mischievously.

"Sometimes I think he forgets that America imports many of its goods."

"One thing America doesn't import is airplanes. We sell them to everyone else," Nick said.

Lily nodded. "Henry often talks about that. He dreams of the day when we will be rich enough to buy such wonders from America. Until then, he'll have to be content with his own designs. And the boys don't mind."

"The insignia on their wings was American," Nick probed.

"You'd know more about things like that than I would," Lily answered.

Nick gritted her teeth. Being diplomatic was a pain in the ass.

Lily rose. "It's time I returned home, and left you to yours." She started down the step, then paused. "Remember what I said about the storm coming. Don't be lulled by the stars in tonight's sky." Without further comment, she disappeared into the darkness.

Once they were inside the house, with the door closed against the constant humming of insects, Elliot adjusted their lanterns until they were producing maximum light.

"Now," he said, addressing Nick, "what was that Lily said about a storm?"

"She told me John Frum is sending us a big one."

Elliot and Buettner exchanged looks that quickly eroded into skeptical smiles.

"I thought Henry spoke for John Frum," Buettner said.

Nick shrugged.

"All right," Elliot said, striking a professorial pose,

"let's hear some interpretations of the ceremony we just witnessed." He nodded to the two students.

Axelrad looked behind him as if he couldn't believe he was being addressed and Tracy, Nick suspected, was on the verge of crying.

"That question's too easy," Buettner jumped in. "After all, what's to interpret? The boys had wings and insignias. They flew in formation. That makes them airplanes."

"Birds fly in formation, too," Elliot pointed out.

"Then, what about their gestures? A hand to the heart is pretty universal, I'd say. A heartfelt welcome is the way I'd translate it."

Elliot chewed at his lower lip for a moment. "That's probably a safe assumption. Even so, we should keep an open mind." He mimicked the childrens' salute, hand to heart and then skyward. "It could be a supplication to the gods, too. My heart to yours, John Frum."

"That's the most obvious," Nick agreed. "The sky, the heavens, the air above us, they're the usual symbols of God's domain."

"Let's not forget," Elliot went on, "that the Baleseans claim to be Christians. They attend Reverend Innis's church."

"Along with John Frum's," Nick pointed out. "Whose symbol is a Christian cross, albeit a bright red one."

Elliot nodded. "Point taken. So we're agreed then. Most likely we've been welcomed, maybe even blessed in the name of John Frum."

"Who is sending us a storm to remind us who's boss," Nick added.

"The rain's stopped and there isn't a cloud in the sky," Buettner said.

"Maybe so," Nick told him, "but I'll stick with Lily's prediction, if you don't mind."

Buettner snorted. "We can always use the radio and get the official forecast from Guam."

23

Nick found herself glad of the excuse to call Coltrane and make certain he'd gotten back to Guam safely. But the radio wasn't cooperating. So far it had produced nothing but static.

Buettner went down on his hands and knees to carefully disconnect and then reconnect every fitting. Once that was accomplished, he settled onto the folding chair and tried again.

The only result was a loud hiss from the speaker.

"Goddammit!" Buettner muttered. "They've got cell phones the size of pocket combs, computer chips you can stick in your ear, and we get this piece of crap. It cost a small fortune."

He grabbed a screwdriver and prepared to attack the radio's supposedly waterproof case.

Elliot intervened. "Here, let me try my hand at that." He commandeered the screwdriver, adjusted the lantern light, and bent over the radio. At the first turn of a screw, he leaned back and shook his head. "This screw was already loose. The seal's been broken."

Buettner glared at his grad students, who looked guilty, probably because they'd been assigned the grunt work of carrying the radio gear from the tent to the house.

Hunching his shoulders, Elliot went back to work. Four screws later, the case slipped off. Something rattled. It was immediately apparent there was a broken part, a wafer-size transistor board that had snapped completely in two.

"I don't want to sound paranoid," Nick said, "but that doesn't look like the result of an accident."

"Don't look at us," Alexrad said, Tracy joining his protest with a nod of her head.

"If you want to get back into my good graces," Buettner told them, "do the honors and fix us something to eat."

Buettner turned to Nick. "Who do you have in mind as chief saboteur?"

She shook her head. "I don't know. One minute life on this island seems idyllic, romantic even, and in the next I feel that something's out of whack. There's a sense of secrecy here that shouldn't be."

"Such as?" Buettner asked.

"According to Sam Ohmura's book the Cargo Cult is proud of its airplanes. Yet here, they're in no hurry to show them off, in case you haven't noticed."

"The weather's been bad, that's all."

"What about Mount Nomenuk being off-limits?"

"All cultures have their taboos, you know that," Buettner said. "Look at America. We're still repressed puritans at heart."

"I still say something's not right," Nick said. "Henry Yali is hiding something."

Elliot groaned theatrically. "Save us from a woman's intuition. My wife was a great one for that, you know. She put more stock in her intuition than anything else.

'Elliot,' she'd say, 'you're groping in the dark. You may have your books and your Ph.D., but I have insight."

"Like mother, like daughter, is that what you're saying?" Nick shot back with more heat than she'd intended. Even now, after so many years, Elaine was still inflicting pain. Or was it her father? All it took was a few words from Elliot to set her off. And yet the father that she still loved had once loved her mother, who Nick still had trouble thinking of with kindness, let alone affection. The guilt rubbed her raw.

Elliot ducked his head apologetically. "Sorry, Nick."

She forced a smile, but the damage was done. She could hear Elaine saying, *I have my insight.*

That was one of Elaine's mantras, uttered time and again.

The words had terrified Nick as a young girl.

I have my insight. It's in my blood, in my very soul. I will pass it onto you, an inheritance, so you will be just like me.

The thought had haunted Nick ever since, causing her to wonder if her genes were like time bombs waiting to explode. Would Nick's world turn black one day? Would she, like Elaine, end her days in dark depression?

Elliot said, "It was a joke, Nick. I've always said gut instinct is important. Without it, an archaeologist had better stay in a museum and leave the field work to those who have an innate feeling for their work."

"Enough already with the family history," Buettner said, holding up a placating hand. "The fact is, Nick is right. Usually, the Cargo Cult welcomes outsiders, especially Americans."

"They've built us a house, haven't they?" Elliot pointed out.

"True enough, but there's something else we should

consider. Maybe Sam Ohmura has ruined Balesin for the likes of us. Remember what happened to the Hopi Indians. They spoke freely to the first archaeologist they encountered and he exposed their private rituals. After that, the Hopi learned their lesson and told so many different stories, no one knew what to believe."

"That's a possibility," Nick conceded.

"On the other hand," Buettner went on, "Ohmura is a good anthropologist. If there'd been some secret agenda here on Balesin, I'm sure he would have mentioned it in his book, even if he hadn't known exactly what was going on."

Elliot spoke up. "There's another possibility. Henry Yali could be a nutcase."

"I've considered that, too," Nick said.

Buettner shook his head. "None of this explains why someone would want to sabotage the radio."

"To cause us grief, if nothing else," Nick said.

"That's not an unusual attitude among primitive peoples," Elliot responded. "Though I'm not at all sure the Baleseans belong in such a category any longer. They've had too much contact with the outside world, especially since the war, to be considered an unspoiled society. There's also the possibility that someone was just plain curious to see how a radio works and opened up the case."

"When could it have happened?" Nick asked.

"Possibly when you were out joyriding with your boyfriend," Elliot replied. "Curt and I were asking around about Walt Duncan, but he seems to be the invisible man." He turned an inquiring gaze on the two students. "As for you two, I thought you were supposed to be sorting things out here."

Tracy flushed a bright red while Alexrad stammered,

"Well, we did go out for a little while. Like we weren't gone very long. I mean, at least I don't think so."

"I'll get the food," Tracy said and hurried toward the rear of the house, Axelrad on her heels.

"Is that how you train your students, Curt?"

"Elliot, give it a rest," Nick said.

"It's moot anyway," Buettner added. "Coltrane won't let us down. He'll be back ASAP if he doesn't hear from us on the radio."

A moment later the rattan rustled as Karen Tracy ducked around the hanging mat carrying sandwiches. "Spam specials," she announced, "with cheese, the last of the cheese actually."

"And warm soda to wash it all down," Axelrad said as he arrived holding cans of cola.

"I ought to flunk you for lack of creativity," Buettner teased.

At Nick's first bite of the sandwich she realized just how ravenous she was. So intense was her hunger, in fact, even the Spam was tolerable.

Between mouthfuls Buettner said, "If Lily's right and a big storm is coming, we should get as much done as possible while the good weather holds. So we'll divide up the tasks. Elliot and I have already put our heads together on this and we're in agreement on a plan of attack, if that's acceptable to everyone."

He glanced around, saw no objections and continued. "Gail and Frank will provide our baseline, mapping the village hut by hut. Each name must be recorded by precise location if we're to verify social strata among the Baleseans. It's true that previous work on the island indicates that we're dealing with a matrilineal society, but prior work should never be taken for granted. So whatever you do, be exact and don't think of this as gruntwork. Without a baseline, anything we publish will be suspect. Understood?"

Wide-eyed, his students nodded one after the other.

"While you're doing that," Buettner went on, "Elliot and I will be recording interviews with as many villagers as we can. We'll be concentrating on origin myths and pre-World War Two customs. We'll also try to get Henry to send some scouts out to round up Walt Duncan. The last thing we can afford right now is a loose cannon."

He paused, taking another bite of his sandwich.

Elliot, by prearrangement, Nick suspected, continued. "That leaves you free to go after your airplanes, Nick."

"Agreed," she said. "As I see it, the key question is whether or not they're based on real aircraft. If we can determine that, we might eventually be able to answer the question of the evolution of John Frum as worshiped on Balesin. Is he based on a real man, as Henry Yali would have us believe, or is he myth?"

Elliot grinned. "That's my daughter. I trained her well."

"All right, Elliot," Nick said. "You're forgiven."

"Did I miss something?" Buettner asked.

Elliot shrugged halfheartedly. "Old family business, that's all."

Old wounds was more like it, Nick thought. Old wounds that never heal. Time did tend to scab them over, though, until now Nick found it easier to remember Elaine's good times, the times when the black shroud had lifted and she had become a loving mother.

"Now to the business at hand, daughter," Elliot went on. "I hope you have a plan of attack."

"I'm getting a guided tour of the airfield in the

morning," Nick said, enjoying the look of surprise on both their faces. "Lily, Yali, and I are meeting in the square and then heading for the Reverend Innis's church. Lily says that's the best place to start."

24

Bathed in sweat, the Reverend George Innis jerked upright in bed, his muscles board-stiff. By force of will he unclenched his jaw to call out, "Jesus Christ!"

Beside him, his wife, Ruth, came awake with a start.

"My God!" he breathed.

"Is it the dream again?" she asked tenderly, reaching out to comfort him.

"Worse."

"Tell me about it."

He sighed, venting air as if it were his last gasp. His heart thumped. That dream would give him a heart attack one day and kill him. Then, at least, he'd be free of it. Maybe. Or would it follow him all the way to hell?

Ruth found his hand in the darkness, took hold of it, and squeezed reassuringly. "You know it always makes you feel better to tell me about it, George. It helps you get back to sleep."

"Sleep," he repeated without conviction. Better to stay awake than to relive something like that twice in the same night.

But he told her just the same. "It started out like it always does. I was at the airfield. There were planes all around me. They looked very real and I kept reminding myself that I must keep clear of their spinning propellers. That if I didn't, it would happen to me like it had to the others. That I would be chopped into pieces like everyone else."

"My poor boy," she murmured. "You'd better tell me everything from the beginning, and be rid of it once and for all."

The reverend nodded in the darkness, swallowing against the lump growing in his throat. The dream was true. It had to be; it was too much like the stories he'd heard from Lily. But to Ruth he said, "It's only a dream."

"You know it will make you feel better if you tell me."

After a long, deep sigh he said, "Henry Yali was there, he and all his followers. At first, I thought they'd come to attend my sermon, so the sight of such a multitude made me very happy. I remember thinking that I'd finally gotten through to him, and that he had turned away from John Frum. But somehow my sermon went wrong. The words coming out of my mouth didn't make any sense, even to me, and Henry kept turning to his followers and shaking his head as if condemning me.

"I remember thinking that I might never get such a chance again. So I tried speaking more slowly. But it was no use, because suddenly the words coming out of my mouth were Henry's, not mine. And I could hear myself promising that John Frum would be here soon to save us all."

"Then what happened?" Ruth probed gently.

"I remember telling myself that I was speaking blasphemy. So I tried to stop, but the words kept coming. I was praising John Frum, the messiah. I was damning myself to hell."

He shuddered.

"My poor dear," she cooed, holding him, rocking him, humming softly.

"Then suddenly everyone changed. They were all wearing Japanese uniforms from the war, even Henry."

"You were only a baby when the war ended," she reminded him.

"Henry was wearing a sword," he went on. "He was an officer. He was the one who gave the order to fire and I . . ." The reverend had to pause for breath. ". . . fired like everyone else at the airfield."

"What airfield?" Ruth asked quietly.

"The one on Mount Nomenuk."

"And then?"

"I kept waiting for John Frum to step out of the plane, but it was Coltrane I saw through the windshield."

"There, you see how silly you're being. Mr. Coltrane's plane can only land on the water."

"The plane had two engines," Innis went on. "It looked like Coltrane's."

"Be calm, dear. It was only a dream. Remember that."

Sweet dreams, his mother used to say when she tucked him in. That was one of Innis's few memories of her. Sweet dreams, not nightmares.

He took a deep breath, steeling himself against what came next. "After we shot at the plane, the real killing started. At first I thought it was the propellers, but it was Henry's sword, whirling like a propeller, cutting off heads and splashing blood everywhere."

Innis squinted, trying to get a better look at the memory inside his head. Was it Coltrane who'd been killed or someone else? He was about to ask Ruth's opinion when he thought better of it. It was only a dream, after all.

He shivered. Or was it a premonition?

"Maybe I should warn Coltrane," he said.

"He'll think you're a fool," she replied. "Besides, he's flown away, so what difference does it make?"

Coltrane told himself he was being a fool, that business was business. But Nick Scott kept getting in the way.

He was standing in the doorway of the metal shed that served as his office, staring up at the sky. The horizon was black and threatening.

Christ, he should have heard from Nick by now. Or from Buettner anyway. But he hadn't been able to raise them on the radio since he left the island.

He shook himself. "You are being a fool. That woman can handle herself."

Besides, she wasn't on her own. She had her father and Curt Buettner, who was an old hand in this part of the Pacific. Even so, the loss of radio contact worried Coltrane. Probably it was nothing more than equipment failure caused by the usual jungle rot, he told himself.

"If you believe that," he added out loud, "why did you turn down that lucrative, short-hop charter?"

So he could fly back to Balesin as soon as the weather cleared, he thought, scanning the sky.

He ducked in the office to check the barometer. It was holding steady on rainy. When he tapped the glass, the arrow dropped to rock bottom.

"Shit!" That's what he got for using a quaint old-fashioned barometer that had markings like stormy, rain, and fair weather. Still, the damn thing was usually right.

Shaking his head, he tried the radio again, but five

minutes of fiddling with the frequency got him nothing but an earful of static.

After that, he locked up the office and headed for the Dai-Ichi Bar on the coast road overlooking Tumon Bay.

As usual, Bob Norris was bellied against the end of the bar, pretending to be drunk. But Coltrane knew, as did all the charter pilots flying out of Guam, that the boilermakers lined up in front of Norris were nothing but near-beer and apple juice. They were part of his act, as were his disreputable beachcomber clothes. He claimed it was his way of coping with all the abuse he took as a weather forecaster, but Coltrane knew that Norris was a reformed hell-raiser who was too proud to admit that an island girl had domesticated him. He flaunted his past only when out of her sight. Despite such quirks, he was still the best weatherman on the island, and most pilots, Coltrane included, trusted him with their lives.

"Still flying that albatross?" Norris asked with an exaggerated slur as Coltrane slid onto the stool beside him. On occasion he'd been known to slump off his stool entirely, pretending to pass out, when he had tourists for an audience.

Instead of taking the bait, Coltrane grabbed one of the shot glasses, downed the whiskey-colored juice, made a face and said, "No more for me, thanks. I'm flying today."

Norris raised the eyelids he'd been keeping at half-mast. "Even ducks wouldn't fly in this weather," he said, the slur slipping somewhat.

"Is that a reference to my trusted Widgeon seaplane?"

"I wouldn't go up in a 747, let alone some kind of moth-eaten bird."

"In case you haven't looked out the window lately, the rain's stopped. There's blue sky overhead."

Norris let out a deep breath. With it went all pretense of drunkenness. "What you're seeing is nothing but a sucker hole, a big one to be sure, but a sucker hole just the same. That rain squall that came through earlier was nothing but a shill for the big one to follow. Kind of like a stand-in warming up the audience."

"How big a storm?" Coltrane asked.

"Like I said, I wouldn't fly anything in the weather that's heading our way."

Coltrane thought that over. He'd known Norris a long time, long enough to know the man never joked about his weather forecasts. "How soon will it get here?"

"I'm a weatherman, not a psychic. Late tomorrow, the day after, it depends on the winds."

"Shit! I've got clients on Balesin."

"We're not talking tidal waves here and even in a worst-case scenario, there's plenty of high ground on that island."

"I've lost radio contact."

"In this climate, it's probably the batteries."

"That's what I figure. That's why I've got fresh replacements on board and ready to go." Coltrane shook his head, remembering Buettner had also taken a generator along.

Norris leaned close. "It's not like you to play nursemaid to a bunch of tourists."

"Tourists on a place like Balesin? You've got to be kidding. They're scientists."

"Then, they ought to be smart enough to take care of themselves."

"You've heard the rumors about the natives on some of these islands."

Norris grinned. "The only rumor I've heard lately is about a good-looking lady archaeologist."

Coltrane shrugged, feigning nonchalance.

"I'd know that sappy look anywhere," Norris said, leering. "I saw it in the mirror the morning after I met my first two wives."

"If I leave at first light, do you think I'll have time to fly in, pick them up, and fly out again?"

Norris shook his head.

"Then I'll beach the Widgeon and stay over." Coltrane spun off the bar stool and headed for the door.

"I hope she's worth it," Norris called after him.

Coltrane waved, acknowledging the comment, but kept going. He wasn't flying in bad weather just for Nick Scott, he told himself. It was his duty; it was an obligation he had to all his clients.

He grinned. Like hell.

25

Nick awoke to bright sunlight stabbing through chinks in the rattan wall. So much for Lily's predicted storm, she thought, and sat up, feeling rested and grateful for a bug-free night. For the first time since leaving Berkeley, she felt free of jet lag.

She grabbed a towel, a change of underwear, and limped to the shower tent, which Axelrad and Tracy had moved into position last night. Thank God for student labor, she thought as she stood under the trickle of cool water, recalling her own years of slave labor. In some ways, she was still a slave, shackled and untenured.

The slow drip was a far cry from yesterday's invigorating dip in the surf. Tomorrow she'd make the walk to the beach and bathe there again, no matter how many bystanders turned up to stare at her red hair.

Nick cut off the flow, such as it was, to lather up. After that came a quick rinse to conserve water, since it had to be hand-carried from the river. Even slave laborers got tired.

Once dressed in lightweight jeans and a workshirt, she slipped her aching feet into their Goodyears. By then, Axelrad and Tracy were waiting outside the tent, with towels draped over their shoulders and wicked grins on their faces.

"We thought we'd save water by sharing," Tracy said the moment Nick ducked under the modesty flap.

"I'm jealous," Nick called after them, joking. Yet even as she'd spoken, Lee Coltrane had come to mind. She wondered what he'd look like in the shower.

She shook her head sharply. Now wasn't the time, she told herself. Stick to business. Stick to airplanes. They might crash and kill you, but they never cheated on you or lied.

Coffee was waiting when Nick returned to the house. There was a note under the cup. *Curt and I have gone for a swim. After that we'll be working in the village. Don't forget to take lunch with you.* No doubt the lunch Elliot had in mind was one of the packets of freeze-dried trail mix stacked next to the butane coffeemaker.

Grimacing, Nick loaded half a dozen of the packets into a lightweight backpack. Next, she zipped a small camera into the pack's waterproof pouch, along with extra film. That done, she tore open one of the packets and munched trail mix, washing it down with coffee. It wasn't exactly a square meal, but it would do.

Nick was on her second cup when she heard a commotion outside. The moment she stepped outside she saw Henry Yali's platoon double-timing away from the flagpole, counting cadence. Children scattered out of their way. When the platoon reached the communal house, Yali barked an order, which Nick couldn't make out. His men dispersed quickly and stacked their "rifles" in front of the porch, where Lily was watching their every move.

The military display was far from reassuring. If Nick was going to succeed in her quest for the origin of John Frum's airplanes, she needed Henry as a peacemaker, not a soldier.

Yali, sounding like a drill sergeant, shouted another sharp order. Instantly, his men were on their way again, still double-timing, though their formation was now somewhat ragged as they disappeared into the jungle.

So much for Henry guiding her to his sacred airfield, Nick thought and started across the square. Lily met her halfway, at the base of the flagpole, where the American flag hung limply. There was no breeze, no sign of a storm. The sky was a blinding blue, the temperature as steamy as ever. Already, Nick felt as if she hadn't showered in days.

"What was that about?" Nick asked, nodding in the direction of the platoon's disappearance.

"Your father has persuaded Henry to look for your missing friend. Henry likes to do things in a very organized way. But don't worry, dear. He has given his blessing to our expedition, but only as far as the old Japanese base. The mountain is forbidden." Lily smiled. "It will be better this way, just the two of us."

Nick sighed with relief.

"I'm ready to leave now if you are," Lily said.

"Just let me get my things," Nick replied before hurrying back to the house to retrieve her shoulder pack.

When she returned, Lily took her arm and led the way across the square to where the Mission Highway began. For the first twenty yards, it was broad enough to justify its name. After that, the road shrank to a jungle path no more than six feet across. Its surface was reasonably firm, considering the amount of rain that had fallen in the last twenty-four hours. Even so, mud clung tenaciously to the treads of Nick's Goodyears. Her protesting feet felt leaden, while Lily seemed totally unaffected.

Without her Goodyears though, Nick would have been completely incapacitated.

Well, that was a debt she owed Todd Parker. To show her thanks, maybe she'd buy something at the man's store, perhaps gifts for the children if such things were available.

"Will there be time to shop at Mr. Parker's?" she asked.

"If we stop there, we'll have to pay our respects at the church. Knowing the reverend, that could take more time than you might want to spare."

"Airplanes first, then," Nick said without hesitation.

Lily nodded and picked up her pace. Nick was hard-pressed to keep up.

The Reverend Innis and his wife, Ruth, were waiting outside the church.

"Sometimes I think the man has radar," Lily murmured while she and Nick were still out of earshot.

What he had, Nick saw, was a watchtower. It was perched on the top of the church, whose entire structure came as a total surprise. She'd been expecting something more traditional, something in the vein of the village's communal building, only with a steeple topped by a large white cross. What stood before her was a metal Quonset hut, original World War Two equipment by the looks of it. Its only modification was the raised, rickety-looking watchtower that had been attached to the hut's rounded, igloo-like roof. The tower had a small platform at its top, a one-man observation post. The only cross in sight was a small one, not much bigger than a crucifix, nailed over the door.

The island store, another corrugated Quonset, was separated from the church by a narrow path, an extension of the Mission Highway that turned north. The store had been painted green once, or perhaps a mottled camouflage color. With the passage of time, the paint had eroded away until only a few spots of color clung to the corrugated crevices like mold. A bright plastic sign, CLOSED, hung from a nail on the front door.

"We never close," the reverend said when he saw Nick eyeing the notice.

"It's not like Mr. Parker to lose business by closing this time of day," Lily observed.

"He'll open up when our children arrive for school," the reverend's wife said, peering expectantly back along the trail. "They should have been here by now. Did you pass any children on the way here?"

"I wouldn't count on them coming today," Lily replied. "Henry's called an alert."

Nick blinked in bewilderment. Why hadn't Lily mentioned that before?

"I knew it," the reverend blurted. "It's always the

same when planes come here and disrupt our lives. I had a dream last night. In it I—"

Ruth laid a restraining hand on the reverend's arm, silencing him, and said, "Is there a problem we should know about, Lily?"

I hope it's not me, Nick thought to herself. But if she were the cause of the alert, why would Lily be acting as her guide?

"Henry hasn't told me," Lily said, "but he's very upset."

Innis nodded. "Do you think I should offer Henry my help?"

"Let's hope it's nothing," Lily answered. "Probably it's best if we all just go about our business, and not worry about things we can't change."

Suddenly, staring at Lily, Nick realized how little she understood the Baleseans. On the one hand, they sought to emulate America; they spoke English; they attended the Reverend Innis's church when it suited them. On the other hand, they worshiped John Frum and were as alien as visitors from another world. She took a deep breath. That was the trouble with being an archaeologist instead of an anthropologist. She preferred dealing with the dead, not the living.

"Whatever it is," Ruth said, "I don't see why the children shouldn't be in school."

Instead of answering, Lily put her hands to the small of her back and stretched, squinting up at the dazzling sky. "When John Frum sends one of his great storms, perhaps it's best that we all stay close to home."

Both the reverend and his wife looked up at the sky and nodded.

"How soon will it arrive?" Innis asked.

"Soon enough so that Nick and I must be on our way if we're to see the airplanes ahead of the rain."

Innis's eyes widened. "You're taking her to the airfield?"

At Lily's nod, Innnis's mouth dropped open.

"If I were you, I'd get ready for the storm," Lily said, then took hold of Nick's arm and guided her along the path that ran between the Quonsets.

"I was here a year before I saw the airfield," Innis called after them.

"Stop by for tea on your way back," his wife added.

"Don't forget your shutters," Lily said over her shoulder. For Nick's benefit she whispered, "There's another way home from John Frum's airfield. We'll take that route."

Within a few steps, the jungle closed in around them as if the Quonsets had never existed. At that point, the path could no longer claim to be a road. It was a game trail, wide enough only for walking single file as it snaked through the trees. Nick had a sense that they were gradually winding their way north, though that could have been an illusion since the thick foliage overhead kept her from using the sun as a reference point.

"Stay close to me," Lily told her. "I know what to watch for."

"Nothing carnivorous, I hope."

Lily laughed and kept going.

According to Professor Ohmura's book, there were no indigenous poisonous snakes inhabiting islands in this area of the Pacific. So the worst that might happen was treading on a coconut crab.

"There are false trails all over this part of the island," Lily said. "We have to be wary of them."

That seemed to imply a system of deliberate deception, Nick thought, but why the laying down of false trails might be necessary on such a remote island she couldn't imagine.

"Lily, how many tourists come to Balesin every year?"

"You are the first in a long time. And none of you are what I would call tourists. You ask more of us than a tourist."

Lily halted and turned to face Nick. "Your eyes reveal you, child. They tell me that you are much like Henry. Like I was, too, when I was younger. You have great faith in your work."

"Have you lost your faith, Lily?" Nick asked cautiously.

"I think maybe you can restore it, child, if anyone can. I pray that's why you've come. Or else . . ." Her eyes glazed over and Nick had the feeling that Lily was now focused on some inward vision.

Suddenly the woman shook herself, as if to cast off her thoughts. "Come. John Frum's base is just ahead."

"And the Japanese and their base?" Nick risked.

"Oh, they're still here all right. They will never leave us."

Lily, as if invigorated, hurried forward. By now, Nick's feet felt like they were on fire. More than anything, she longed to soak them in cold water. Or any kind of water.

Minutes passed. Lily's "just ahead" stretched into a quarter of a mile, maybe more. Nick checked her watch. Though supposedly waterproof, the crystal had steamed up, totally obscuring the hands.

Nick caught a glimpse of the sun. It had yet to reach its zenith.

Abruptly, Lily broke free of the jungle. For a moment, Nick thought it was only a small clearing. But when she moved forward to stand beside Lily, she realized that the trees had been felled all the way to the sea and that they were standing on the runway itself, the one she'd seen from the air.

The runway was half a mile long, perhaps longer. Its unpaved surface sprouted ankle-high grass. Considering the lushness of the vegetation and the year-round growing season, the runway had to have been mown quite recently.

"This was the main Japanese landing strip on the island," Lily said. "They built two when they first arrived. They had great expectations, but they never had the need for more than one place to land airplanes."

"Where is the other strip?" Nick asked, expecting confirmation that it was the one she and Coltrane had flown over on the slopes of Mount Nomenuk.

"Swallowed up by the jungle long ago," Lily replied as she laid a hand on Nick's arm. "Child, let me give you some advice. Sometimes it's best to let the past die."

"Looking for the past is my job."

Lily sighed deeply. "I know that. It's why I brought you here. But I want you to remember that to me this past was once my present. And it wasn't a happy time."

Lily pointed south, toward the sea. Nick could see the remains of a man-made structure. "You see that lighthouse. It's abandoned now, but more than fifty years ago, the Japanese built it to warn their fleet of the reefs that surround our island. But it was a wasted effort. Their ships never came again in great numbers after that first landing, not even to evacuate their soldiers at the end. They were left here to die." Lily shook her head slowly. "It is a terrible thing to die alone and abandoned. Let us hope that such things never happen again."

Staring at the lighthouse, Nick realized that it looked in remarkably good condition. "Is the lighthouse still used?"

"There's no need for it. The only ships we ever see know better than to come in close. They anchor offshore, beyond the reefs, and send in small boats. Mind you, the Japanese knew what they were doing, building the lighthouse there. It marks the most sheltered cove on the island. That's where they kept their shallow-draft landing craft. In the end, they were sunk there, too, not by the weather but from bombs."

Nick turned back to the runway. More than anything, she wanted to ask about the airstrip on Mount Nomenuk, but decided it would be better if she could somehow coax the information from Lily without direct questions.

"Did you see the airplanes that landed here during the war?" she asked.

Lily nodded. "They seemed gigantic to me, but then I was a young girl. The soldiers seemed like giants, too. I hated them. We all did. They and their airplanes. Their planes were not from John Frum."

"It would be a great help if you could describe the planes that landed here."

"Which planes?"

"The Japanese . . ." Nick caught her breath. "Were there other kinds?"

"American planes came too, but that was later."

"Lily, anything you can remember will be helpful."

"You can see them for yourself in a moment."

Nick peered up and down the runway. There was nothing man-made in either direction, not even a rusting war relic, though the northern end of the runway was obscured by a fold in the landscape.

"I don't see anything," Nick complained.

Lily smiled reassuringly. "From here, neither do I."

She headed north. As Nick followed, a surge of adrenaline shot through her like an electric shock. Her fingers tingled in expectation. The thought of touching an artifact, a piece of history, had her short of breath. A true find, her father liked to say, put sex to shame. She wondered if he had sublimated his feelings as his marriage disintegrated. Or was she the one sublimating?

The heat, added to Nick's flush of excitement, was oppressive. Sweat flooded her eyes. Distantly, her feet throbbed, but she didn't care. A real airplane, even if only in pieces, might be enough to provide the template for John Frum's air force. And even if such a template didn't coincide with the models she'd seen on Mount Nomenuk, finding a Japanese plane would be a feat in itself. Few had survived the war, and those that did had been quickly destroyed by the occupying forces. The one or two that remained were in museums.

They topped the rise.

"My God!" Nick whooped, elated.

Two planes stood at the head of the runway, twin-engined, twin-tailed, which made them Mitsubishi G3M2s, nicknamed Nells, the Japanese Navy's long-range bomber. Nearby lay the rusted hulk of a Japanese tank.

But the moment she wiped the sweat from her eyes, elation gave way to disappointment. She'd been guilty of wishful thinking. The planes weren't real. They were mock-ups. "Dammit!"

"What's wrong?" Lily asked hurriedly.

"It's not your fault, Lily. I was fooled there for a minute, that's all." Fooled just like the followers of John Frum intended. It was a good thing she wasn't a pilot.

Otherwise, she'd have killed herself landing for a closer look. "Is it all right if we see them close-up?"

"Of course. Touch them if you'd like, but be careful. Henry is very proud of all the hard work that went into building them."

"May I take photographs?"

"I didn't ask Henry about that, but I don't see why not."

After snapping several long-shots, Nick moved in for a closer inspection. The detail work amazed her. Leaves, branches, and mud bound with hemp twine had been worked together to achieve surfaces that looked almost metallic. The wings and tail were properly tapered. White leaves, almost silver in color, simulated the cockpit glass. Underneath it all had to be some kind of wooden skeleton, much like the models she'd built as a young girl. The only jarring note was the undercarriage. Instead of wheels, the airplane rested on wooden struts that had been driven directly into the ground. Even so, the achievement was stunning.

Nick shook her head, annoyed with herself for giving way to even a moment's disappointment. The mockups in front of her were as good as the dummy aircraft the allies had used to fool German aerial reconnaissance during the war. Had these two mock-ups been here during the war, our own P-38s might easily have mistaken them for Nells and strafed them, she thought.

Despite their twin-engine, twin-tail configuration, Nick was a long way from proving that the mock-ups had been fashioned after the Nell. For instance, why would the Baleseans use a Nell as a model when they hated the Japanese? It didn't make sense, especially since John Frum seemed to love everything American. That left Nick with only two other twin-engine, twin-tail

American possibilities, the P-38 fighter, and the B-25 medium bomber. But the P-38 had distinctive twin booms behind the engines, while the mock-ups didn't. She racked her brain for other planes with similar configurations. Only three came to mind, the British Manchester and two German planes, the Dornier and the Messerschmitt 110. And none of them had been used in the Pacific, as far as she knew.

"I need to know what planes were Henry's models for building these replicas," Nick said.

Lily tapped the side of her head. "He flies them in his dreams."

Nick clenched her teeth in frustration.

"The planes come from John Frum," Lily went on. "They belong to him as we do. As does everything. Even Jesus is a part of John Frum's plan."

"I'm not sure the Reverend Innis would agree," Nick said.

Lily smiled, a perverse glint in her eyes. "The reverend does John Frum's work. He just doesn't know it."

"Did Henry admire the Japanese airplanes when they were here?"

"Not during the war."

"And now?"

"There are those who say the Japanese didn't really lose the war. They say the Japanese are richer than America even. They say that we should look toward Japan, not America, because it is a much closer neighbor."

"Does Henry say these things?"

"Henry speaks for John Frum."

"That doesn't answer my question, Lily."

Lily closed her eyes. "When Japanese planes were stationed here . . ." She opened her eyes and pointed at the runway beneath their feet. ". . . the American planes dropped bombs on them. After a while, the Japanese gave up bringing their planes here. Or maybe they had none left to spare. After that, the Japanese came here only in very small ships, but as the war went on even those stopped arriving. Finally, the soldiers could only be supplied by air. Their cargo was dropped by parachute at night. Not all went to the Japanese. John Frum saw to it that some of the cargo drifted inland, where we could find it."

"What type of cargo?" Nick asked.

"Young women do not go looking in the dark for such things."

Nick decided to try another approach. "Why did Henry choose this spot to build John Frum's air force?"

"We built them for you, of course, because we knew John Frum would send you here to us. And we were right. Your coming has proved John Frum's power. Soon, even more cargo will arrive."

"Do I count as cargo?" Nick asked.

Lily smiled. "Only if John Frum sent you."

"Do you believe he did?"

"I think Henry does."

26

April 18, 1942
The North Pacific

He couldn't get his wife out of his mind. They were already an hour into the mission, an hour away from the *Hornet*. Or where the *Hornet* used to be, Johns corrected himself. She'd cut them loose and run. The only thing she could do. And his wife, would she cut loose and run? Johns imagined her waiting for him when he came home. All smiles, as if nothing had happened.

He was jolted out of his reverie by an anxious call on the intercom. "Smoke on the horizon!"

The B-25 dove so suddenly Johns was thrown against the bulkhead. Through the Plexiglas nose, he could see the ocean coming up at them at an alarming speed. The navigator held on, praying the pilot would be able to pull up in time.

"Christ," he breathed with relief as the bomber leveled off at the wave tops and turned away, off course, but a necessary maneuver to follow orders. Avoid contact. All shipping was to be considered enemy shipping.

"Navigator, come to the cockpit," the pilot snapped.

Johns, still swallowing hard to get his stomach back under control, grabbed his maps. As soon as he poked his head into the cockpit, the pilot said, "I've done a one-eighty. I'll hold her on this course for another three minutes and then climb into the clouds. Once under cover, we'll circle well clear of the smoke before coming back onto our course. Will you still be able to get us there?"

"Leave it to me."

"Bombing Tokyo with the others would have been easier," the copilot said.

Johns started to nod, then caught himself. At least we'll have enough gas to get home, he thought, even with the added weight of two passengers.

He eyed the solid cloud cover above them and crossed his fingers. "I'll get you there, skipper." He tried to instill confidence in his voice. They had to believe in him or they might panic.

He hustled back to his cubbyhole and began running

a clock as soon as the skipper turned north and began climbing. At thirty-two hundred feet exactly they were socked in and flying blind. From now on their survival depended on his ability to account for every deviation from their original course. Time, speed, wind drift, a mistake in calculating any one of them would get them killed. He no longer thought about his wife.

27

By the time Nick and Lily reached the village square, Yali's platoon was drawn up beside a bonfire that had been built near the flagpole. A rolled tarp, with a small lump inside, lay at the foot of the pole. For an instant Nick was reminded of a snake that had just swallowed its kill.

Everybody, including her father and Buettner, were staring at it. Karen Tracy was sobbing hysterically in the arms of a pained-looking Frank Axelrad.

At Nick's approach, Elliot looked up and shook his head. "Bad news. There's been a death. Henry found Walt Duncan, or what's left of him."

Nick stared at the small bulge in the tarp. "What happened?" she asked.

"God knows," Buettner answered, revealing stricken eyes. "Henry says the crabs got at him, but . . ." He seemed to run out of words.

Nick, eyeing Yali intently, said, "Henry, are you saying the crabs killed him?"

The shaman's casual shrug belied the furtive look in his eyes.

"What about you, Chief?" Nick turned her gaze on Jim Jeban. "Do you think that crabs attacked a man?"

Jeban's fearful eyes betrayed him completely, and made Nick reassess Yali's reaction. What she'd taken to be a furtive look was much more than that. Yet whatever she'd seen in his eyes was now gone, replaced by a steely look of determination, not to mention a clamped jaw. Both men were hiding something. She felt certain of that. Judging from Elliot's raised eyebrow, he agreed with her.

She was wondering how to pry loose their secrets when Buettner spoke up. "I blame myself for this. Walt Duncan was once my student. He . . ." Buettner's eyes shimmied away from the tarp. ". . . he wouldn't have come here if it weren't for me. His death is on my hands."

"Duncan's student days were long gone," Elliot reminded him. "He was faculty and a professional. He came here hoping to make a discovery just like the rest of us. Remote locations have their dangers. He understood that."

"Christ!" Buettner muttered. "More fools us, then. We all think fame is just around the corner, but sometimes, when we turn that corner . . ." He looked down at the tarp. ". . . something else is waiting for us. In Walt's case, he was trying to prove my theory about an Anasazi connection. So that makes him my responsibility, whatever you say."

Elliot shook his head. "If I remember correctly, you told all your students the same story. Not all of them were crazy enough to believe you."

"You're here, aren't you?" Buettner shot back. "So is Nick. Does that make you two crazy?"

"Probably," Elliot answered.

Buettner opened his mouth as if to fire another salvo, but ended up nodding in agreement. "You're right, Elliot. This is no time to feel sorry for myself. We've got work to do."

"Did you examine the body?" Nick asked.

Buettner looked away. It was Elliot who said, "Thanks to the crabs there wasn't much to see."

"Maybe you need another opinion," she said.

Elliot answered with one of the long-suffering sighs that had once driven Nick's mother wild. Then he forced a smile and said, "We're in your hands, daughter." His nearly invisible wink, however, said he had his suspicions about Duncan's death.

Nick drew a bead on Henry Yali. "What do you think happened?"

He wrinkled his nose to indicate the faint smell that was already in the air and shrugged.

"As a duly authorized magistrate of the United States Government I am authorized to issue a death certificate," Chief Jeban said.

"And what are you going to put down on the certificate, 'Death by Crabs?' " Nick spat.

Lily grasped her arm, squeezing hard, whether for support or to send some kind of warning Nick couldn't tell.

"I told your father that the crabs got to him," Yali said matter-of-factly. "I didn't say they killed him. If you ask me, your friend was there for the taking, on the ground, dead or dying, and unable to defend himself. Such things happen. It's the way of nature and the will of John Frum."

"How did you know where to look?" Nick asked, recalling how Yali and his platoon of men had trooped off into the jungle only a couple of hours ago, their movements too precise for those of a random search party. Surely, searchers would have spread out rather than stay in formation.

Yali shrugged. "We came across him by accident."

Nick glared at Yali, hoping to spot a crack in his composure, but the shaman merely folded his arms and smiled back.

Lily was now gently tugging on Nick's arm, but Nick persisted, "Where did you find the body?"

"Where it shouldn't have been."

"I saw you and your men march off this morning. You knew where to look, then, didn't you?"

"We found him in one of John Frum's places. It has no name that you would recognize."

Nick looked to her father, who spoke up. "We'd like to see it for ourselves."

Yali shook his head. "There is nothing to see. And even if there were, the coming rain would soon wash all signs away."

As if on cue, the first drops began falling, drumming against the tarp.

"Just a goddamned minute," Buettner blurted. "Walt Duncan was a young man, no more than thirty. He'd been on any number of field expeditions and knew how to take care of himself. Even if he had broken a leg or some such thing, he would have been able to cope."

Lily released Nick and said, "What would you have us do? We have no police here on Balesin. There was no need until you and your people came here. As soon as possible, we'll notify the authorities on Guam. Until then, all we can do is pray for your Mr. Duncan."

Lily nodded at Yali, who in turn gestured to his men. Four of them immediately detached themselves from the platoon and took up the tarp, hoisting it onto their shoulders.

"We'll bury him immediately," Jeban said. "And since tomorrow is Sunday, we'll ask the Reverend Innis to hold a memorial service."

28

The Reverend Innis stared accusingly at his wife. She was sitting in the front pew, peering up at him as he practiced his sermon. Never before had she interrupted him to say such a thing.

He blinked. Maybe he'd misunderstood her. Maybe it was his own wishful thinking he'd been hearing. With an exaggerated gesture, he inserted a pinkie finger into his ear as if clearing away the wax.

"You heard me all right," Ruth said. "There's no call to hold services for that man just because he died on the island. He was an outsider."

"We have to consider his soul," the reverend responded. "To do otherwise would be . . ." He raised his hands, then dropped them to his side. The thought of a lost soul, unattended, made his heart ache. And on this island of all places, with its secrets and its unaccounted dead. Well, maybe not unaccounted, he thought to himself. Not anymore. He'd seen to that a long time ago, conducting his own private, one-man service for the forgotten dead. It was all recorded in his diary, the one thing he'd kept secret from Ruth all these years.

"Listen to me," she said, interrupting his thoughts, "we don't even know the man's beliefs. Holding services might even be a violation of his faith, or his last wishes." She shook her head slowly. "I've never known Chief Jeban to ask you to hold any kind of services before. The plain fact is, he and Henry would be happy if we disappeared from Balesin altogether."

The reverend sighed with relief, but not too loudly. Ruth had given him a way out, but he couldn't take it. A man's soul was at stake. His, too, maybe.

She smiled as if reading his silence as indecision. "Mr. Duncan might be a Muslim or a Jew," she went on quickly. "In that case, our service might be an affront, or maybe even sacrilegious."

"Surely, his friends would know," the reverend replied, thinking it was about time he dug out his diary from its hiding place and made a new entry covering recent events.

His wife, not pausing to listen, continued. "It would be just like Henry to get up to mischief like that, getting us into trouble with your bishop. Besides . . ." She rose from the pew and approached the reverend's raised dais. ". . . I have this terrible feeling that he's up to something. I can feel the tension in the air."

"Now, Ruth," he consoled. "That's to be expected when someone dies."

She folded her arms across her bosom and glared at him, a sure sign she was upset.

"Have you been talking to Lily again?" he asked.

"I wouldn't discount a woman like Lily. If you ask me, she knows just about everything that goes on."

"She also knows every old wives' tale, most of them good for nothing but frightening children."

Her glare closed down to a condemning squint. "You shouldn't scoff at things you don't understand. Where would we be if everyone demanded proof of the miracles that we take on faith."

The reverend sighed. Somehow, they'd strayed from the point, that they were both uncomfortable with the chief's request for a memorial service.

"What would you think if Henry and I got together to say a few prayers instead of a formal ceremony?" the reverend said.

"Where?"

"The village square maybe, if it doesn't rain."

Her eyes widened, a sign that her mood was brightening. "You know what Henry will say."

The reverend nodded. "The same thing he always does, that John Frum is coming. No one pays attention anymore. Henry's been saying that since the war."

"I heard him say John Frum is here already."

The reverend twitched. That was something new. "Are you sure?"

"He said John Frum is here to drive out the unwanted." She opened her arms to him. When he stepped down from the dais to hold her there were tears in her eyes.

She spoke against his chest. "To Henry, we're unwanted, too, I think."

The reverend shuddered. Balesin had a terrible history when it came to unwanted outsiders.

Coltrane cursed his luck. The point of no return was coming up, and he was screwed either way. If he turned back, he'd be heading directly into the teeth of the storm. If he continued on toward Balesin, he'd be flying through one squall line after another. The one he was in now had visibility down to half a mile. He switched the Widgeon's windshield wipers to high and leaned forward, squinting through the Plexiglas. All he could see was an angry, wind-whipped ocean below and clouds above.

Coltrane gritted his teeth. Turning back was out of the question. Continued loss of radio contact with Balesin had seen to that. A ferry pilot had responsibilities to his passengers, he told himself, an unwritten code. He couldn't leave them stranded. Besides, continuing on to the island gave him a tail wind. That was worth considering.

He snorted. Who was he kidding? He had Nick Scott on the brain. He smiled in spite of himself. Scott on the brain sounded like some kind of rare disease.

Wind shear bounced the Widgeon. When the plane steadied, he checked the heading, just as he had been doing every few minutes since leaving Guam. On course, the satellite navigator said. Well, by God, it had better be right, considering the small fortune he'd paid for it. The gear had put Coltrane Airlines into the red for months.

Without thinking, he reached out to tap the dial, then caught himself. Electronic gear could be touchy. Tapping the fuel gauge or oil gauge was one thing, messing with the gods of electronics quite another.

He'd already had one run-in with those gods. A faulty warning light had delayed his takeoff from Guam by more than an hour. Otherwise, he would have been ahead of the storm. The problem turned out to be a short circuit, triggering a light bulb on the temperature gauge. It had happened before but couldn't be ignored.

Coltrane tried radioing Balesin again, got no reply,

then switched to Guam's frequency and asked for an updated weather forecast.

It was Bob Norris who answered. "Only a lunatic would fly in this kind of weather."

"It takes one to know one," Coltrane replied, aware that Norris was out of shift, and should have been home in bed instead of manning the radio. "I thought you told me it was going to be bright sunshine all the way to Balesin."

"I told you not to fly, for Christ's sake. Where are you, anyway?" The concern was obvious in Norris' voice despite the background static.

Coltrane checked his watch. "Just passing the point of no return, if my calculations are correct."

"That would be a first."

"So would an accurate weather forecast."

"Enough bullshit," Norris said, his language flaunting protocol and FCC regulations. "What's your situation?"

"I've got a fifty-knot tailwind. Visibility is maybe half a mile, but not getting any worse at the moment. So I figure, I'm still running ahead of the nastiest part of your storm. Over."

"I'm looking at the map," Norris said. "If you're halfway, with that kind of tailwind, you ought to make landfall with plenty of daylight to spare. But once you get down, haul that goose of yours up on the beach and tie her down. This is going to be one humdinger of a blow."

"What about wind direction?" Coltrane asked.

"From the north. Seventy-five knots, maybe more."

"I'll land on the south side of the island."

"Watch your clock. If you don't spot the island on time, turn back."

To where? Coltrane wondered, but kept the thought to himself. They both knew that if his navigation was off in the least, he'd miss Balesin and be as good as dead.

He signed off the radio feeling sweat trickle from his armpits. If he was going to fly across the island to land on the south side, he'd have to watch out for the volcano, Mount Nomenuk. It was two thousand feet high, but he couldn't afford to fly at that altitude and risk missing land altogether. Instead, he'd have to stay low and hope he spotted that damned mountain in time to fly around it.

In Honolulu, Sam Ohmura entered his well-appointed den, furnished to perfection by his wife, closed the door behind him, and approached his radio as if it were a time bomb. Gingerly, he switched on the set and waited for the promised message.

Promised, he murmured to himself, playing the word over and over again inside his head. His surfing career had shown great promise at one time, with sponsors lined up offering money for his endorsement. His academic career had shown similar promise, only to be eclipsed by the likes of Curt Buettner, and even Walt Duncan. Only his bank account continued to show promise. More than promise, actually. All that money paid in for contingencies, options as Kobayashi liked to call them. Options that so far had never been exercised. Money for work never done, for being on call, for being a sleeper who'd hoped never to be awakened, until his fateful call from Guam.

Only now, Ohmura suspected, he was about to be awakened from a nightmare. One over which he had no control, or no knowledge for that matter, other than that he was being held responsible for events on a remote island. A useless island as far as he was concerned, despite its unique Cargo Cult religion.

The trouble was, Ohmura had been away from his homeland, Japan, for a long time now. In the eyes of a man like Kobayashi that made Ohmura suspect, subject to the corruption of the western lifestyle.

Beware of the good life, Kobayashi had once told him. *Never allow it to cloud your judgment or your loyalties.*

Ohmura tucked his chin against his chest and stared at the radio. He loved the good life and could think of nothing worse than being called home.

A gentle knock told him that his wife had brought tea. He hurried to the door, relieved to have something to do, and opened it for her.

She carried a tray set for two, complete with bud vase and rose blossom.

"Alice," he began, then caught himself. He'd been about to ask her how she'd feel if they were called home, but that was a question better left unasked. He knew how much she loved Hawaii. Here she was somebody, the wife of a department head at the university. In Japan, she would be an outsider, and never completely trusted.

"Yes, dear, what were you saying?" she said.

Before he could respond, the radio crackled to life.

29

Kobayashi shook his head in despair. If he had been the head of the family he would have never allowed Haruko, Alice she now called herself, to marry a *nisei*. But his father had been weak, arguing that the Ohmura family had been in service to the Tokugawa family while Kensai's family did not come into prominence until the Meiji restoration two hundred years later.

Kobayashi thought of his grandfather, so proud of the sword presented to him by Prince Asaka. As a boy, he remembered his father telling him that the sword was one of the famous *Soshu-den* works of Masamune from the Kamakura era. It was an honor for the family to own it. Later, when Kobayashi had it examined by experts, the sword had turned out to be a later *utsushi-mono*, a reproduction, by Yasutsurgu. The sword dated from the seventeenth century and although Yasutsugu had been patronized by the Tokugawa, he was an inferior swordsmith. The sword was a fake. It was made from *namban tetsu*, foreign steel. Even then, the corruption of Western culture was making itself felt.

And now here was this fake, this Sam Ohmura, married into the family. Now, I am the head of the family, Kobayashi thought. The honor of the family rests with me, but it balanced on an edge as sharp as his grandfather's sword. In 1946, Iwane Kobayashi had escaped the International Military Tribunal for the Far East, the Tokyo War Crimes Trial, Westerners had called it. But he had lived in shame, nevertheless. He had erected a shrine and placed in it a statue of Kanon, the Buddhist Goddess of Mercy, made of clay mixed with soil from Japan and China. To this day the family paid for a priestess to chant prayers and weep for the Chinese war dead.

There are other dead we must weep for, Kobayashi muttered to himself. Whatever his grandfather had done in Nanking could not compare to what had happened on Balesin, and Sam Ohmura was a poor weapon to save the honor of the family.

30

Nick shifted her weight, trying to make herself comfortable. Beside her, Elliot and Buettner did the same. But the Reverend Innis's rough-hewn pews defied comfort. Their backs were straight, their seats unforgiving. Sitting on them was pure penance.

Even "Amazing Grace," sung by a choir of women, Lily among them, failed to soothe Nick. She clenched her teeth against the growing kink in her spine. Making matters worse was the heat, intensified by the Quonset's corrugated-metal walls. The place reminded her of a bake-oven, not a church.

She was about to throw caution, not to mention protocol, to the wind and make a dash for freedom when the reverend strode to the pulpit. He was carrying a bible festooned with multicolored ribbons as bookmarks. With a flourish, he opened it to the first marker, then looked over his audience, a full house now that Yali's contingent had arrived.

"Amazing Grace" ended. The ladies of the choir, glistening with sweat, took their seats in the front pew that had been reserved for them. They immediately began cooling themselves with reed fans. Nick glanced around. All the islanders had similar fans. She nudged her father, who nodded his acknowledgment that they should have been forewarned and forearmed.

The Reverend Innis cleared his throat. " 'I *am* a stranger and a sojourner with you; give me a possession of a burying place with you . . . ' So says the good book. Could we do less, even though this man, Walt Duncan, was unknown to us? Certainly not. We have buried him in full hope of resurrection."

The reverend shimmered, then lost focus as sweat flooded Nick's eyes. She mopped her face.

" 'I am a stranger in the earth: hide not Thy commandments from me.' "

"Amen," the congregation murmured.

Nick rubbed her stinging eyes, then closed them.

" 'I have been a stranger in a strange land,' " the reverend went on.

A stranger in need of a fan, she added to herself, losing track of what Innis was saying. She felt sorry for the preacher. His voice was strong, passionate even, but he couldn't compete with the oppressive heat.

Her head sagged. Sleep threatened to overwhelm her.

" '. . . hast Thou taken us away to die in the wilderness?' " Innis intoned.

Wilderness, Nick echoed to herself, the Baleseans were living in a kind of wilderness. They were living on the wrong side of the island. She should have realized that before.

She shook her head. Dummy. On an island like this, one with a dominating mountain, there was a wet side and a dry side, depending on which way storms tracked. In this part of the Pacific, they usually tracked from east to west. That made the west side of Balesin the dry side, but the village was east of Mount Nomenuk.

The question was, why? Even if it were only a matter of a few inches of rain, the islanders should have known better. Maybe Lily could explain it.

Nodding to herself, Nick tried to concentrate on the reverend's words. But he'd given up quoting from the bible to extol the virtues of Walt Duncan, a man he'd never met. Neither had the rest of the congregation. Among those assembled, only Buettner had known the man. Maybe Tracy and Axelrad had been acquaintances too.

My God, Nick thought, remembering what Duncan's remains had looked like. What a way to die. And for what? For Buettner's so-called Anasazi connection? That was something else rotten about Balesin.

Out of the corner of her eye she saw Tracy and Axelrad leave their seats at the end of the pew and slip outside. Their departure drew a barrage of condemning stares, but Nick envied them just the same. It had to be cooler outside, and Nick thought she had a good idea why they wanted to slip away. So much for Buettner's standards of professionalism, she thought.

"Let us pray," Innis said.

Nick sighed with relief. In this kind of heat, a short sermon made sense.

"Amen," Innis said a moment later, a signal for everyone to begin filing from the church.

Outside, Nick took Elliot aside.

"The whole place is upside-down," she began. "If you ask me, the culture has been contaminated by too many outside influences. Fifty years ago we might have made some interesting discoveries. But now? Curt should have realized that before organizing this snipe hunt."

Elliot nodded in agreement. "I know. I'm not sure what Curt is up to. In the past he's been prone to rush to judgment, but I feel I owe it to him to let him come to his own conclusions, however long it takes."

"So how long are you going to stick with this goose chase?" Nick demanded.

"What makes you think it's a total goose chase? I find that there are some very interesting features in this island culture."

"You mean, like they live on the wrong side of the island," Nick snapped.

Elliot's eyes lit up. "Daughter, you do me proud. I was beginning to think you hadn't noticed."

31

Axelrad squeezed Karen's hand. When they'd started out, he thought they could stop along the way to make love. But the bugs made that impossible. They were out in force, swarming like frenzied dive-bombers. If anything, there seemed to be more of them than ever. Perhaps they were desperate for blood because the rain had kept them from feeding.

He opened his mouth to expound his theory but swallowed one of the little bastards. It reverberated all the way down his throat.

He coughed so hard Karen pounded him on the back.

"Someone went down the wrong way," he managed finally.

"I know what you mean," she answered, keeping her teeth clenched, her lips barely moving.

"I'm sorry," he said. "It was stupid of me not using the native bug potion, but it made me itch."

"You broke out in red spots."

"You didn't have to stop using it and suffer with me."

She winked at him. "I figured touching me might bring your spots back."

"I love you," he said.

They kissed briefly.

"One thing's for sure," he said, breaking contact. "It was something a lot worse than bugs that got to Professor Duncan."

"Are you having second thoughts about us going off on our own like this?"

"I'm walking, aren't I? Besides, we've already agreed. The only way to prove ourselves is to make a find that's ours alone. If we do that we'll be home free, with our doctorates handed to us on a platter."

She smiled weakly. "Then, I say it's worth the risk."

"It was probably an accident, you know. Professor Duncan should have known better than to wander around on his own. You need a buddy system. That's why I've got you."

She snuggled against him.

"If you ask me," Axelrad continued, "Duncan probably died of natural causes, maybe a heart attack. Once you're disabled in a place like this, things eat you. Remember that last dig we were on." He grimaced. "God knows what got to those people."

"Yeah, but in their case they'd been dead for a thousand years," she reminded him.

"Dead's dead."

She punched his shoulder playfully.

"One thing's for certain," he went on, "that shaman puts on a good show. Saying it was Frum's will and that Professor Duncan had broken some sort of taboo. Curses don't work unless you believe in them, for God's sake."

By now they were both breathing hard as they headed uphill toward Mount Nomenuk, sacred ground according to the shaman. Dangerous ground, as Professor Duncan had learned the hard way.

"It stands to reason that anything worth finding is on this mountain," Axelrad said out loud, to justify the risk they were taking.

"Stop worrying," Karen told him. "Everyone's still at the service, so we ought to have the mountain to ourselves."

He hoped she was right. Besides, as far as he was concerned, Yali was the man to worry about and he and his men were sitting in church right now.

"What do you think about the model airplanes Nick keeps going on about?" he asked to clear his mind.

"Somehow, I don't think Buettner's Anasazi flew them here."

Axelrad snorted. The path was growing steeper with each step. Scrunching his neck, he trudged forward, head down, scratching at himself.

"That only makes it worse," Karen told him.

He kept going, ignoring her.

"You'll get an infection," she said after a while.

Angrily, he lurched to a stop and turned to face her. "I don't want to hear—" The sight of her bite-swollen face made him wince sympathetically. "Dammit. I'm sorry. Maybe we ought to forget this and get you back to base for a shower and heavy dosing of the local bug juice. Besides, we haven't seen a damned thing."

Her puffy lips managed a grin. "Why don't you raise your sights?"

"My God!" he blurted. He'd come out of the trees without realizing it. They were standing at the edge of a clearing that ran as straight as a highway for half a mile. At the other end stood an airplane that looked poised for takeoff. It looked too real to be one of the usual Cargo Cult counterfeits pictured in textbooks.

Karen jabbed him in the ribs. "Maybe the Anasazi flew across the ocean after all."

The sight of the runway cut into the jungle, and the work taken to build it, awed him. In a climate such as this, where the growing season never ended, a closely cropped runway like this one would have to be tended constantly. Axelrad took a deep breath, not caring how many mosquitoes went with it. His adrenaline kicked into high gear and he started jogging forward. Karen ran alongside, practically dancing for joy.

Two-thirds of the way down the runway, he saw the plane for what it was, an elaborate mock-up, and started to slow. Another model plane stood to one side and slightly behind the first.

She grabbed his arm to keep him going. "In the trees," she shouted.

My God, she was right. A hangar was hidden beneath the overhanging branches.

The hangar wouldn't be visible from the air, he realized, which seemed odd. The whole purpose of the Cargo Cult was to use fake runways and airport facilities to lure planes and their cargo. So why hide the hangar?

"We've got to get back and report this," he said breathlessly.

"Hold it," Karen said as a man appeared in the hangar's open doorway. "Who's that?"

By then they were close enough to see his military gear.

"He's no native. That's for sure," Axelrad said. "Better yet, what the hell is he doing here?"

32

Nick crossed her fingers and offered a silent prayer to the gods of technology, hoping the batteries in her laptop computer had survived the steam bath that passed for atmosphere on Balesin. At the sound of a healthy beep, she sighed with relief and angled the computer screen toward Henry Yali, who was sitting beside her. The two of them were perched cross-legged on the floor of the new house. Everyone else had left for their assigned chores after promising not to disturb Nick until mealtime.

That gave her plenty of time to interview Yali, as long as the laptop cooperated. Its manual promised two to four hours of use before recharging was necessary. She'd settle for one.

Yali claimed to have seen computers before, though

he shook his head skeptically when she told him that this one could show him all the airplanes that had flown during World War Two.

Like a magician preparing a trick, she held out a compact disk for inspection, showing him both sides before inserting it into the drive. At the click of a button, the title page, *Aircraft of World War Two*, filled the screen. Icons showing options according to country of origin ran along one side of the screen.

Using the track-ball, Nick centered the cursor on American Bombers and clicked. A B-29 Superfortress appeared against a vibrant blue sky.

Yali's jaw dropped open. "Frum be praised," he intoned, reaching out to touch the screen. "This is truly wondrous."

She clicked again and the in-flight B-29 gave way to a full-scale cutaway drawing.

"It's like a miracle," he said.

She explained the plane's finer points, remote-controlled gun turrets, pressurized bulkheads, and crew bunks, all of which distinguished it from earlier, smaller bombers.

"How do you know so much about planes that flew so long ago?" Yali's tone verged on reverence.

"Airplanes are my first love. I've been building models of them since I was a girl."

He stroked his chin and stared at her in open appraisal. "John Frum himself would welcome you," he said finally.

Now was her chance, Nick thought. She had his respect, or so she hoped. "Henry, do you remember the planes that came here during the war?"

He nodded at the B-29. "Nothing that large ever landed on Balesin."

"How old were you when the first planes came?"

"I remember them clearly enough, if that's what you're asking. When you get to be my age, it's the old memories that stay with you, while the rest fades away."

"Did American planes ever land here?" she persisted.

His eyes shifted away. "During the war, only Japanese."

"What about after the war?"

"By then there was no need for them to come. American soldiers landed, but the Japanese were gone by then."

"When did you build your first airplane?" she asked.

"John Frum's airplanes, you mean?"

She nodded.

Yali smiled. "John Frum's power goes back long before I was born. My people have been building monuments to him for a very long time."

"The airplanes that you've built have two engines," she observed. "Was that always the case?"

He nodded absently, his eyes fixed on the computer screen.

Nick repositioned the cursor and called up a twin-engine B-26 Martin Marauder, known as the widow-maker because of its unforgiving flight characteristics. "Have you ever seen a plane like this?"

Yali touched the screen tentatively, his finger tracing the full-color image. "No."

"What about this one?"

A keystroke turned the B-26 into a twin-engine Mitchell B-25. Yali removed his finger.

"I have seen photographs of such planes," he said, "but they've never come to Balesin."

"Lily told me that American planes came here after the war."

Yali shrugged. "All planes that come here do so at John Frum's bidding. Even your American seaplane."

"But it belongs to Lee Coltrane," she pointed out.

"Only through the grace of John Frum."

Nick took a deep breath and called up another view of a B-25. This one had teeth painted on its nose.

"Wonderful," Yali breathed, his finger caressing the sharp, white teeth.

Both the B-25 and B-26 had seen extensive service in the Pacific during the war. But Yali's unfamiliarity with them seemed to indicate that Frum's air force had been inspired by Japanese aircraft. That left Nick with the Mitsubishi known as the Nell.

She manipulated the track-ball until a side view of the Nell came on screen. It became famous early in the war for sinking two British battleships, the *Prince of Wales* and the *Repulse*. The bomber's success was due to its extremely long range, something the British navy hadn't expected. That range also meant that Nells could have flown from the Japanese mainland to Balesin without refueling.

Yali leaned close to the screen, started to reach out, then hesitated. "I don't remember seeing anything like that before."

He looked too calm and too sure of himself to be telling the truth.

She closed her eyes and revisited the airstrip near the old lighthouse. Certainly, the mock-ups there could have been replicas of the Nell. For that matter, the B-25 wasn't that dissimilar. To refresh her memory, she opened her eyes and called up the B-25 one more time. Seen in side view, its fuselage was bulkier than the Nell and the B-26 Marauder. Otherwise, it had comparable features, two engines, two tails, and a top turret.

"John Frum tells us that America is the promised land," Yali said abruptly. "We must look there, not east."

"Is that your way of saying that John Frum's airplanes are based on American models?"

He smiled indulgently. "John Frum may create planes in any image that suits him." Yali tapped the screen, then immediately transferred the tapping finger to the side of his own head. "I have flown such planes in my dreams. Our goal is always America."

Nick stared at him, probing for any sign that he might be trying to mislead her. But the look on his face seemed smugly sincere. Certainly, Yali worshiped the American way of life. His flag-raising ceremony was a celebration of Old Glory, as was his ritual red, white, and blue body painting. So, why wouldn't his air force be American?

She sighed. Chances were, the best she could ever do was speculate on the type of airplane that served as a model for Balesin's mock air force. Of course, much of archaeology came down to speculation, a great deal of it built on shaky evidence. Such conjecture was well and good when dealing with sites thousands of years old. But guesses dating back a mere fifty or sixty years could be career killers.

"Our planes will fly one day," Yali said abruptly. "To come to life, they await only the touch of John Frum."

"When will that happen?"

Yali smiled. "Sooner than you think."

Nick swallowed a groan. Over the years, she'd interviewed any number of shamans. To a man, they delighted in responding to questions with enigmatic comments that sounded as if they'd been gleaned from fortune cookies. Henry Yali was no exception.

"Sooner doesn't help me much," Nick told him.

Still smiling, Yali closed his eyes and nodded at something only he could see. Whatever it was had his eyeballs shimmying behind their lids.

"I can see him now," Yali exhaled. "I was there, you know, to welcome John Frum when he arrived on Balesin. Now I have sent for him again. This time he and his followers will arrive in a great ship. He will lay hands upon us and his planes and we will be as strong as America is."

Pure shaman-speak, Nick thought, promising everything without being too specific.

"You have no facilities to accommodate such a ship," Nick remarked, remembering that before airplanes the Cargo Cult had built fake docks.

Before Yali could reply, Chief Jeban appeared in the doorway. "We must go," he said to Yali. Addressing Nick, he added, "Two of your people were seen climbing Mount Nomenuk."

Yali clenched his fists. "I saw them in the night. I flew above them. I'd hoped it was only a nightmare. Now, they have broken John Frum's law and will have to pay."

22

April 18, 1942
The South Pacific

He imagined what the bomb run must have been like
Had they caught the Japs with their knickers round their
knees or had the Japs been waiting for them? Those poor
bastards, bad weather and not enough fuel to get home
and maybe not enough fuel to make it to mainland
China either. Still, he felt a momentary regret for having
been diverted from the *Hornet*'s main mission. Every
body's going to remember the guys that dropped the first
bombs on Tokyo. Nobody's going to remember us. Hell
nobody was even supposed to know. If they got out of
this alive, he wondered what would happen to the crew
Probably they'd be sent on some high-risk mission and
given a chance to die as heroes. As for himself, he'd
gotten to the point where he no longer cared.

They'd been flying for eight hours now and he knew
that the crew was getting nervous. He looked at his map
again as if to gain reassurance. Their target was what was
called a high island, not some strip of sand barely twenty
feet above sea level. Still, it wasn't very big. You could
probably walk from one end to the other in a day, and it
wouldn't make much of a blip on the horizon. An error
of even half a degree in his calculations would put them
hundreds of miles off course. He'd had to compensate for
the magnetic variation as well. He rechecked his calculations, then went back to the map.

He examined the markings that indicated two separate airstrips. The one on the west side of the island had been built by the Japs. They would have to come in low from the north to avoid it. He'd been told that the other strip, the one cut into the mountainside, was pretty crude. In fact, it was just dirt with the undergrowth scraped off by the natives. A B-25 was no Piper Cub, he thought. Even coming in low, they were bound to make a racket. It was impossible to keep two 1700-horsepower Wright Cyclone engines quiet.

The pilot's voice came through the intercom. "Navigator, where are we?"

The name is Johns, you bastard, he thought. "On course, skipper," he replied, swallowing his resentment. "Landfall anytime now."

He could feel the pilot ease back on the throttle. Not too slow, he hoped. Their speed couldn't be much above the B-25's stall speed of eighty-five miles an hour, and at their low altitude they couldn't possibly recover from a stall.

"I'll be damned," he heard the copilot say.

"Landfall," the pilot announced.

The top turret gunner let out a whoop.

Johns asked, "Do you see the landing strip?"

"Right where it should be. I've got a straight approach. You did a good job, Bob."

Johns was surprised that the captain had actually remembered his name. He felt the wheels come down and the first bump as they touched ground. The plane taxied for what seemed like forever and then swung around. Good landing, he thought. Now all we have to do is take off again. He hoped the jungle wasn't crawling with Japs.

He eased into the cockpit and peered over the pilot's shoulder. "Cut the engines," he ordered. The co-pilot looked like he was going to protest, but the pilot feathered the props.

"I hope you know what you're doing," he said.

"Listen," Johns replied.

"I am listening," the pilot said, sliding open his side window. "I don't hear a damned thing."

"I don't either," Johns said. "That's what's got me worried."

34

Nick joined Elliot on the porch, where he'd been pacing sporadically since Yali and his men marched out of the village, intent on finding the missing couple.

"Look at this!" he complained, leaning over the porch railing to thrust a hand into the rain that was growing heavier by the hour. "This place is nothing but damp and mildew, while my Anasazi sites in New Mexico haven't been rained on in years."

"A desert drought would feel good about now," Nick responded.

"At least the desert mummifies the dead," Elliot went on, not the least bit mollified. "But this climate. Nothing survives here that isn't shrink-wrapped."

"What's really bothering you?" Nick asked, though she figured she knew the answer already.

"Curt and his wandering students, what else?" He wiped his wet hand on his trouser leg. "Hell, Nick, I' sorry I got you into this. I've been putting up with Curt's eccentricities for years, but that's no reason to inflict them on you."

"Hey, you know me and airplanes. I wouldn't have missed it for the world. You don't think they'd be foolish enough to climb the mountain?"

"Curt's the one who ought to be out there searching for them."

"Come on, Elliot, you're not being sensible. Henry didn't want help. He made that clear. We were all ordered to stay here and wait."

Elliot groaned. "You're right. It's just . . ." He spread his hands in a gesture of helplessness. "Curt can be rather erratic. Right now, he's probably worried sick about those two and won't admit it. That's one of his foibles. He's a specialist in foibles. That's what his cover stories are all about. Take this Anasazi theory of his. No one's expected to take it seriously, so nothing nasty sticks to his reputation when nothing materializes. But take it from me. If the Anasazi actually turned up here, Curt would say he never doubted the connection for a minute. I learned a long time ago that behind that easygoing facade of his, is blinding ambition. Ever since I've known him, he's talked of making a truly great discovery. Something not only to rival my Anasazi work, but surpass it."

"You make him sound a little crazy," Nick said.

"Aren't we all? But he got worse when we were competing for a fellowship. When I won, he shrugged it off, saying he'd expected to lose. But I could see even then it was eating him up."

While Nick was thinking that over, Lily arrived, half-hidden beneath a huge umbrella. "Prepare yourselves," she announced immediately. "Henry is right behind me." She climbed onto the porch and folded away her umbrella. "Here they are now."

A line of men came out of the rain. A body was slung beneath a pole carried on the shoulders of the first four men in line.

"My God!" Elliot gasped. "That's Karen Tracy."

With each step the men took, the girl's head bobbed loosely as if her neck were broken.

"Curt!" Nick shouted over her shoulder. "You'd better get out here."

Axelrad's body came next. He, too, was slung grotesquely beneath a long bamboo pole. Henry Yali was walking beside him.

Nick grasped her father's arm as the thought swept through her mind that Yali had killed them for breaking John Frum's law.

"Let's get them out of the rain," Buettner commanded. Until he'd spoken, Nick hadn't realized that he'd come out of the house.

Once the bodies had been laid out side by side on the porch, Nick took a deep breath and left the comforting sanctuary of Elliot's arm. Within a few seconds, only Yali and Lily remained behind. The rest of the shaman's men had faded back to their houses.

Nick knelt beside Karen Tracy. "There are no obvious wounds," she said, struggling to maintain a professional tone of voice.

"I concur," Elliot said, kneeling across from her.

It was a procedure Nick and her father had used before, cross-checking one another at field autopsies. Only in those cases the dead had been gone for a century at least.

Nick looked up at Henry Yali, whose bare chest glistened wetly. "Is this how you honor John Frum?"

Yali shook his head violently. "This is not my work. They were dead when we found them. I swear it."

"Where did you find them?" Buettner asked.

Yali gestured vaguely toward high ground. "On John Frum's mountain."

"Do you know what happened?" Nick asked.

"Only that it must be the will of John Frum."

Nick glared at the shaman, but he pretended not to notice. Clenching her teeth, she went back to work, unbuttoning Axelrad's sodden shirt.

"I don't see any . . ." She broke off to lean closer to Axelrad's chest. "My God, his neck's been broken."

"How could that be?" Buettner asked.

"Maybe they fell while they were climbing the mountain," Yali offered.

Nick examined the girl's arms. "Look." She pointed to faint bruises on both arms. "These were made before she died."

Elliot nodded and placed his right hand on the girl's left arm. His thumb and fingers covered the bruised areas. "Someone grabbed her by the arms," he said. "Hard."

Nick rotated the girl's head from side to side. "Her neck's broken, too."

Nick's fingers trembled slightly as she examined Karen's blouse. One look and Nick rocked back on her heels. Bile surged up her throat. Most of the buttons had been ripped away. The blouse was mis-buttoned and hanging loose.

She swallowed convulsively.

"Do you want me to take over?" Elliot asked softly.

Nick shook her head. "I think Karen deserves some privacy."

"I'm sorry," Elliot said. "Another time I might agree,

but two broken necks rules out accidental death as far as I'm concerned. Do you agree?"

Nick nodded.

"Then, prudence comes before privacy. We all have to know what we're up against."

As gently as possible, Nick loosened Karen's shorts and pulled them down.

"Goddammit! Her panties are missing."

"We don't know that she was wearing any," Elliot said.

"Trust me. In this climate, with these bugs, a woman's going to wear panties to protect herself."

"Are you saying she was raped?" Buettner asked.

"It's a possibility," Nick answered.

"Before we jump to any conclusions," Elliot put in, "let's check Axelrad's pockets for lover's souvenirs."

When they found none, Nick stared straight at Henry Yali and said, "May God strike down whoever did this!"

Yali's mouth dropped open, but no words came out. He looked to Lily for support.

Lurching to her feet, Nick lunged across the porch to jab a finger against the shaman's bony chest. "I want to know what happened on that mountain."

"Lily?" Yali implored. "You must help me convince them."

"Of what?" Nick snapped, turning her anger against Lily, who raised a hand as if to ward off a blow.

Tears, or maybe rain from her matted hair, ran down Lily's face. "You must understand, child," she said in a shaky voice, "I . . . we are cursed."

"Curses have nothing to do with this. Someone killed them, and maybe raped Karen."

"John Frum," Yali intoned.

"Since when does God break necks?" Nick shouted, pinning him with her finger again.

"Easy, Nick," Elliot said.

"Your father's right," Buettner added, coming to stand beside her. "This isn't doing any good."

"They brought it on themselves," Yali blustered. "They were struck down as a punishment for their transgressions. There's no other explanation."

"What transgressions?" Nick demanded so forcefully that Buettner grabbed her arm.

"They were on Mount Nomenuk. You were all warned. The mountain belongs to John Frum."

"That won't do," Nick said, her voice shaky. "I want to see the place for myself. I demand that you take us there now."

"In case you haven't noticed," Buettner said, "the weather is getting worse."

"It is a holy place," Yali added. "Outsiders are not allowed."

"Henry," Lily said softly, "maybe this one time an exception should be made."

Shaking his head, Yali looked away, but not before Nick thought she detected fear in his eyes.

"When the authorities hear of this," Nick said, forcing herself to speak as calmly as possible, "you'll have to show them where you found the bodies."

"She's right," Buettner jumped in. "They were my students and my responsibility. The police on Guam have to be notified. The best thing to do until then is to investigate what happened ourselves." He stretched a hand toward Lily. "Surely, you'll help us?"

"Listen to him, Henry," Lily said, her eyes pleading. "Sooner or later someone will have to climb Mount Nomenuk to see what happened."

Yali folded his arms across his chest. "John Frum has not spoken to me on this."

"Then there's nothing I can do," Lily said. "On matters of John Frum, Henry's word is law."

Elliot said, "Tell us, Henry, since you won't guide us, will you stop us if we climb Mount Nomenuk on our own, without your consent?"

"You do so at your own peril."

"We understand that."

"Understand this, then. I will raise no hand against you."

"What about your people?" Elliot persisted.

"You have only John Frum to fear."

Elliot turned to Lily. "Is Henry right?"

"Are you calling me a liar?" Yali shouted.

"I have a daughter to protect," Elliot answered.

"That is a father's duty," Lily said. "Isn't that right, Henry?"

Yali glared but said nothing.

"I don't know what's happening up on that mountain," Lily added. "I'm not sure Henry does either. So maybe it's best if we all stay on low ground for now. In the meantime, we must do something for these two departed souls."

"I'll have no part of it," Yali said.

"Then I will ask the Reverend Innis to conduct another service," Lily told him.

"I'm afraid a burial is out of the question," Nick said. "We're going to need autopsies. The quickest way to do that is to fly the bodies to Guam as soon as Coltrane gets here."

"I turn my back on all of you," Yali said. Like a soldier at attention, he pivoted sharply and marched down the steps and started across the square toward the communal buildings.

"Henry's a proud man," Lily said. "If he gives his word, he'll stand by it." She moved to Nick's side. "You can believe him if he says he won't raise a hand against you."

"We can worry about Henry later," Elliot said. "Right now, we've got to make a decision about the bodies. Do we fly them off the island? If we do, the authorities might raise hell."

Nick said, "I don't think we have a choice."

"I hate to bring this up," Buettner put in, "but we really ought to dig up Walt Duncan and send him back too."

"Then, you're going to need body bags," a voice said, startling them all.

Todd Parker had seemed to appear out of nowhere, though quite obviously his arrival had been masked by the sound of falling rain. A glistening black poncho that had been fashioned from a plastic trash bag enveloped him.

"I don't have real body bags," he said, tugging at his makeshift rain gear, "but I have plenty of these." He pulled a box of them out from under his poncho.

"Christ," Buettner muttered, looking squeamish.

Nick knew how he felt. Chances were that body gases would inflate the bags long before they reached Guam. If one burst . . . My God, that didn't bear thinking about.

"I brought duct tape too," Parker said, "though I thought you'd be needing rain gear, not shrouds."

Nick accepted the offering with a grim nod and then they all went to work wrapping the bodies.

The moment they finished the job, Parker lit a cigar,

blew smoke at the nearest swarm of mosquitoes, and said, "Take my advice. Leave Balesin while you still can. With three people dead already . . ." He glanced at the plastic bags and shook his head. ". . . there's no telling what might happen next. I've been here a long time and there's never been violence before. Isn't that right, Lily?"

"Certainly not in your time," Lily answered. "But you are young to Balesin. You weren't here during the war."

Parker dismissed her comment with a flick of ash. "There are no soldiers here now, and no war."

"Tell Henry that," she said. "He is a soldier in John Frum's army."

Parker rolled his eyes.

"And what about you, Mr. Parker," Elliot said. "Are you planning to leave?"

The man shrugged. "You're the outsiders. You're the ones dying."

"Maybe he's right," Buettner said. "You all came here because of me. Duncan, Tracy, Axelrad. I couldn't bear having anyone else on my conscience."

"If we decide to leave," Elliot responded, "we're going to have to make a choice. Do we leave the dead behind, or do we send them on ahead? I don't think that Coltrane's Widgeon will hold everybody at once."

"If the dead go first," Nick said, "I'll have another day to ID my airplanes."

Elliot looked to Buettner. "What about it, Curt? How do you vote?"

He took a deep breath and let it out slowly. "I'll go with Nick. It's better we fly out Tracy and Axelrad first. I think we'd better hold off on Duncan until we have a more substantial container."

"You're making a mistake," Parker said, condemning them with a sharp shake of his head.

Lily laid a hand on Nick's arm. "They're under my protection, Mr. Parker."

"Is that good enough?"

Lily didn't answer. She was already on her way down the steps.

"Is it?" Parker called after her.

But by then she was invisible in the rain.

35

Kobayashi paced the room. The sight of his beloved horse no longer served to calm him. *I know why the tiger paces in his cage*, he thought. *It had been a mistake to let Farrington supply the agent, but who else could he have turned to?*

The voice came through the receiver. "This is Tarzan, calling Jane. This is Tarzan calling Jane. Come in Jane."

Kobayashi felt a churning in his stomach. He hated the American penchant for theatrics. He felt that they were mocking him, making a game of his predicament.

"Report," he commanded. He refused to use their foolish code names.

"The pistol is primed. I repeat, the pistol is primed."

"Stop speaking gibberish," he nearly screamed into the transmitter. "Did you destroy the evidence?"

"Uh, not exactly," the agent replied.

"What do you mean, *not exactly?*" Kobayashi realized that an icy calm had overwhelmed him. He felt that he was floating somewhere high above the island where the evidence of his grandfather's shame rested. If he could not get this stupid fool to carry out orders, there were always others.

The agent must have heard the change in his interrogator's voice because his answer was straightforward. "I set the charges, but I was interrupted."

"It's been discovered, then." Kobayashi sat down. It was all over. The patient years of waiting, planning, researching the site were all for nothing. His grandfather's crime, Kobayashi's shame, had become known.

"Don't get your knickers in a twist," the agent replied. "I took care of it."

"Who interrupted you and how did you take care of it?" Kobayashi almost didn't want to know.

"It was those two kids from the expedition. They caught me with my pants down, so to speak. I thought everyone was over at the services for the other geek, that Duncan guy that pegged out before I got here. Let's say they've been effectively silenced."

Kobayashi closed his eyes. "Why did you not destroy the evidence after you had killed them?"

There was a long pause. Finally, "Uh, it took me longer than I had expected." There was another pause, then, "I've been on this island for three fucking days and, shit, a man's got to have a little relaxation, if you know what I mean. In any case, a bunch of natives came tearing up the trail and I had to hightail it out of there. I didn't even get a chance to hide the bodies, but the charges are out of sight so unless someone goes poking around in there, they won't be noticed. With any luck

I'll be able to just mosey on back later tonight and finish the job."

"Tomorrow, at the same time," Kobayashi replied. "May your luck hold," he added, and broke the connection.

Kobayashi was not a believer in luck. I am cursed with bad luck and poor tools, he thought. He had placed Todd Parker on the island to keep a watching brief and he had failed to meet the rendezvous. He claimed that he'd been sick, but Kobayashi suspected drink. As for the agent Farrington had supplied, the man gave priority to his animal needs over the mission he was supposed to carry out. The man would ruin them all. Farrington would just have to take care of him.

It was up to Ohmura now. A college professor on a mission such as this. Kobayashi shook his head. Even if Ohmura was successful, Kobayashi would have to make certain that Huruko would be in need of a new husband. As head of the family he would choose more wisely than his father had.

36

Nick heard the plane but couldn't see it. Low clouds and pelting rain obscured everything beyond the village square. My God! What was Coltrane thinking about, flying in weather like this?

For an instant, the thought crossed her mind that it

might be someone else up there, but that seemed un-
likely.

The engine sound faded, then abruptly grew loud
again as the wind shifted slightly. In the center of the
square, the American flag snapped like a towel in gym
class.

Nick winced sympathetically and squinted at the
impenetrable sky. Behind her, the door banged open and
Curt Buettner joined her on the porch. "I told you Coltrane wouldn't let us down," he announced before
thrusting his head through the curtain of water sluicing
from the roof. "Damn, I can't see shit."

"I know," she said, hugging herself. "That means
Coltrane can't either."

"It sounds like he's getting closer." Buettner retreated to the back of the porch, shaking his head like a
dog drying itself.

"He should have waited for good weather," Nick
said. "He'll never be able to land in this stuff."

Buettner gave up shaking himself to mop his face
with a soggy handkerchief. "Maybe the visibility's better
up there."

"And if it isn't?"

"Coltrane's an experienced pilot. He knows what
he's doing."

Sure, Nick thought, remembering her first impression of the man, not to mention his disreputable
Widgeon. They were both throwbacks, relics. The image
made her smile. After all, she'd made a career of un-
earthing relics.

The engine pitch changed, growing louder until it
sounded as if the plane were directly overhead.

"Jesus Christ!" Buettner muttered. "I hope he
doesn't try to put down here."

Nick crossed her fingers.

"If he's missed the beach," Buettner went on, "he's had it."

"You'd better try the radio again," Nick told him, even though she knew it had given up the ghost.

"But—"

"We've got to do something. He's flying blind."

Buettner jerked open the door and launched himself across the threshold just as Elliot was coming out. The two collided momentarily.

"Is that Coltrane I hear?" Elliot asked as soon as he'd untangled himself.

Nick nodded. "It sounds like the Widgeon's engines to me."

"You're the expert."

"But I'm no pilot. If I were, I think I'd head for shelter." She was about to start down the wooden steps when Elliot caught hold of her.

"I know that look of yours," he said. "You get it every time you're around airplanes. It makes me nervous. It'll be pretty rough on the beach where he landed us the last time."

"He'll probably head for the mouth of the river. It's possible that the waves and the river current will just about cancel each other out. If he does land there, he might need help getting ashore."

"Listen to yourself," Elliot said. "We're standing in the middle of a monsoon. What can you do?"

"I'm going."

Elliot groaned. "Then I'd better come with you."

"I don't have time to argue. I jog three times a week, you don't." She caught her breath to listen. "I don't hear the engines anymore, so he's either down safely or he didn't make it. Either way, it'll be dark soon and I can get there faster than you."

Elliot looked hurt.

"I also know where I'm going," she added.

"Then take someone from the village with you."

"Just round up some villagers and send them after me in case more manpower is needed."

Before Elliot could respond, she grabbed her backpack and first-aid kit, ran down the steps and headed across the square. As soon as she reached the trail to the river, she discarded her sandals, which were slowing her down.

The wind was in her face, howling and hurling the rain with staggering force. The footing was treacherous, slick in places, muddy in others. Time and again, she fell headlong into the goo, but each time she struggled to her feet and kept going. But she was no longer running. The foot-clogging mud made that impossible. Instead, the best she could manage was a kind of stumbling jog.

Soon she was sucking air through clenched teeth. Her feet felt cold and on fire at the same time. God, she should have kept the sandals. Or better yet, retrieved her desert boots, anything to protect her tender feet.

Idiot, she thought. What good was she going to do anybody if she crippled herself?

And maybe this was for nothing. Maybe Coltrane didn't need help. Had she guessed right or was she heading the wrong way?

She was gasping now, mouth wide open, her lungs burning, but she knew she had to go on. Coltrane, whatever his macho, soldier-of-fortune image, had kept his promise and come back rather than leave them stranded.

By now, she felt as if she were moving in slow-motion. Her legs were leaden, her feet encased in burning concrete. She had to stop; she had to rest. If she didn't, she'd be no use to anyone.

Gasping for breath, she dropped to her knees and closed her eyes. At least the ever-present mosquitoes were gone. The wind seemed to be too much even for them. It may be too much for me, she thought.

When she looked up, the river was only fifty yards away. It was racing to the sea in a dark oily torrent in the fading light. She realized that the blinding rain and wind had disoriented her and caused her to take a course too far upriver. She needed to veer down toward the beach.

She tucked stray hairs under her soggy baseball cap, lurched to her feet, and trotted forward. From now on, she had to be careful. The jungle was dense along the riverbank. It would be hard to pick her way downriver. There was the added danger of getting too close to the water's edge and falling in.

As soon as she lost sight of the river and moved into the heavy foliage, wind-whipped branches stung her face. She stubbed a toe on a tree root, felt a stab of pain, and looked down to see blood mixing with the mud between her toes. Visions of gangrene danced in her head. If Buettner hadn't thought ahead and put in a supply of antibiotics, she could be in big trouble.

She gritted her teeth. Antibiotics were part of any archaeologist's standard field kit. Elliot had taught her that. For that matter, she should have brought along her own first-aid kit. But she'd forgotten about it in her haste to leave Berkeley. She imagined what Elliot would say. *You haven't got any more sense than your mother.* Maybe he was right. Maybe she'd been crazy to go after Coltrane on her own. Why had she done it anyway? Was it Coltrane she was thinking of, or his airplane? *Crazy like your mother*, Elliot answered in her imagination.

"Damn you," she answered, "you have no right to compare me to Elaine."

Listen to yourself, she thought, shaking her head sharply. Don't lose it. Keep your mind on where you're going.

In that moment, she realized how dark it had gotten. There wasn't more than a few minutes of light left. If darkness fell while she was still in the jungle, she might lose her way. Then she'd have to stay awake all night waiting for the coconut crabs.

So turn back, common sense told her, or at least wait for the villagers to catch up.

She was about to take her own advice when it suddenly grew lighter ahead. A moment later she was out of the trees and into the open. At the mouth of the river, the ocean churned angrily, but the river current and the tide had formed a small inlet that remained relatively calm. But the beach was empty. She'd made the trip for nothing.

Exhausted, Nick doubled over, resting her hands on shaky knees as she fought to catch her breath. The wind, with no trees to break its force, staggered her.

"For Christ's sake!" Coltrane shouted. "Are you going to help me, or just stand there?"

Nick lurched around as Coltrane stepped from behind a palm tree around which he was wrapping a rope. The other end was attached to the Widgeon that was still out to sea, obscured by mist and bobbing violently. Coltrane had missed the sheltered waters by no more than a hundred yards.

"We've got to get her up on the beach," he said as soon as she joined him.

She took hold of the rope that was wrapped around the tree trunk. "I'll cinch while you pull."

Coltrane nodded, took a deep breath, braced himself and hauled on the line while she took up the slack. It was an inch-by-inch effort. Minutes went by and the Widgeon looked no closer to the shore, though she knew that to be impossible because the rope was lengthening at her end.

The muscles in her shoulders and arms quivered under the strain, and she felt herself growing weaker by the moment.

"It's taking too long," he shouted over the wind. "She must be caught in the current. Let's tie her off and take a rest."

They secured the rope and squatted side by side on the leeward side of the tree. Nick closed her eyes, raised her head, and opened her mouth, quenching her thirst with rainwater.

Coltrane leaned close. "We're running out of daylight. I'm going to have to swim back out there and get another line on her."

"It's too dangerous."

"It's my fault. I miscalculated. I nosed her in close to shore, then bailed into the surf to tie her down. But the current swept her back out before I reached the trees. It's just lucky I didn't lose the Widgeon completely."

"That's no reason to kill yourself now."

"The weather boys say the storm's going to get worse. When it does, one rope's never going to hold her."

Nick leaned around the palm tree to check the surf. The waves were already crashing hard enough to sound like thunder. Only fifty yards to the north, at the mouth of the river, the water wasn't nearly as rough. A swimmer might make it from that direction, though the overall distance to the Widgeon would be much greater. But Coltrane looked as exhausted as she felt.

"Once I get to the plane," he shouted, "I'll start her engines and bring her in slowly under power, while you tighten the mooring."

"Look at that surf. The undertow will turn you into shark bait."

"I can't leave her out there, Doc. She's all I've got."

"Isn't she insured?"

"She's pushing fifty, Doc. You know insurance companies. They'll pay me replacement value and I'll be lucky to be flying a paper kite."

Looking at him, she realized his devil-may-care image was nothing but a facade.

"Help should be here soon," she told him, hoping she was right.

"Who knows where you are?"

"My father does."

His shoulders sagged in obvious relief, though she couldn't help wondering how long it would take the villagers to arrive. Considering the weather and growing darkness, maybe they wouldn't budge from the village until daylight.

Coltrane nudged Nick's shoulder. "What do you say, Doc? There's no use sitting here getting waterlogged and doing nothing. Let's get back to work. Maybe we can drag her in yet and save someone else the trouble."

He got to his feet and pulled her up after him.

"Easy," she said. "I hurt all over."

"I know how you feel, Doc."

"And I'm never going to get dry again."

"Think of my poor Widgeon. She's getting drenched out there, and you have no idea what saltwater can do to an engine, let alone the fresh batteries I brought you for your radio."

It was dark by the time Chief Jeban arrived leading a small contingent of men, including Elliot and Buettner, both of whom were armed with battery-powered flashlights. Yali's men carried butane-burning lanterns, which flickered precariously with each wind gust.

After their arrival, it took only a few minutes to drag the Widgeon onto the beach by the mouth of the river. With the plane out of the water, everyone worked to tie her down.

Nick watched in exhaustion.

"You haven't been this helpless since you were a baby. It makes me feel young again," Elliot said.

"You don't look it."

He snorted. "That's my daughter. What would you have done if I hadn't gotten the chief to come?"

"That never crossed my mind," she lied.

Under the chief's direction, the plane was quickly secured. Once that was done, he circled the plane slowly, inspecting the work. Coltrane and Buettner accompanied him.

When the circumnavigation was complete, Chief Jeban gestured at Coltrane and said, "Your plane will be safe here. This is a safe haven. The waves never come higher than here."

With his toe, he drew a line in the sand well short of the Widgeon. "In a great storm, the only place safer would be on the other side of the island."

Just then Henry Yali stepped forward. "We do not go to that side of the island," he said.

"Then maybe we should all be on high ground,"

Nick said, hoping the weather might change Yali's mind about allowing them a look at the sacred mountain.

Yali raised his head as if assessing the heavens, though there was nothing to see but blackness. "John Frum isn't that angry."

"But it will be a very bad storm," Chief Jeban put in.

With that, he turned to the villagers, nodded, and led the way back toward the village.

37

Nick came awake with a groan. Every muscle in her body ached. Dimly she realized that someone was shaking her. It was Coltrane.

"Go away," she managed to mumble.

"You've got to wake up," Coltrane insisted.

Some part of Nick's mind desperately wanted to slip under again. The swaying of the hammock she was in was lulling her back to sleep. She bolted upright. There was no hammock. She was in a sleeping bag on the floor of the house and the entire structure was swaying.

"When you come awake, you really do it with a vengeance, don't you?" Coltrane said. "Remember that line Chief Jeban drew in the sand?"

Nick nodded mutely.

"Remember how he said that the waves never came any higher?"

Nick groaned. "Don't tell me," she replied.

"Okay, I won't tell you. But I've got to get the Widgeon out of there. If I don't, the waves will toss her into the trees."

Just then Elliot pushed aside the privacy screen. "The natives are abandoning the village. The chief tells me that they're going to the dry side of the island. I think we'll all be safer there."

Nick realized that she was still fully clothed. So much the better, she thought, now all she had to do was find her boots.

"Dad, I've got to go with Lee. He needs help." She recovered her boots from under a pile of dirty clothes and jammed her feet into them. She felt a stab of pain from where she'd injured her foot. Thank God Buettner had brought along antibiotics.

"I don't think the plane can be saved," Elliot said. "I won't be able to get the villagers to help this time. They're busy salvaging what belongings they can. A family has already been injured by a collapsing house. Most of the spare men have already gone to the church with the injured."

"I've got to try," Coltrane replied.

"And I've got to help him," Nick said.

"There's no arguing with you, daughter. I know that. Curt and I will collect as much of our gear and notes that we can carry and head down the Mission Trail. We'll meet you at the church."

Nick threw her arms around her father. "Be careful," she said.

He smiled. "Funny, I was just going to say the same to you." He turned and left quickly.

"Let's move," Coltrane said.

The journey back to the plane was worse than the

previous trip. Nick wasn't sure if they would have the strength to do anything once they got there.

By the time they reached the plane, water was lapping at her and the wind was so fierce that Coltrane had to shout in Nick's ear to make himself heard. "It won't be as hard to unleash her as it was tying her down. The big worry is that the wind will pick her up and flip her. Wait here." He staggered to the Widgeon.

Nick braced herself behind the trunk of a palm and wondered how her father and Buettner were doing. She hoped the wind wasn't as ferocious toward the interior of the island. Suddenly Coltrane was back.

"Here," he said, handing her an axe. "I'm going to start up the engines. Count to ten after I've started both engines, then cut the ropes. Got that?"

She nodded. "What happens after that?"

"She's already floating, so I'll use the river current to get me out to sea while you skedaddle back to the Mission Trail. The villagers are right about the church. It's built on the more protected side of the island."

"You can't fly into that storm," she protested.

"I don't intend to. I'll taxi her around the island. The Japanese knew what they were doing. The lagoon by the lighthouse is where they anchored their ships. If I can reach there, the old bird just might make it through the storm."

"I'm going with you."

"For Christ's sake. Risking my life is one thing, but yours . . ." He shook his head and stared at the sea.

Nick followed his gaze. Out there the angry wind was whipping up waves twenty feet high. The rain was nearly horizontal and hard enough to hurt bare skin.

"She's going to bob like a cork," Nick shouted. "You're going to need help to beach her again."

"I don't want to have to worry about you and the Widgeon too."

"I can take care of myself. Besides, I'd rather be with the Widgeon than go back the way we came on my own."

Wiping rain from his eyes, he stared at her. "Good God, woman, you are stubborn." He grinned. "Just be ready with the axe when you hear the engines."

Bent over against the blasting wind, he plunged toward the Widgeon and was soon knee-deep in white water. By the time he reached the plane the waves were waist-high and strong enough to bang him against the fuselage.

Nick caught her breath. It was going to be hell when her turn came. She wasn't as tall as Coltrane, and not as strong either. Strength aside, the Widgeon was going to be loose when Nick's turn came. That meant Coltrane would have to hold the seaplane in place with the engines. If he put on too much power, Nick would find herself swimming for her life. If he didn't power up enough, the Widgeon would be swept back onto the beach.

So now's the time to back out, she reminded herself. Otherwise . . . Otherwise didn't bear thinking about. She clenched her teeth. She was committed.

As she watched, Coltrane latched open the fuselage door so it would stay put. Then he looked back at her, gave her a thumbs-up, and disappeared into the Widgeon.

Nick sighed with relief. At least she wouldn't have to struggle with the door. And by leaving it open, he'd committed himself, too. He didn't intend to leave her behind, not on purpose anyway.

The port engine coughed. Nick crossed her fingers. The waves seemed to be growing by the moment, but so far the Widgeon was riding them like its namesake.

The prop began to turn, then caught.

"One down," she muttered, her fingers crossed more tightly than ever. "Come on, Lee. Show me what kind of pilot you are."

The starboard engine belched smoke. Its prop spun and roared to life. The ropes went taut as the Widgeon strained to be free.

Nick counted to ten, sucked a deep breath, and swung the axe, once, twice. Then she ran for the plane. Halfway there a wind gust pinned her in place. Her legs felt as if they were churning uselessly. All the while the engines revved and idled as Coltrane fought to keep the seaplane in one spot.

Clenching her teeth, she struggled to move. Just as her strength started to wane, the wind shifted. The change sent her surging forward into the surf. A moment later, she grabbed the door frame, pulled herself aboard, and closed the door behind her.

From the cockpit, Coltrane acknowledged her with a nod and opened the throttles. Nick didn't know which grated more, the engine roar or the sound of the storm. By the time she reached the cockpit and dragged herself into the copilot's seat she felt exhausted. But one look through the windshield rekindled her adrenaline. Against a black sky, an even blacker ocean roiled and seethed. The waves looming above them reminded her of oily, obsidian canyons.

Somehow, Coltrane managed to keep from being overwhelmed by the breakers as he used one engine against the other to steer through troughs. Only when they were far enough out to sea to be free of the surf action, did he turn toward the lighthouse cove.

"Now aren't you sorry you came with me?" he shouted.

"I'll tell you if we live through this," she replied.

28

With the lighthouse just coming into sight, the storm worsened. The sky grew as dark as if the sun had been eclipsed. The sea churned, bouncing the Widgeon as if it were nothing but a piece of flotsam. Wind-whipped spray, or maybe rain, it was impossible to tell, engulfed them. The windshield wipers couldn't cope. Nick couldn't see more than a few feet. She shuddered at the thought of what would happen if they missed the lighthouse.

"I've never been in anything this bad," Coltrane said. "We must be near the eye of the storm!"

The Widgeon was bouncing so hard Nick felt each impact through the soles of her feet.

"The wind is shifting," he told her. Even as he spoke, the plane's nose sank as it plunged through a wave. Water swept over the windshield.

"We're fucked," he said. "We're going to have to get out of here."

"Where to?"

"We'll run the other way, with the wind. If we don't, we'll be swamped."

At that moment, the plane shuddered violently as a wave struck it head-on. Coltrane immediately cut back on the port engine, and slammed the throttle to emergency power on the starboard. The seaplane rolled and for a moment Nick thought they might turn-turtle. Another wave hit them broadside. The port engine, already weaned to idle, sputtered and began missing badly.

"Help me hold her!" Coltrane shouted.

Nick grabbed the yoke in front of her and felt a shimmy strong enough to resonate through her entire body. "What now?"

"Just hold on." He freed his right hand to work the throttle and choke, fighting to smooth out the port engine. But it failed to respond, backfiring once before quitting altogether.

"Hold her tight!" he snapped and let go of his yoke completely as he tried to restart the engine. After a few seconds, he hit the off switch and grabbed his yoke. "It's no use. We don't have any more time. We've got to beach her before we lose the other engine. If we can't make the beach, go for the life raft in back."

He glanced at her, smiling or grimacing, she couldn't tell which. Either way, his eyes said the raft was all but useless in this kind of sea.

"Put on a life jacket," he told her. "Then bring one for me."

She bounced from side to side as she fought her way back through the fuselage to where the life raft and jackets were stored. She struggled into her jacket, then battled her way back to the cockpit. A quick glance through the windshield showed nothing but black ocean.

She held Coltrane's jacket while he worked himself into it. That done, she eased back into the copilot's seat and rubbed her shoulders where they'd slammed against the bulkhead. She was going to be black and blue tomorrow, she thought, then had to smile. You had to be alive to be black and blue.

She peered out her side window, straining to see land, but there was nothing but angry water. Leaning across Coltrane gave her a similar view on his side of the plane.

"Where's the island?" she shouted.

"To port, I think. On my side."

"You think?"

"I saw it for an instant while you were in back, from the top of a high swell."

"And now?"

"Now," Coltrane said through clenched teeth, "I turn to port and give her everything she's got left. If we're lucky, we hit land."

In one piece? Nick was tempted to ask but bit her tongue.

Gingerly, Coltrane began maneuvering the plane. Once he completed the turn to port, the wind was at their back and they picked up speed quickly. As a wave crested beneath them, Nick saw land dead ahead. Coltrane's navigation was perfect, except for the fact that Balesin was rushing at them at an alarming rate. Nick suddenly felt as if she were riding a surfboard.

"Look for someplace soft!" he shouted.

She leaned forward, straining to see between swipes of the wiper blade. Her breath misted the glass. She wiped a hole in the mist.

"Anything?" he said. He, too, was leaning forward over the yoke to get a closer look.

"Not yet." She wiped the Plexiglas again. "My God, Lee, there's land on both sides. We must be heading for Balabat, not Balesin."

"I don't think we have a choice."

"It's one of John Frum's sacred places."

"Well, he's going to have visitors. Now look for someplace to land."

Nick knew that wasn't likely. Her first overflight of the islands had shown her that. While Balesin had tourist-white beaches, Balabat had trees growing close to its shoreline.

Nick blinked. Were her eyes playing wishful tricks? No, there was a strip of beach, not deep certainly, but with enough sand to cushion their impact. She pointed it out to him.

He nodded. "Say your prayers."

But all Nick could think about was how mad Elliot was going to be if she got herself killed in what he called, "One of her damned airplanes."

"Brace yourself!" Coltrane bellowed.

Balabat couldn't have been more than fifty yards away. A wave rose beneath them and they rode its peak like a surfer. Only then did she see the cauldron of frothing white water that made up the last twenty-five yards.

For an instant the froth subsided, exposing Balabat's teeth, outcroppings of sharp coral close into shore. She screamed a warning.

"Christ!" He revved the engine trying to veer away, but it was too late.

The Widgeon shuddered as the coral ripped open her belly. The impact threw Nick forward against the yoke but she'd managed to keep her hands in front of her face.

"We're hung up!" Coltrane yelled. He jammed his hand against the throttle. "We've got to get her loose." The engine screamed.

Metal screeched. Beneath her, Nick felt the

Widgeon tearing itself to pieces. Water was pouring inside.

"Lee!" she shouted over the roar of the engine. "We've got to get out."

He shook his head violently. "We'll be torn to pieces on that coral." He cut back the power, but only momentarily before returning to full throttle. The Widgeon rocked, or maybe it was more of a wallow, Nick decided. He kept at it, adjusting the power and rocking the seaplane. And all the while Nick could hear metal scraping against the deadly reef.

Then suddenly, the Widgeon slid to one side and was free of the reef and heading for shore, where she hit nose-in and slowly began to sink.

Coltrane cut the power just as the Widgeon's belly touched bottom. By then water was sloshing knee-deep inside the cockpit.

"Christ!" he shouted, banging his fist on the yoke. "She's a write-off."

"All she's got is a hole in her bottom. She can be salvaged."

"Maybe," he conceded. "But if this storm gets any worse, she might not stay put."

He was probably right since the Widgeon, as waterlogged as she was, creaked and shuddered as each incoming wave crashed against her.

Coltrane took a deep breath and ran his hand over the control yoke. "Come on, Doc," he said finally. "Let's get out of here. And watch where you step. That coral's as sharp as glass."

Nick eased into the water. By the time she was waist-deep, her feet touched a soft bottom. Squinting against the wind-whipped rain, she looked up at Coltrane, who was kneeling in the doorway.

"We're through. The reef's behind us," he said, grimacing. "Just my luck, though. I have to hit the last piece of coral."

"You saved our lives."

Shrugging, he handed her a watertight plastic container the size of a small suitcase. "Emergency supplies," he said. "You get that one ashore." He slid an identical case into view. "I'll bring the food."

They dragged the supplies onto the narrow beach and Coltrane said, "Stay here."

"Oh no you don't," Nick shot back. "If you're going to try to tie her down, I can help."

"Don't say I didn't give you an out," Coltrane said, smiling, and waded back to the plane.

He retrieved a line and the two of them began to work. It was brutal and Nick wondered if their feeble attempts to anchor the plane weren't futile, but the effort seemed to give Coltrane some kind of emotional lift.

When they had finished, they took cover beneath the palm trees that grew close to the water. But by that time they were no match for the rain, which was pelting them with the intensity of a high-pressure showerhead.

"We've got to find ourselves some real shelter," she said.

"Where? This island can't be more than half a mile across. You saw it from the air. It's nothing but a fly speck."

"High ground, then."

He snorted. "Whatever you say, Doc. It's going to be a short trip."

They staggered inland.

Farrington, his feet braced against the warship's plunging deck, smiled at Ohmura and said, "There's nothing like an ocean voyage." He sucked a deep breath and gestured theatrically at the seething ocean. "Now aren't you glad I intercepted you? You would have had to fly in. Now we've got shipboard accommodations."

"What I am is seasick," Ohmura said, holding tight to the ship's rail with both hands.

That was part-time agents for you, Farrington thought. Soft and spoiled. "Your Mr. Kobayashi . . . ," Farrington began, enjoying the way Ohmura bowed his head at the mention of the name, ". . . told me that he wanted to be represented on this mission and you were his choice."

"Mr. Kobayashi is a wise man."

"How was I to know about the storm? But don't worry. The weather boys tell me it will blow itself out by the time we reach the island. Then we'll catch a few rays and maybe get ourselves a tan."

Ohmura swallowed experimentally. "How long until the sea calms?"

"Tomorrow morning. Trust me. In the meantime, though, we've got to coordinate our actions."

Ohmura looked at him with ill-concealed hate.

"Did he also tell you that I asked him to keep this operation simple? Instead, we've got a Chinese fire drill on our hands. There are so many people involved now that the cleanup is going to look like an ethnic cleansing."

Ohmura widened his smile, wondering if that was some kind of backhanded racial slur. Probably not, he decided. Americans were just plain self-centered and insensitive.

"Tell me how many other agents Kobayashi has on the island?" Farrington asked bluntly.

"I don't know."

Farrington squinted at him. "What the hell. I know old Koby likes to play things close to the vest. I'm glad you're here anyway. This way, there won't be any second-guessing later on."

"Mr. Kobayashi isn't the kind of man to second-guess," Ohmura said, appalled that anyone would dare refer to Mr. Kobayashi as Koby.

"You'd be surprised what people do when the shit hits the fan." Farrington winked. "That's when our bosses start washing their hands faster than Pontius Pilate."

Ohmura winced.

"Now tell me, have you ever run an operation like this?" Farrington asked.

Ohmura dry-swallowed a Dramamine before responding. "I am an anthropologist."

"Of course you are. That's a good cover too. But that doesn't answer my question."

"I do what Mr. Kobayashi tells me."

"I'll take that as a no," Farrington said.

"What about you, Mr. Farrington?" Ohmura asked, deciding to risk impertinence to gain information for Mr. Kobayashi.

"Me what?"

"Do you have agents on the island? And have you been on such missions before?"

"Sorry. That's strictly classified on a need-to-know basis."

Ohmura bowed his head.

Farrington clapped Ohmura on the back. "I don't blame you for asking. Now why don't you run along and make certain the helicopters are lashed down properly."

"Wouldn't your navy take care of such things?"

"It never hurts to be careful."

Farrington smiled as Ohmura lurched along the deck toward the helicopter pad. Once he was out of sight, Farrington cracked open the sea door and entered the bridge to brief the captain.

40

Half-blinded by the pelting rain, Nick thought she was seeing things for a moment. She shook herself but the vision remained. Tucked beneath a writhing canopy of breadfruit trees at the center of Balabat Island stood another Quonset-like structure built of corrugated metal. How it got on Balabat she couldn't imagine. There was no easy access to the smaller island, separated as it was from Balabat by a shark-infested channel.

She nudged Coltrane, who, head down in an attempt not to drown in the deluge, was trudging beside her.

"I hope you believe in miracles," she shouted in his ear.

He looked up, grinned, and replied, "I do now, if you're supplying them. From now on, Doc, you lead, I'll follow."

The metal door was padlocked. The lock itself looked new, showing no sign of rust, which was unusual in the island's corrosive climate.

She put down the plastic case she was carrying and tested the lock. The feel of it told her it had been oiled recently.

"You wouldn't happen to have a crowbar handy, would you?" she asked Coltrane.

"I've got a .45 automatic in one of these cases. Will that do?"

"Have you ever tried shooting a lock off?"

"They do it in the movies."

"They'll know we've been here, that's for sure. But I say it's better risking John Frum's wrath than spending the night outside in this weather."

"I'm with you." Using his body to shield his emergency kit from the rain, Coltrane opened the case. He took out a .45, fed in an ammunition clip, and jacked a shell into the firing chamber. "Now stand back, Doc and let me do my job."

Four shots later, the padlock snapped apart. Gingerly, Coltrane opened the door and peered inside. "It's pitch-black in there. I can't see a thing."

"I hope you've brought along a flashlight."

"I came prepared, Doc, like a Boy Scout. But let's not dig them out here in the rain. Follow me." He grabbed his case, stepped across the dirt threshold, and disappeared into the dark.

Nick picked up the case she'd lugged up from the

beach and went after him, leaving the door open to provide what light there was. By now Nick had no idea what time it was, nearing noon probably, though the heavy cloud cover and constant downpour made that only a guess.

Inside, the rain thundered against the metal roof, creating an incessant din. Nick shuddered. Until that moment she hadn't felt cold. But now, despite a temperature that had to be somewhere in the eighties, gooseflesh climbed her spine.

She dropped to her knees and began rummaging in the case for a flashlight.

"Let me do that," Coltrane said, kneeling beside her. "I know where to look."

"A fire would be nice," she said.

"There're matches in here too, but I don't think we're going to find anything dry enough to burn."

The flashlight's beam hit Coltrane in the face. As soon as it swung away to probe the darkness, Nick gasped, "My God!"

Bones were piled in the center of the Quonset, a pyramid of them taller than Nick. Human bones.

"Christ almighty!" Coltrane breathed. "Look at the skulls. There has to be a hundred of them. Maybe the stories are true. Maybe the Baleseans really are headhunters."

"They've kept more than heads. It looks like everybody bone is here. Give me the light."

Coltrane handed it over. "I've got another one in here somewhere," he said, and went to rummaging.

Nick moved to get a closer look. Headhunters, she recalled, preferred their heads intact. But many of these had holes in their skulls, some round as bullets, others jagged. She'd never heard of headhunters piling bones in pyramids. Of course, this could be a shrine dedicated to some kind of ancestor worship.

No, she thought with a shake of her head. That didn't make sense. The holes proved that many of these people had not died from natural causes. You don't do that to your ancestors.

Coltrane joined her, shining a second light onto the six-foot pile. "This place gives me the creeps, Doc."

Nodding, she turned her light on the far wall. Its beam revealed a half-dozen wooden crates stacked waist-high. Their sizes varied, as did their markings. A few were stenciled U.S. Army, but most had Japanese ideograms designating their contents, whatever that might be. She suspected they all dated from World War Two. Certainly, the Japanese helmets placed in rows along the top of the cases did.

"Look over there." Coltrane flashed his light on the other end of the Quonset.

Bolt-action Japanese rifles were stacked carefully along the corrugated wall. The rifles, unlike the lock outside, had been allowed to rust.

"We never invaded Balesin, or Balabat," Nick said. "They weren't considered important enough. So our invasion forces passed them by on their way to more strategic targets. The Japanese were trapped here. They had no way to evacuate their forces, or resupply them either for that matter."

"So what are you saying?"

"That whoever these people were, they didn't die of old age."

"Are we talking cannibalism?" Coltrane asked though his heart didn't sound in it.

"More like some kind of massacre."

He whistled.

"I could be wrong," she added. "It could be an undiscovered offshoot of the Cargo Cult, though that doesn't seem likely."

"Even if you're right, why make such a big deal of this place. Back then, the Japs were the enemy. Killing them got you medals."

"Not if the war was already over."

Coltrane shrugged. "That was a long time ago. Nobody cares anymore."

Maybe, Nick thought to herself. But if no one cared, why was Balabat so high on John Frum's taboo list? Many cultures believed that unburied bones kept souls in limbo. Perhaps this was the Baleseans' way of getting even with their Japanese invaders. There was also the possibility that they were an offering to John Frum.

"Let's check the cases," she said.

Together they opened the crates. All but one contained rotting Japanese uniforms, insignias, ceremonial swords, and assorted military memorabilia. The last crate held a tea box containing a small package wrapped in oilskins. With shaky hands, Nick lifted it out and waited while Coltrane replaced the lid so she could use it as a desktop. Only then did she carefully unwrap the package. Archaeologists lived for such moments, the chance to touch a piece of history.

Don't anticipate, she told herself. Let the facts speak for themselves.

Her breath caught at the sight of the old, leatherbound notebook. Except for its expensive binding, it was similar to those she and her father used to record site data. Please God, she thought, don't let it be in Japanese. Coltrane added his flashlight to hers so she could read more easily.

Nick opened the notebook and sighed with relief.

The inside cover was inscribed *Balesin Island, 1947*. Beneath the inscription two names were written: *Nathan and Jessie Innis*.

"Who the hell are they?" Coltrane asked.

"At a guess, I'd say they were related to the Reverend Innis. But guesses don't count in my line of work."

Nick's legs felt suddenly weak. The harrowing ride in the Widgeon had drained her more than she realized, that and the excitement of her discovery inside the Quonset. "I've got to sit down."

Coltrane quickly rearranged the crates so she could sit on one and use the others for a backrest.

"I'll hold the lights, Doc, you read."

"Do you want me to read it to you?"

"Make it easy on yourself. Just give me the highlights."

It didn't take long before Nick realized that the notebook had belonged to an anthropologist, two of them actually, a husband-and-wife team. Judging by the date, 1947, only two years after the war, they'd been lured to Balesin by tales of the Cargo Cult carried home by returning GIs. Their analysis of Balesin's culture coincided with many of Nick's observations, that the society was matrilineal, with most powers, other than religious, held by the island's matriarch. Sacred duties were the domain of John Frum's priest, Thomas Yali. Possibly, he'd been Henry's father, Nick decided, or at the very least a close relative of the present shaman.

Something else occurred to her. Quite possibly Nathan and Jessie Innis had been the only members of the so-called "lost" expedition. The dates were right and there was no mention of any other scientists.

As Nick turned the pages, she became more and more convinced that her assessment was correct. What bothered her, though, was finding the journal here among the Japanese dead. Were Nathan's and Jessie's bones also among those so carefully piled in the center of the Quonset?

As she turned a page, an underlined comment caught her eye. She read it out loud. "*All primitive cultures have taboos, but those on Balesin seem extraordinary. We have been warned constantly where we may go and where we may not. John Frum is known to many peoples throughout the Pacific. But here he rules with absolute authority. A frightening authority, we're tempted to say, though that would be unprofessional.*"

"I know how they felt, Doc," Coltrane said. "The whole damned place spooks me, but it must have been a lot worse back in those days. Hell, if you weren't military, the only way in here was by boat, unless you wanted to parachute."

Nick hugged herself. "Look around for something to make a fire."

"I already did that. There's nothing, unless you want to break up these crates."

"Not a chance. They're artifacts."

"Sure, whatever you say."

"Not mine, John Frum's."

"I guess we're going to have to eat cold food, then."

"What have you got?"

"Spam and energy bars."

"I'm not that hungry yet," Nick said, and went back to reading to herself.

After a few minutes, Coltrane said, "I'm getting tired of standing here holding these lights for you."

"Sorry, I lost track of time."

"Well, take a break and rest your eyes. We ought to

rest the batteries, too, at least in one of the flashlights. God knows how long we'll be stranded here."

"We can inflate your life raft as soon as the storm passes."

"Sorry, Doc, but the coral cut it to pieces."

Nick put down the notebook and sighed. "You can switch them both off for a while."

When he did, she realized it had grown completely dark. In the darkness, something else struck her. Rain was no longer thundering on the roof; it had become a gentle dripping.

"The storm's easing," she pointed out.

"It figures. This time of year, they don't last long. But in the monsoon season watch out. That's when I dry-dock my Widgeon for safekeeping. Or did," he added sadly.

"Stop feeling sorry for yourself and switch on the light again," she said.

Coltrane grumbled but complied.

"There," she told him, waving the flashlight, "don't you notice anything?"

"Like what?"

"Light attracts bugs and there aren't any."

They'd probably been blown out to sea, she thought, or flat-out drowned. Either way, they ought to have a couple of days' respite before the next batch hatched out.

"That calls for a celebration, Doc." He dug into one of the cases and handed her a limp energy bar. "You better eat, whether you're hungry or not. We've had a rough day."

Holding the flashlight for herself, Nick ate while she read. Because of the bar's consistency, it stuck to the roof of her mouth like peanut butter. But she forced it down and immediately began to feel better. All she needed now was a hot shower and a real bed. For a moment, she thought about taking off her clothes and standing in the rain, but that would be a bit provocative considering the circumstances. She glanced at Coltrane, who grinned back as if he'd been thinking about the romantic possibilities when a man and woman find themselves alone and stranded.

She forced herself to read on. Two pages later she hit an entry that needed sharing. "Listen to this, Lee. *My wife and I have spent many weeks gaining the confidence of the people here. Today, our hard work finally paid off. They have agreed to take us to one of their holy places, the airfield on their sacred mountain. There, they say, John Frum himself landed during the war. We begin to believe that John Frum may have been a real person after all. If so, identifying him would be an important milestone in the history of the Pacific Islands. Unfortunately, we are not allowed to take a camera with us. We have also been sworn to secrecy and not to reveal what we see. As scientists we feel such a lie on our part is justified.*"

Nick paused to think that over. Over the years, Indian tribes in America had learned not to trust anthropologists with their secrets. As a result, many Indians had started making up myths and stories, until now fact and fantasy were often impossible to separate, making scholarship virtually useless.

"*We've also been told that we can't take our son, George, with us,*" she read. "*He must stay behind in the care of the village women.*"

"I'll be damned," Coltrane said. "You were right. That is the reverend they're talking about."

"It seems likely," Nick said, and went onto the next entry. "*They have shown us pieces of a real two-engine war-*

plane, or what's left because of battle damage. The pieces have been carefully collected and appear to be in the process of being moved. Our guess is that the shaman intends to build a shrine somewhere. In any case, we are told this is the airplane that brought John Frum to Balesin. He came disguised as a flier, they say, but he was mortally wounded, so that he could die and be resurrected again."

Coltrane interrupted. "Those people sound a little nuts to me. But then a place like this would do it to anyone."

Nick turned the page. It was the final entry in the notebook. *"We must break our promise and return to the site alone. We intend to document it with photographic evidence. With luck, we'll be back in the village before anyone misses us and no one will know we have broken their most sacred taboo."*

Nick sighed and put down the notebook. "Apparently they were found out. The diary ends here."

"The islanders killed them, you mean."

"Who else?"

"I wonder if the Reverend Innis knows," Coltrane said.

"I don't think we should be the ones to tell him," she replied. "It all happened more than fifty years ago, so chances are that whoever killed them is long gone."

"So what! I'd still want to know, if I were the reverend. Besides, aren't you forgetting something, Doc? History's repeating itself on this damned place. Three more people have died wandering around where they shouldn't have."

He had a point. Even so, annoying as Yali was with his obtuse shaman-speak, she couldn't imagine him as a killer. Chief Jeban either, for that matter. And Lily was unthinkable as a suspect.

"I think it best that we keep quiet about this journal until we find out more."

"No way. These bastards are killers."

"Dammit," she said, "let me talk to my father and Curt Buettner first. Maybe we can figure out a way to soften the blow. Remember, these people are the reverend's parishioners. What would happen if every time he looked at them, he saw them as killers?"

"Aren't they?"

"Just keep quiet about it."

"You make that sound like an order, Doc."

"Just remember you're working for Curt Buettner."

"Let me tell *you* a story. When I was a kid, I lost both my parents. They were rear-ended by a goddamned drunk driver, who got off with a few months in jail. For years after, I dreamt about tracking that bastard down and killing him for ruining my life."

"But you didn't, did you?"

"I never got the chance. The bastard drank himself to death."

Shaking her head, Nick wrapped the journal back into its oilskins and replaced it in its wooden crate. "This is an artifact, a piece of history, whether you like it or not. It stays here with everything else, at least until we sort out the situation."

She asked, "Do you think the Widgeon's radio is still working?"

He pursed his lips. "Swamped the way she is, I wouldn't bet on it."

"Then we're just going to have to swim for it."

"Not with sharks I don't," Coltrane said. "Buettner warned me that the waters around here are infested."

"When was that?" she asked, unable to recall any such conversation.

"It was months ago, when I flew him here the first time. He said the sharks were everywhere. I'd forgotten all about that until now. I flew him in, dropped him off, then picked him up a few days later."

He walked to the door and peered out. "It's stopped raining."

When he stepped outside, she joined him. She looked up, expecting to see nothing but blackness, but stars were showing in patches.

Thank God, she thought, and touched him on the arm.

"It's time we got some rest," he said, pulling away. "We're going to need it in the morning."

As they went back inside, she realized he'd stopped calling her Doc.

41

A growling stomach woke Nick. She'd been sleeping with her head propped against one of the wooden crates, leaving a painful crick in her neck. Bones, or maybe cartilage, crunched when she sat up and stretched.

"Lee?" she muttered, looking around the Quonset and finding it empty.

"Out here!" Coltrane's muffled call came from outside. A moment later, the door banged open and blinding sunlight spilled inside. "I was about to go down to the beach and take a look at my Widgeon."

Breakfast first, she thought, then remembered all

they had left was Spam. Ignoring her aches and protesting stomach, she scrambled to her feet and hustled outside. The brilliant sky dazzled her. She took a deep breath. The air smelled of rich, wet earth. The temperature, though warm, was pleasant. There was still no sign of mosquitoes.

"Are you coming?" he asked.

"I'm right behind you."

The walk to the beach, winding through palms and breadfruit trees, refreshed her. In such weather these islands really were tropical paradises. Even the sea had calmed, its breakers more picturesque than dangerous.

Coltrane planted his feet at the water's edge, folded his arms over his chest, and shook his head at the Widgeon. He was again wearing his leather flying jacket, she noticed, zipped up despite the warm day.

"Maybe it's not as bad as it looks," Nick offered. "At least it stayed put." Which was an understatement, since the Widgeon looked more like a sunken ship than an airplane. "Nothing seems to be broken off," she added.

"Shit, woman. Use your eyes. That's the end of Coltrane Airlines."

He still wasn't calling her Doc, she noticed.

"Surely something can be salvaged," she said, trying to sound upbeat.

He squatted in a catcher's stance, picked a piece of shell from the sand at his feet, and hurled it at the plane. "Hasn't it sunk into that brain of yours? I'm now a pilot without a plane."

"While you're deciding on a new profession," she said sarcastically, "why don't we see if the radio's in working order, or were you planning to take up permanent residence here?"

"When you say *we*, you mean *me* wading in and getting soaked again, don't you?"

"Men," she muttered, and waded in herself.

"Hold it."

When she looked back he was folding his jacket and stowing it on the sand.

She reached the fuselage door ahead of him.

"For Christ's sake, woman," he snapped. "Look at her. You're wasting your time. She's half-full of water and her electronics will be shot to hell."

Irritated, she tugged on the door latch but it wouldn't budge.

"Ease up," he said, plunging past her. "I locked it."

Good thinking, she said to herself, since a crowded place like this had to be rife with thieves.

"It's no good you sloshing around in there," he went on. "You'll just make a mess of things. I know where everything is and what to look for."

"Such as?"

"Stay behind me and maybe you'll learn something."

She clenched her teeth to keep from swearing.

Inside, the water was waist-deep. Even the cockpit's instrument panel was partially submerged. So were the seats, except for their flotation cushions that were bobbing against the windshield.

"Just stay out of the way," he said, taking a deep breath before plunging beneath the surface.

A moment later an airtight cylinder-shaped container sprang to the surface hard enough to bang into the ceiling. A second followed, barely missing her.

Coltrane came up for air. "Flare guns," he announced breathlessly.

"What about food? Is there anything else in here to eat besides Spam?"

He started to say something, then submerged again without a word. This time he popped to the surface along with yet another yellow plastic case. He thrust it at her. "More energy bars and some trail mix for madam. Now let's get out of here and phone home."

While Nick chewed on a bar the consistency of road tar, he loaded a flare gun, aimed it toward Balesin, and fired. Its smoky trail culminated in a disappointing burst that wouldn't have passed muster at a Fourth of July celebration.

"Do you think they'll be able to see something that small?" she asked with her mouth full.

"If they're looking for it."

That wasn't exactly comforting, though Nick knew Elliot would have organized some kind of search by now. The problem was, anyone in the jungle, no matter how alert, wasn't likely to see an airborne signal.

"What about the church tower?" she asked. "Could you see it from there?"

"How far's that?"

"Miles."

"Only if they have binoculars."

Nick sighed and counted energy bars. There were a dozen, eleven now she'd eaten one. "Maybe we should ration these in case help's a long time getting here."

Coltrane shrugged. "We're going to run out of fresh water before we do food."

"If we have to, seawater can sustain us for a while."

Fifteen minutes later he fired another flare. "I think we'd better save the rest for tonight. You can see them for miles in the dark. Any objections?"

She shook her head.

While he retrieved his jacket, she sat on the sand and stared toward Balesin. The thought struck her that tourists paid small fortunes to land on tropical beaches like this one.

Behind her, she heard the metallic thud of another flare being loaded into its pistol. But when she turned to check on Coltrane's intentions, he had a strange look on his face and his head was cocked to one side, listening.

She jumped to her feet and listened, too. For a moment she heard nothing but the lapping of waves. Then suddenly there was the distant but distinctive thumping of helicopter blades.

Nick scanned the horizon, but couldn't see anything.

Coltrane fired another flare. A moment later the sound of a chopper grew louder.

"There!" Nick pointed out to sea. The chopper was coming in low, and not from the direction of Balesin, which surprised her.

"Buettner must have gotten the radio working," Coltrane said.

Even if true, a helicopter didn't have the range to fly in from Guam. She was about to say so when she saw the U.S. Navy markings on its side. Their flares must have been seen from a ship, though what the hell one might be doing out here she couldn't imagine. Only yesterday the ocean had been like a cauldron.

The chopper hovered directly overhead for a moment, giving them time to scramble out of the way. Once they were clear, it settled slowly onto the beach. The man waving at them from the open doorway looked familiar. She was about to ask Coltrane if he recognized him when she realized where she'd seen him. Sam Ohmura's photograph had been on the back cover of his book on Pacific Island cultures.

Head down to avoid the whirling rotor blades,

Ohmura jumped out and came to meet them. Two sailors accompanied him.

"You must be Nick Scott," he said, offering his hand. "And you're Lee Coltrane. It's good to see you both. We were afraid your plane had been swept out to sea."

"I didn't know the Navy was looking for us," she said.

"Your father sent us. He's waiting at the church with my partner. Come, we'll ferry you over there."

42

"What took you so long?" Elliot demanded as Nick climbed out of the helicopter.

"Glad to see you, too, Elliot," Nick snapped. "It's nice to know that you were as worried about me as I was about you."

"Of course I was worried about you, daughter. But I had the advantage of receiving Sam's message when he found you. And he, no doubt, told you that I was well."

He stepped forward and enfolded Nick in a bear hug, which surprised her, it was so uncharacteristic.

"Watch what you say," he whispered in her ear.

"What's wrong?" she whispered back.

"I don't know for sure. Just be careful."

Buettner took a turn hugging her. Over his shoulder she saw a line of villagers trudging along the Mission Trail, carrying their belongings back home now that the storm had passed. Of the locals, only Yali, Chief Jeban, and Lily remained behind. With them, waiting their turn to greet Nick and Coltrane, were the reverend and his wife, and a man Nick had never seen before. Probably he was the partner Ohmura had referred to, though why a professor would need one, she couldn't guess. Especially a partner who had a Navy officer hovering close by like an aide-de-camp. For that matter she couldn't understand why a professor would be giving orders aboard a U.S. Navy helicopter.

"I'm Reed Farrington," the stranger said. "Lucky for you Sam Ohmura and I came along." Farrington wore a loose-fitting linen jacket over a bright Hawaiian shirt and rock-washed jeans. He looked to be somewhere in his mid-thirties.

Ohmura came over to stand beside him like a second aide-de-camp, smiling and nodding reassuringly whenever Nick looked his way. She didn't really know the man, but it seemed to her that beneath the reassuring veneer there was a sense of strain and anxiety.

"I can see by the look on your face," Farrington continued, "that you're wondering how we happened to be here. It was luck, pure and simple. We were on a training mission."

"In this kind of weather?" Nick responded.

"I'm not Navy myself, you understand, just temporarily attached for this mission. But the ship's captain assured me that the storm was absolutely fortuitous. 'Training can never be too realistic,' he told me, 'because you never know when you're going to war, in which case you can't stop for the weather.'"

"A ship!" Yali interrupted excitedly. "Have you come in a great warship?"

Farrington nodded.

"Where is it?"

Farrington pointed in the general direction of Mount Nomenuk, but Nick assumed he meant north of the island. "She's steaming just over the horizon."

Yali raised his hands to the heavens. "John Frum be praised. He prophesied that one day great vessels would visit Balesin, and that they would be carrying wondrous cargo."

"Frum be praised," Jeban echoed. "How soon will you be docking?"

Farrington shook his head. "No can do. The captain says there's too many reefs in this area. He intends to stay well clear."

Jeban looked crestfallen. Yali's chin dropped onto his chest. Lily took his arm as if to steady him.

Elliot spoke up. "I still don't know how you knew that we were in trouble, or even that any Americans were here."

"You have our captain to thank for that," Farrington answered. "Since we were close by, he decided to send in a chopper to check for storm damage. This island is an American protectorate, you know. We have to take care of our own."

"Your story sounds like bullshit," Buettner blurted. "Why would you and your so-called training mission include my department head?" He glared at Ohmura. "What do you have to say about that, Sam?"

Farrington answered for him. "We needed an expert on this area of the Pacific, what else?"

Judging from the expression on Buettner's face he didn't believe a word of it. Nick glanced at her father. He, too, looked skeptical. Elliot tended to be a cautious man, except when in hot pursuit of his beloved Anasazi, but at the moment that natural caution seemed tinged

with alarm, if she was reading him correctly. Judging by
the look on Lily's face, she also shared Elliot's concern.

Elliot forced a smile, the condescending kind that
used to infuriate Nick's mother, and turned it on Farrington. "Well, Mr. Farrington, it's not really important
how you got here. I'm just thankful you were on hand to
rescue my daughter."

"Actually, it was Mr. Ohmura who did that."

At the mention of his name, Ohmura bowed. Elliot
bowed back.

"We found her and Mr. Coltrane on Balabat,"
Ohmura told him somberly.

"Balabat!" Yali burst out. "What do you mean?"

"That's where their seaplane washed ashore."

"That is one of our most sacred places," Yali said, his
voice trembling with rage. "You had no right violating
it."

Chief Jeban nodded in agreement.

Ohmura started to bow, then seemed to think better
of it and merely shook his head. He had to know about
the taboos, since he'd included Balesin in his book.

Yali turned on Nick, pointing a trembling finger at
her. His mouth opened and closed but no words came
out.

"I'm sorry," she told him. "But we had no choice.
The waves took us there. If they hadn't we would have
been washed out to sea and lost."

"Maybe it was John Frum's will," Lily offered.
"Please, listen to me, Henry. It's done now. We must
accept it."

Yali sputtered. "You don't know what you're talking
about, woman." He looked to Jeban for support, but the
chief turned to Lily as if weighing his options.

"No," Coltrane said, speaking for the first time since

stepping out of the helicopter. "You're not getting away with it anymore, Yali." Coltrane unzipped his flight jacket and took out the journal still wrapped in its oilskins. "We found this on Balabat, not to mention the bones of all the people you and your ancestors murdered."

Jeban looked stricken, Yali worse.

"You had no right, Lee," Nick said, angry at herself for leaving without checking that the journal was still tucked away safely in the Quonset. "We agreed—"

"You're a scientist, aren't you?" Coltrane's voice took on a pleading quality. "You must want the truth to come out."

"Calm down," Farrington said, his tone sounding like a military commander. "I think we'd better hear more about what you found."

Instead of responding, Coltrane handed the journal to an astonished Reverend Innis. "This has the name *Innis* on it, Reverend. It was written by your parents before they died."

Innis looked as if he'd just been handed a live grenade.

Stepping forward, Farrington said, "You'd better let me have that, Reverend."

Innis, who was studying the flyleaf, shook his head. "You're a stranger here, Mr. Farrington. This has nothing to do with you. It belonged to my parents."

"Who were here under the auspices of your government at the time, I seem to remember," Farrington snapped.

Nick blinked with surprise. The Innis expedition had come to Balesin in 1947, long before Farrington had been born. And even though their disappearance must have been big news at the time, Nick suspected that only the locals and a few anthropologists in the field would remember the incident.

She was about to say as much when the reverend said, "Now if you'll excuse me, I want to be alone when I read this."

"But George—" his wife began.

He cut her off. "I'm sorry, dear. All my life I've been waiting for this moment. Maybe now, my questions will be answered. Maybe now, I'll understand my nightmares."

"It's for the best, Doc," Coltrane said. "When we get back to Guam, you'll see."

But it was Farrington who had Nick's attention. He and Ohmura were exchanging glances that made her wonder if they weren't about to take the journal by force.

Finally Farrington shook his head and shouted at the reverend, who was retreating into his church. "I can wait."

43

The Reverend Innis sat in the tiny windowless sacristy that served as his office and stared down at the journal on his desk. Gravely, he ran his fingers over the note-book's cover. To touch something they'd actually handled themselves, was like . . . Words failed him. Like having your faith rewarded, he decided finally.

He lit a votive candle and placed it beside the notebook. The act was as much a gesture of worship as it was a need for light.

After bowing his head and saying a quick prayer, he opened the leather-bound volume and gazed through moist eyes at the handwriting on the flyleaf. The script was precise and easily readable, much like his own. Whose writing was it, his father's or his mother's? he wondered.

Solemnly, he turned the page and began reading, forcing himself to go slowly, to savor every word. He'd been hoping, longing, for personal revelations, but the first few pages of the journal were devoted exclusively to his parents' work. After several pages, the sense of disappointment became overwhelming. Tears filled his eyes, making it impossible to continue reading.

Innis sat back and fought to calm himself. Think about Jesus, he told himself, and squeezed shut his eyes. But flame shapes from the candle came through his lids; the images reminded him of hell.

His eyes snapped open. He wiped them with trembling fingers and turned the next page. Midway down, a comment hit him like a physical blow. *We've also been told that we can't take our son, George, with us. He must stay behind in the care of the village women.*

Carefully, so as not to smudge the ink, he ran his fingertip over the word *George*. Memories flooded back. Real or not, he couldn't tell. Maybe they were only the stories told to him by the village women, but he wished them real.

He'd been three, going on four, when they'd come to Balesin. *You're going to have to stay close*, his parents had cautioned him. He remembered those words clearly even now. *Mommy and daddy wouldn't want you to get separated from us in a place like this. Do you understand?*

"Yes," he answered out loud, his voice as shaky as the flickering shadows on the sacristy wall.

If only he hadn't been kept behind with the village women, maybe then he could have saved them. The guilt of not being there was like a pressure inside his head, though reason told him that a child would have been powerless to help.

But if he'd been left behind why had Lily, then a very young woman herself, found him wandering in the jungle, hungry and ravaged by mosquitoes?

Back then, only two years after the war, the Pacific was in chaos. Backwaters like Balesin, though an American protectorate, were ignored. Because of that, Innis had lived the next five years on the island, raised by Lily.

He buried his face in his hands. Did he really remember any of it? Or were his memories only those stories Lily and the others had chosen to tell him? Maybe it was all a fantasy.

He shook his head. Some memories were just too vivid to be ignored. He remembered blood, or at least he thought he did, though Lily had never filled his head with such images.

What else did he remember? Blades. Yes, he was certain of that, though they weren't always the same. Sometimes they were machetes and bayonets, other times spinning propellers. Whether or not they'd cut down his parents, he was never certain.

What was certain was that Innis had lived on Balesin until he was nine, until missionaries landed. It was the missionaries who sent him back to America for schooling, but not before he'd promised Lily that he would return one day. He'd kept that promise twenty-five years ago and had been on Balesin ever since. During that time not a week had gone by that he hadn't gone looking for his parents' graves, but his respect for the islanders' taboos had limited his search. As a result he'd found nothing, no sign they'd ever existed.

Innis clenched his fists in frustration, took a deep breath to steady himself, and went back to reading.

He smiled at his parents' portrait of Henry Yali's father, a man obsessed by John Frum's taboos. Like father, like son, Innis thought, since Henry was no different.

A sound startled him. Something scuttled on the other side of the sacristy's metal wall. Whatever was making the noise had to be larger than a gecko. A coconut crab came to mind. He clenched his teeth. Those damned crabs were everywhere, scavenging. He hated them with a passion, an un-Christian thing to do, since they were one of God's creatures. Yet their purpose appalled him. Most likely, they were the reason his parents had never been found.

He turned the page and his breath caught at the sight of an underlined passage. It was written in another hand, the script much more elaborate. It had to be his mother's. *At first I welcomed the stifling heat, with its cleansing effect. It seemed to burn away all the cares and worries. But I should have known better. Here, the tropic sun intensifies everything it touches. Here, old secrets, like old sins, cast ever-lengthening shadows.*

What did she mean by that, he wondered. Perhaps it was merely a romantic observation. But that hardly seemed likely for a scientist.

He quickly turned the page, looking for more such passages. But he'd reached the end. His eyes skipped to the final paragraph. It chilled his heart.

We must break our promise and return to the site alone. We intend to document it with photographic evidence. With luck, we'll be back in the village before anyone misses us and no one will know we have broken their most sacred taboo.

Stunned, he backtracked, reading the entire page. His parents had gone alone to Mount Nomenuk.

"God almighty." His nightmares were true. The blades he'd dreamed about night after night were machetes. Machetes in the hands of Henry's father, and God knows how many other men.

His parents's blood was on their hands, on the souls of every Balesean. "May God forgive them. I cannot."

He opened the desk drawer and took out the revolver that Ruth had insisted upon when she first come to Balesin. He'd told her then she was being foolish, that there was nothing to fear on the island. He should have known better.

He cracked open the cylinder, fed in the cartridges, and smiled. It was noon now, when no shadows were cast. His timing was perfect. He'd erase Yali's shadow forever, along with all the lies.

He laid his hand on the bible, quoting from memory. " 'I will render vengeance to mine enemies.' "

44

In the strained silence following the reverend's retreat into his sacristy, Nick's stomach reasserted itself, growling for food. As hungry as she was, even Spam would have been welcome.

She glanced around the compound but saw no sign of food or a cook fire, either. Even the store was closed.

"Elliot," she said, holding up crossed fingers, "tell me you salvaged something to eat when you abandoned our house?"

He shrugged sheepishly. "Sorry. Between us and the villagers we practically cleaned out the store."

"My dear," Mrs. Innis said, "what am I thinking about? You must be famished. You too, Mr. Coltrane."

He nodded. "We've been living on energy bars ever since my Widgeon went ashore."

"You're in luck, then. I managed to bake bread before the storm hit. I'm sure there's enough for everyone. We'll get you out of the sun and I'll make sandwiches." Ruth Innis gestured toward the church's open door. "Please, come inside. We can picnic in the pews. Considering what you've all been through, I'm sure my husband wouldn't mind."

Yali stepped forward to bar her way. "Before anything else is done, you must tell your husband that I have to speak with him. He must hear my side of the story, otherwise . . ." The shaman licked his lips and clapped his hands like a man who'd burned himself on his own words.

"Now, Henry," Mrs. Innis said gently, trying unsuccessfully to capture one of his hands in hers, "you know I can't disturb George when he's in his sacristy. In your own way, you're a man of God yourself, so you must understand."

"I will confront him myself, then. What I have to say cannot wait."

"Would you accept such behavior in John Frum's church?" she asked him.

"Henry," Lily said, intervening, "Mrs. Innis is right. Perhaps it's best we leave and come back later."

Yali shook his head defiantly.

Mrs. Innis began shooing them inside. "You'll all feel better once you've had something to eat."

The Quonset was divided into living quarters at one end, the sacristy at the other, with the church portion in the middle, six pews deep, all facing a raised wooden pulpit. The only windows were small, with one on either side of the pulpit.

As soon as Mrs. Innis left to make sandwiches, Nick, her father, and Buettner took the pew in front, nearest to the pulpit. Jeban and Lily slipped into the pew behind them, while Coltrane commandeered the back pew for himself, where he stretched out. Yali refused to sit. Instead, he paced back and forth in front of the pulpit like someone eager to confess and get on with his penance.

Farrington and Ohmura took up positions on either side of the door. Their naval aide had stayed outside with the helicopter.

In the silence that followed all that could be heard was Yali's heavy breathing and the occasional rattle of dishes from the Innis's living quarters.

Nick leaned against her father and whispered, "Does Farrington know what's been going on around here?"

"Yes, but not from me."

"Who told him, then?"

"The only person I've seen him huddling with is Ohmura. They both seem to know a great deal for the accidental visitors they claim to be."

Nick twisted around to look Farrington in the face. "I'm still confused, Mr. Farrington. Since you came in a military ship, do you represent the authorities?"

"In what sense?"

"People have died here, two of professor Buettner's students, along with an associate of his."

"We'll be taking the bodies off the island, if that's what you're asking."

"And?" she prompted.

"I'm sure an investigation will be launched in due course, Ms. Scott. Where are the bodies, by the way?"

"We bagged the two students. The other is buried," Elliot answered. "Lee Coltrane was going to fly them out, but that was before the storm hit. Now I'm not quite sure where they are."

Buettner thumped himself on the forehead. "In my rush to evacuate I forgot about them. For obvious reasons we stored them well away from the houses. I just hope the storm didn't disturb them."

"Don't worry," Yali said. "They are safe. They are with John Frum."

"Henry means they've been taken to our church," Lily said.

"John Frum's church," Yali added.

"Not actually inside," Chief Jeban amended, "but well sheltered."

"How did they die?" Farrington asked.

"They were killed," Elliot said. "Their necks were broken."

"Excuse us for a moment," Farrington said, and led Ohmura to the far end of the church, where Ohmura immediately began gesturing heatedly. Farrington's response was to shake his head. Finally, though, he nodded once and they rejoined the group.

"I'd better go take a look at the dead for myself," Farrington said. "Mr. Yali, I'd appreciate it if you'd show me the way to your church."

"I am here on John Frum's business. I cannot leave now."

"Wouldn't you like a ride in my helicopter?"

Yali's mouth dropped open as he stared through the window at the helicopter outside. "I . . . I . . ." Finally he shook his head. "To fly like John Frum would be a wonder, but I cannot leave."

"I'm afraid I'm going to have to insist."

Chief Jeban spoke up. "Henry's right. His place is here. I'll show you the way."

Farrington's eyes narrowed and for a moment Nick thought he was going to press the point and insist on Yali as his guide. Instead, he shrugged and said, "Professor Ohmura will remain behind."

"I'll tag along, if you don't mind," Coltrane said.

Farrington raised an eyebrow.

"It's getting a little chilly in here," Coltrane added, no doubt, Nick thought, for her benefit.

Farrington smiled and shrugged his shoulders. "Why not?"

The men were halfway to the waiting helicopter when Mrs. Innis came through the door at the back of the Quonset, carrying a platter of sandwiches. "Don't you want to eat first?"

Before anyone could answer, the helicopter's engine whined to life. Conversation became impossible. Shaking her head at the din, Mrs. Innis moved along the pews dispensing sandwiches.

At Nick's first bite, she sighed with relief. Though she'd been hungry enough to eat Spam, Mrs. Innis had worked a miracle, coming up with something that tasted like a tuna-salad sandwich. Everyone ate, even the pacing Yali.

"There are seconds for everyone," Mrs. Innis announced. "So eat up. We can't have any leftovers, not in this heat." She sat beside Nick in the front pew.

Until that moment Nick hadn't realized how hot it was. The noontime temperature had soared, well into the nineties if she was any judge. The Quonset's corrugated walls radiated heat like a microwave. Yet part of her felt chilled to the bone by what was happening on the island. If the past was repeating itself, Yali had to be responsible for Tracy and Axelrad, just as his ancestors were responsible for the Innises. Or was she missing something? One way or another she had to know. But with Ohmura hovering nearby, she hesitated to confront the shaman. Yet this might be her last chance now that Farrington and his Navy helicopters were clearly in charge.

She took a deep breath and began. "Henry, there's something you ought to know."

Yali stopped pacing but didn't respond.

"I read the journal," she went on. "I know about Mount Nomenuk."

Yali moved behind the pulpit as if wanting a barrier between them. "The mountain belongs to John Frum. It is his pathway from heaven."

She nudged her father to let him know something was coming. "I don't believe that someone from heaven would demand the spilling of blood. John Frum must be the devil."

"Blasphemy!" Yali spat.

Elliot laid a restraining hand on Nick's arm but she ignored it. "What kind of God would kill people because they walked on his mountain?"

Yali grabbed the pulpit so hard his arms shook. "Frum's hands are clean."

"If that's true," Nick persisted, "then yours aren't."

Yali's frantic eyes sought Lily, who immediately left
the pew to stand beside the shaman.

"A god didn't kill the Innises," Nick said calmly.

"Is that what my husband's reading?" Mrs. Innis
asked. "About the death of his parents?"

"I'm afraid so," Nick told her, thinking that Coltrane had a lot to answer for.

"And the people on this island did that?" Mrs. Innis
asked. "That's what's in the book?"

"Unless Henry can prove otherwise, that's what I
think."

Mrs. Innis leaned against Nick and began to sob
quietly.

"This must end," Lily said suddenly. "It's time,
Henry. The truth has to come out."

"I am John Frum's priest. He spoke to me personally.
He touched me, anointed me. I will not turn against
him."

"Henry," Lily pleaded, "this isn't about John Frum
anymore." She reached out to him. He shuddered beneath her touch. "I'm begging you, Henry."

His shoulders sagged. "I must do my duty. I must—"

The sacristy door banged open.

"Yali!" Innis screamed as he charged through the
door, brandishing a revolver. Yali danced away, putting
the pulpit between them.

With a swipe of his arm, Innis sent the pulpit crashing to the ground. "Judgment day," he spat, and pointed
the gun at Yali's head. Lily moved between the two men.

"My hands are clean," Yali protested.

"You must pay for your father's sins," the reverend
replied.

Out of the corner of her eye Nick saw a gun appear
suddenly in Sam Ohmura's hand, not a move you'd ex-

pect from a middle-aged professor. The gun stayed at his side, beyond Innis's field of vision.

Yali bowed his head. "If it is the will of John Frum, so be it."

Innis gestured Lily out of the way. When Lily didn't budge, Nick grabbed her arm and pulled her out of the line of fire.

"George," Mrs. Innis said. "Don't do this." She leapt from the pew and took Lily's place. "Remember your commandments. Thou shall not kill."

" 'I will render vengeance to mine enemies,' " Innis answered, his voice as shaky as the rest of him.

"Give me the gun, George." His wife moved toward him, reaching out, placing herself between Yali and her husband.

Inside the metal hut, the explosion was deafening.

45

Innis fell to his knees beside his wife, whose staring eyes told Nick that help was useless. Innis flung the revolver against the wall, where Ohmura scooped it up.

"Please, God," the reverend moaned as he pressed both hands against her wound. "Help me!"

Nick searched for a pulse and then said as gently as he could, "I'm afraid she's gone."

Innis looked up at her with pleading eyes.

"I'm sorry," Nick told him.

Innis blinked, then laid his head against his wife's bloody breast.

"Enough," Lily blurted, her eyes filled with tears. She pointed a finger at Yali. "Do you hear me, old man? Too many have died already. No more secrets."

"Lily, I—"

"Don't," Lily snapped. "No more talk."

"Please," he said.

"I won't listen, Henry. We have lived in fear too long. We have become prisoners of our past."

"As John Frum's priest, I beg you."

"My ears are closed to you." Lily turned her back on him to look at Nick. "Child, if you found the diary, you also found the bones. They are what's left of the Japanese soldiers that our fathers killed."

Yali gasped.

Lily nodded. "There, it's said. It's done."

"It was the war," Yali pleaded.

"The war was over, old man."

"They invaded our island. They killed our people They deserved no better."

Tears were running down Lily's cheeks. "Listen to yourself, Henry. They were cut off and forgotten. They'd run out of food. They were weak and starving. It was a massacre."

Nick looked at Ohmura, wondering how a man with his obvious Japanese ancestry would react to such a revelation. But he was only nodding as if he already knew the truth.

"All we did," Yali went on, "was save the American the trouble."

"We, Henry?" Lily responded with a shake of he head. "You're acting like you and I did it, but we wer only children, then. I refuse to shoulder the blame any longer."

"I touched John Frum," Yali said, as if that superseded blame.

Lily's shoulders sagged. "You never change, old man." She collapsed onto the pew and bowed her head.

"Lily," Nick said gently, "I can understand your people's anger, even their need for revenge against the Japanese. But what about the reverend's parents?"

"They had discovered part of our secret. So old Thomas Yali and my father, all of the men, decided to kill them and add their bones to those already at Balabat. There was a price though. The village had to be moved away or it would have been poisoned by the souls of the dead."

"And that's why your village is on the wet side of the island?"

Lily nodded.

"You still haven't told me what the Innises found on Mount Nomenuk," Nick said.

"Come with me," Lily answered, taking Nick's hand. "I'll show you and put an end to the secrets once and for all."

"No!" Yali screamed frantically.

Lily glared at him. "My mind is made up."

Yali lunged at her, but Elliot caught him from behind.

"What about the rest of us?" Buettner asked. "Can't we go too?"

"I'm sorry," Lily told him. "Only Nick may come. It is proper. She is the forerunner."

Nick looked to Ohmura, questioning him with a glance.

He shrugged. "Do what you want. I'm sure there will be plenty of time for the rest of us to go sight-seeing later."

46

The hard-packed, winding trail up Mount Nomenuk was obviously well traveled. It was clear of vegetation and solid underfoot despite the rain. For a while it was wide enough for Nick and Lily to walk side by side. But halfway up the two-thousand-foot slope, the trail narrowed, becoming snake-like as it doubled back upon itself to reduce the angle of ascent. They were forced to trudge single file. Lily took the lead, setting the pace.

All around them heavy growth, dominated by walls of bamboo, reduced visibility to only a few yards. If an outsider like herself wandered off the trail by accident, Nick thought, it was doubtful she'd ever find it again.

By the time Lily called a halt, Nick was gasping for breath, the sweat dripping from her like rain. Even the brim of her Cubs cap was soaked. But Lily looked fresh. Or maybe placid would have been a better description.

"Are you okay?" Nick asked, wondering if she was misreading the woman's appearance.

"For once I feel as light as a feather. A heavy burden has been lifted from me at last."

Nick swung her cap around like a catcher and looked back the way they'd come. But there was nothing to see but bamboo.

"John Frum's place isn't far now," Lily said.

To Nick, the ground slope looked unsuitable for a landing field. "Did you see John Frum?" she asked.

"Not to talk to." With that, Lily started climbing again.

For the next few minutes, Nick walked with her head down, watching where she stepped. The ground seemed to be leveling out somewhat, and around them the bamboo thinned.

"There," Lily said suddenly.

Nick looked up to see a long, straight clearing, lush with knee-high grass. A quarter of a mile of it stretched out before her, ending in a stand of breadfruit trees. For the briefest moment, seeing it from ground level, she didn't recognize it for what it was. In the next instant, she felt triumphant. She was looking at the airstrip she'd seen from the air, one still usable if the grass were mown.

"Is this where John Frum landed?" Nick asked.

Nodding enigmatically, Lily started down the runway, with Nick hustling after her, marveling at the older woman's stamina. But then she no longer felt tired, either. Her archaeologist's adrenaline had kicked in.

Yet as impressive as the strip was, cut into the mountainside by hand, she felt a growing sense of disappointment. A quarter of a mile wasn't much of a takeoff run for a real airplane. Yet it didn't make sense that Lily would have challenged Henry Yali's authority if all that was at stake was just another make-believe airstrip.

Lily stopped suddenly, shading her eyes against the sun, and pointed toward the trees directly ahead.

"I see them, Lily. They're beautiful."

"No, child, what we seek is beyond Henry's airplanes."

Nick spun the bill of her cap around to shield her

eyes. "Is it a real hangar?" she asked, failing to mention that she'd already seen it from the air.

"Yes," Lily said. "John Frum shares it."

With whom? Nick thought, but didn't waste time asking. She wanted to see for herself. Now she led the way, with Lily struggling to keep up.

At the edge of the trees, Nick stopped dead in her tracks. Before her, tucked beneath overhanging tree limbs, stood something she hadn't expected. The wasn't one of those round prefab Quonsets, but a square, high-roofed structure. Obviously, it had been built by hand to take full advantage of the natural camouflage.

Blinking, Nick wiped the sweat from her eyes. Not a working hangar, she decided, since there was no door to accommodate an airplane. There was no opening at all that she could see.

Lily pulled up beside her and bowed her head as if in prayer. To show her respect, Nick did the same, though she could barely contain herself. Her heart thumped excitedly; she tingled with expectation.

"You said John Frum shares it," Nick said.

Lily nodded. "With the forerunner. Come. You'll meet them both."

Lily led her to a small door at the side of the building. Like the walls and roof, the door had been hammered together from pieces of metal siding, war salvage judging by the olive-drab paint that still clung to some of the crannies.

Lily pulled a chain from around her neck. "Henry and I are the only ones with keys." She hesitated. It was clear that the door had been forced.

"Who has been here?" Lily cried, and thrust open the door.

Even with the door open the gloom inside remained

impenetrable. Remembering her grim discovery inside the Quonset on Balabat, Nick hesitated.

"I must see what has happened," Lily said, and disappeared inside.

Nick held her breath, straining to catch the slightest sound. "Lily?"

"Patience, child."

A moment later light flared, accompanied by the hissing of a kerosene lantern. "It's all right," Lily called. "Nothing appears to have been touched."

Nick stepped over the raised threshold, gazing in wonder. This was no mock-up in front of her. This airplane was real, a twin-engine, twin-tailed bomber. It had to be the original template for John Frum's air force.

A second lantern blazed to life, this one near the bomber's nose.

"My God," Nick murmured reverently. Seen head-on the plane was unlike any other she'd ever encountered. She moved closer, reaching out tentatively to touch this piece of history. Her hand found a seam, a ragged seam without rivets. She circled the plane, finding more such seams, examining them carefully to make certain she wasn't jumping to the wrong conclusion. All right, she told herself, think. The nose looked like a B-25, though the Plexiglas portion of the nose was missing. The tail looked right, too. But there was something subtly wrong.

"Are there more lanterns, Lily?"

Lily came forward with two more. Their combined light dispelled most of the shadows. It was only then that Nick saw there was no machine-gun turret atop the fuselage, and no opening to show there ever had been one. So it couldn't have been a warplane like a B-25.

She checked the engines. They were Wright Cy-

clones sure enough, like the ones that powered B-25s.
Only one of the propellers was real, the other an inge-
nious hand-carved replica.

She raised one of the lanterns high enough to get a
better look at the cockpit. The badly cracked Plexiglas
windshield appeared to have been glued back together
like a jigsaw puzzle.

She examined the port wing and shook her head in
awe. It was pockmarked with bullet holes. The starboard
wing was relatively undamaged; but then she realized it
didn't match. It had to have come from a separate kind
of airplane.

She moved closer to the fuselage door, which was
held in place by a piece of heavy wire looped around a
rivet.

"Go ahead," Lily assured her. "It can be opened
safely."

The moment Nick thrust her lantern into the fuselage her knees wobbled. Her hand shook at the enormity
of her discovery. The lantern light pitched drunkenly.
Despite that, she could see the reason for the ragged
metal seams outside. The plane had been recreated by
hand, each piece held in place by wrappings of wire.

Directly in front of her, a scrap of jagged metal lay
on the fuselage floor. Reverently, she picked it up and
held it to the light. It was a foot-long piece of Alclad
with a line of rivet holes along its one smooth side.
She'd need calipers to prove what she already knew intu-
itively, that it had been ripped from a larger sheet of
0.032 Alclad.

Shakily, she backed away from the plane and collapsed onto the hard-packed earthen floor, the Alclad
clutched in her hand. Lily came over to sit beside her.

Nick dropped her head between her knees and

willed herself to relax, while Lily gently stroked her back. Finally Nick was calm enough to sit up and ask, "There are two planes here. You put the pieces together, didn't you?"

"We salvaged them, yes."

"And one came during the war, is that right?"

"It was John Frum's plane. But the Japanese hit it with a shell and it exploded. But John Frum got away, at least for a while."

"And the other plane?"

"That was the forerunner's. She came before John Frum, as it is hoped you have come before his return."

Get a hold of yourself, Nick thought. She was jumping to conclusions. Elliot would have her head. She silently repeated his mantra, never make assumptions.

"How far ahead was the forerunner, Lily?" she asked. "Do you know the year?"

Lily shook her head. "I was a small child. I have been told that it was two, maybe three years before the Japanese came."

It couldn't be possible, Nick thought. Balesin was too far north, but the time was right.

"And her name?" Nick asked, silently praying for what she considered must be impossible.

"Her name was *Mis'a'putam*. In your language it means she who comes before. In those days we didn't speak much English like we do now."

"And the English name?" Nick asked.

"I was never told. Perhaps Henry knows."

Nick let out the breath she'd been holding. It was enough. With Lily's statement, along with Alclad, and the other pieces in the patchwork plane, she could prove what was now obvious. That there were two separate airplanes here, one a B-25, the other a Lockheed Electra.

Both had looked very much alike. Both had two engines, twin tails, and similar wing and cockpit configurations. But the Lockheed, a civilian plane, had no gun turrets. Which brought it down to this. It was possible that John Frum, or whoever he was, had flown here during the war in a B-25. Why had he come? Had he been looking for this woman, the forerunner? And if so, why? What was so important about this woman that a B-25 would fly to this flyspeck in the ocean? And even if the B-25 didn't have anything to do with the previous plane, what was important was that Nick had pieces of a Lockheed Electra five hundred miles north of Howard Island. And Howard Island was where in 1937 the Navy had looked for the world's most famous aviatrix.

Nick said, "There should have been a man with her, with the forerunner."

"There was," Lily answered. "He is buried with her."

"Where?"

"Very near where we're sitting."

"How did they die?"

"When the Japanese came we hid them. The forerunner made many promises, but there were some who did not believe. She told us that she was Mis'a'putam, the one who comes before, and that Mis'ta'putam, the one who comes next, would do many wonderful things for us. We all knew that she meant John Frum, but Thomas Yali, Henry's father, grew tired of waiting. He betrayed them as he betrayed John Frum. The Japanese captured them and made them talk. That's how they knew John Frum was coming. That's why they killed everybody."

Nick was dumbfounded. By a quirk of language the islanders had misunderstood what they were being told. She didn't have the heart to tell Lily that Mis'ta'putam had nothing to do with John Frum. Instead she hugged Lily and said, "Balesin is going to be famous. Rich and famous just like John Frum promised."

"I don't think so," Sam Ohmura said from the doorway.

Nick had been so intent on questioning Lily that she hadn't seen him slip across the threshold. He still had a gun, only this time it was pointed at her.

"You don't realize what I've found." She gestured toward the airplane. "See for yourself. It's two planes, part B-25 and part Lockheed Electra. Amelia Earhart was flying the Electra when she crashed."

"You don't have to convince me. It's the reason I'm here. It's a shame really, to obliterate history, but think of the embarrassment if people learned that we Japanese had killed Miss Earhart."

"Embarrassment," Nick repeated, stunned. "What are you talking about? There was a war on."

Ohmura smiled. "We have placed a very powerful explosive inside the plane. It will be over in the blink of an eye. You shouldn't feel any pain. If you do, I apologize for it. Now, if you'll both stand up and step inside the aircraft."

Lily said, "This is a sacred place. You have no right to be here without invitation."

"Please, inside." He showed them a small remote detonator no bigger than a cell phone.

"You're a scientist," Nick said. "How can you do this?"

"Believe me, Dr. Scott, this is very painful, but I am very loyal to my people and my family. Besides, there are certain obligations of a financial nature that are owed by my wife's family. It is all very distasteful. Perhaps you would prefer that I shot you where you sit?" He gestured them to their feet.

As Nick helped Lily stand, she weighed her chances of jumping him. Slim, she decided, but she had to try anyway. The alternative was to let herself and Lily be led to the slaughter. Tightening her grip on the Alclad, she was about to hurl it at him when she saw movement in the doorway. Even against the dazzling sunlight she recognized Buettner's silhouette.

Buettner pointed a pistol at Ohmura, causing a shadow to fall across Nick's face. Ohmura pivoted, but his reflexes weren't quick enough. The pistol touched his head and went off. Ohmura collapsed instantly, dead before he hit the ground.

"Dear God," Lily intoned. "This is John Frum's ground. Blood must not be spilled here."

"He was going to spill yours," Buettner shot back, stooping quickly to retrieve the detonator from Ohmura's hand. "Besides, that's my plane he was messing with."

"Yours!" Nick and Lily exclaimed in unison.

"Certainly. Discovering it is going to make me famous."

"In case you haven't noticed," Nick said, "I was here first. Your gun doesn't change that."

"Unless, of course, I intend to shoot you like old Sam was about to do." He nudged the body with his toe. "Which I do actually. Lucky for me he followed you here, because now I can tell everyone that he shot you two ladies. And lucky for me that I followed him, wouldn't you say?"

"What the hell is going on?" Nick asked.

He shook his head at her. "You asked the wrong

question. You should have said, 'what's gone wrong?' To which I would have answered, 'everything.' "

"You're crazy."

He winked. "All I've ever wanted to do was make an important discovery."

He stepped over the body to get a better look at the plane. In the lantern light, his eyes shone greedily. "Ain't she a beaut. She'll make me the most famous anthropologist in the world."

"Are you saying you knew the plane was here all along?" Nick asked.

"Yep. Finders keepers, as they say. I stumbled across it on my first trip. I walked right in on Henry Yali. That's when I made a deal with him. I conned him into thinking that I'd help him turn Balesin into a resort. I told him he'd be as rich and powerful as any American."

"I don't believe it," Lily said. "You're lying."

"It took some doing, but I finally convinced him that it was just a matter of time before America's satellites spotted this place." Buettner chuckled. "He actually believed that our satellites have X-ray cameras that can see through anything."

"Poor Henry," Lily murmured.

Nick said, "I still don't get it. You didn't need me or my father for any of this."

"You're as naive as Henry. The instant I laid eyes on this baby, I thought of your father, the Anasazi king, and you, the airplane virtuoso. I figured I could kill two birds with one stone. You could verify my find and I would finally eclipse your father's reputation, with him looking on so I could rub his nose in it."

"I thought he was your friend."

He snorted contemptuously. "You should know better than that. You've been living in the great man's shadow all your life. Well, not me, not anymore. I want the spotlight to swing my way for once."

"And your so-called Anasazi connection?" she asked.

"For Christ's sake. It's been my own personal joke for years. It was my way of poking fun at dear old Elliot. I never dreamed it would finally pay off and give me an excuse to get you here."

"My father never believed it. He only agreed to come here because you're his friend."

Buettner shrugged. "Maybe so, but Walt Duncan bought it. The silly fool came looking for the Anasazi and got too close to my airplane."

"And Tracy and Axelrad?"

He shrugged. "Who knows. Probably Henry got them when they were looking for a place to fuck. Well, I'm the one who fucked you all. Now, if you don't mind, you're holding a piece of my eminent fame in your hand. I want you to put it back where you found it."

Nick glanced at Lily, who had her eyes closed. And who could blame her? No one wanted to see death coming. But she'd be damned if she'd give up without a fight, especially to a crazy bastard like Buettner. She hurled the Alclad at him. He ducked it easily, but in so doing he swung the pistol off target. She dived for his gun hand, forcing him to fling aside the detonator to fight her off with both hands.

"Run!" Nick screamed at Lily, knowing she wouldn't be able to hold off Buettner for long.

Buettner pulled her close, snarling, his face a mixture of rage and delight. She tried to knee his groin, but she was off balance. Her knees hit his. Pain shot up her leg. She clenched her teeth, hoping he felt the same agony she did.

Nick gasped as Buettner swung her off her feet and slammed her against the metal wall. A burst of light flashed behind her eyes. Her vision dimmed. Not long now, she thought distantly. One more jolt like that and she'd be as good as dead. Yet she refused to make it easy for him, and dug her nails into his wrist. Hold on, she told herself. Hold on or die.

Buettner growled in her ear. "Shooting's too good for you." He wrenched free of her grip and wrapped his arms around her, squeezing her in a bear hug. His crushing grip raised her off the ground. Her feet dangled uselessly.

Nick couldn't breathe, yet somehow her eyes focused again, and she saw Lily hesitating in the doorway. What was the woman thinking about? Did she want to die?

As if in answer to Nick's unspoken question, Lily shook her head sadly.

Frantically, Nick sank her teeth into Buettner's arm. He screamed and whirled around as if intent on throwing her off.

In the next instant, Nick found herself looking Lily in the face with Buettner holding her from behind, his back to the plane. Lily was backing away from the hangar, the detonator in her hand.

Nick couldn't breathe at all now. Her vision narrowed to a single point, the detonator in Lily's hand.

The explosion hurled Nick out of the hangar and into total darkness. She was wondering if she'd died when she landed on her face. Pain was good, she thought, trying to get her mouth open to scream. Pain meant she was alive.

Distantly, she felt hands on her back. Christ, not Buettner again.

"Child," Lily said. "Are you all right?"

Nick rolled over. With the dirt no longer in her face, the sun was agonizing. She groaned.

Lily felt her from head to foot. "There's nothing broken, child."

The pain ebbed. Nick blinked at Lily and said, "Are you hurt?"

"John Frum was with me, with us both."

With Lily's help, Nick sat up. She'd landed on the runway, where the long grass had cushioned her.

Buettner lay close by. He looked peaceful. He might have survived too, if it hadn't been for the propeller blade protruding from his back.

47

"Hey, old buddy, bet you didn't expect to hear from me," Farrington's voice boomed into the office from the radio receiver.

Kobayashi felt as if a hand were squeezing his heart. Where was that fool Ohmura? They had arranged to make contact at this hour. He steadied himself so that his voice betrayed no emotion.

"It is always good to hear from you, Farrington-san."

Farrington let out a whoop. "Koby, you must be sweating bullets. You always hide behind that Japanese *san* shit when you're stressed. I guess you're not too happy right about now."

Kobayashi closed his eyes as if willing Farrington to go away.

"Well, I've got good news and I've got bad news, old buddy. Which do you want to hear first?"

"It is of no importance to me, Farrington." Kobayashi paused for a moment and then deliberately added, "san." He fairly hissed that last word. "I am certain that you will tell me what you wish."

"Might as well get the bad news out of the way then," Farrington replied. "I'm afraid your boy Ohmura's bought the farm."

For a brief moment in time Kobayashi did not understand. Then the realization dawned and he bowed his head. There was a brother-in-law that would have to be informed, but he felt no personal loss. However, there was a sense of dread growing in the center of his being that would not be denied.

"How did this come about, this buying of pastureland?" he blandly asked.

"Koby, you are a kick. Your boy got shot, and by an amateur, to boot," Farrington said bluntly. "But then your boy was an amateur himself, wasn't he? You really should have let me know in advance that he was coming. I had the devil's own time intercepting him."

"Considering the professional that you recommended, I preferred someone I could trust," Kobayashi retorted.

"I admit, that was a mistake. People that exceed orders are nothing but trouble. All that killing, what a mess. But I took care of that. He won't be around to tell tales. And you've got to admit, there were some tales to tell. In any case, now for the good news. I think I said that Ohmura got killed by an amateur? That anthropologist, Buettner, shot him to protect the you-know-what."

"That is the good news?" Kobayashi said coldly.

"No, the you-know-what got blown to smithereens." Farrington started to laugh. "Don't know exactly how it happened, maybe your boy just managed to pull it off before he died."

Kobayashi felt as if he might faint. After all this time he was free. The evidence of his grandfather's behavior had been obliterated. No longer would he live in fear that it would be discovered that his grandfather had killed so important a woman.

"Of course, there is a little bit of more bad news," Farrington's voice cut into his thoughts. "The woman archaeologist did get a gander at the you-know-what, before it blew."

"It was a plane," Kobayashi spat out. He dug his nails into his palms to regain control. "This thing, this you-know-what, was a plane."

"And we both know whose plane it was, don't we, old buddy. In any case, she has no proof, and she didn't have all that much time to examine it. Hell, most of it was B-25 anyway. Oh, and there's one thing more that I need to mention. I took a roll of film off our mutual friend, before I had to, shall we say, clean up loose ends. Seems he made an extensive record of the, uh, plane, before he set the charges. I know you're kind of sensitive-like about all this. Now you can rest assured that the evidence is in good hands. You'll be hearing from me again, old buddy. Real soon."

The connection was broken and Kobayashi was left to stare at the communications equipment. He looked up and the Tang horse was sitting on its pedestal, serene as ever.

He had his grandfather to thank for this one piece of beauty in his life and also for his enduring shame. His grandfather had served honorably at Nanking, although the world might condemn him now. But there was no honor in what he had done at Balesin. He had condemned that woman for a spy, and perhaps she was, but what honor was there in killing an unarmed female? And now Farrington had proof which could be used against him. Proof that Kobayashi's family had been responsible for the death of . . . No, it didn't bear thinking of. He couldn't say the name, even to himself.

He looked once more at the horse. The eyes seemed knowing, reading the future as confidently as they had witnessed the past. Honor must be preserved. He would not become a pawn of Farrington. He turned his back on the horse and went to look for his grandfather's sword.

48

Nick's ears were still ringing as she and her father sat in front of the church and watched their gear being loaded aboard the helicopter. They were seated on camp stools borrowed from the store. Farrington had declared the church off-limits.

Spots danced in front of her eyes as her headache, aggravated by the sun, grew worse by the minute. Even pulling the brim of her Cubs cap all the way down to her eyebrows failed to help.

She closed her eyes. The spots became explosive flashes. "I hope Lily feels better than I do."

"While I was seeing to your cuts, Henry's men came and carried her back to the village," Elliot said.

Nick sighed through pain-clenched teeth. If the helicopter hadn't come to investigate the explosion, she and Lily would still be on Mount Nomenuk, too weak to walk back on their own. Lily, who'd seemed untouched by the blast at first, had quickly collapsed on the grassy runway and refused to move. She just sat there, hugging herself, and staring at the scorched earth and dying trees that had been consumed by the fireball. She was, Nick had suspected, overwhelmed by the enormity of what she'd done, the total destruction of John Frum's airplane. But then Nick had felt the same way.

"You look like you need more aspirin," Elliot said.

Her stomach was already queasy, but the pain was definitely getting worse. She held out her hand. Elliot pulled a bottle out of his pocket and shook two tablets into her palm.

"I'll get you some water," he said, and headed for the store.

She raised her palm to eye level. Sweat was already dissolving the tablets. She licked them into her mouth and swallowed as best she could, intending to wash them down after the fact.

A shadow blotted out the sun. When she looked up, Lee Coltrane was standing in front of her. "Your father sent me with this." He offered her a bottle of water.

She drank deeply to rid herself of the taste of aspirin.

He said, "I just wanted to tell you I'm sorry. I had no way of knowing what Innis would do."

"Didn't you?" Nick replied coldly. "Did you hear a word I said to you on Balabat, or did you decide that because you're a man you know best? You didn't even have the decency to tell me what you were going to do."

"Come on, Doc, it wasn't like that. I just didn't want to argue with you. Can't we get past this? The Navy is lending me a hand at salvaging the Widgeon, so I'm going to be staying behind for a while. If you took a long layover in Guam, I could catch up. We could have a real date."

"Mr. Coltrane," Nick said, biting off every word, "I only go out with real men, not boys who feel they have to sneak around."

His face went white. "Well, if you ever change your mind, you know where to find me. I'd better get over to the Widgeon now." He turned and left, his back braced as if he were on parade.

She nearly called him back, but the momentary impulse quickly faded. Dammit, she said to herself. She'd had such high hopes for him. He was funny and brave and she had to admit to herself that she'd been attracted by his good looks and the fact that he lived his life flying. I dig in the dirt while he soars, she thought. But he had been the cause of too much pain to others because he was self-absorbed and uncaring. She now had no desire to ever see him again although she realized that they had faced death together and she would never be totally free of him.

She stood up, wincing in expectation, but the aspirin had kicked in. The pain was no more than a distant ache. Or was that her breaking heart she was feeling?

She shook off the mood. Hell no, she told herself. Sure, she'd been attracted to him, but then, she had a weakness for airplanes and all the men who flew them.

She eyed the waiting helicopter. No romance there. It was too new and too functional. She'd take a B-25 or a

Lockheed Electra any time. To her surprise, Elliot climbed out of the huge chopper, with Farrington right behind him.

"Nick," Elliot called, "I see you're on your feet again."

When they reached her, Elliot raised an eyebrow and said, "Everything that belongs to us is loaded on board." She translated his eyebrow's unspoken message as *we're up to our asses in alligators.*

Farrington smiled. "I've just had a nice chat with your father, Ms. Scott. Lily, I debriefed earlier. The facts seem clear enough and undisputed. Now, it's only a matter of tying up the loose ends. Before we do, I just want to let you know that I'm on your side."

Nick held her breath. Her department head, Ben Gilbert, had said the same thing to her once, while all the time he was slipping a knife into her back.

"As you know," Farrington continued, "Balesin is under United States protection. Since I am the senior government representative present, I'm acting as ambassador. Which means I'm here on your country's behalf, Ms. Scott. And right now, your country needs your cooperation."

Nick cringed inwardly. "What exactly are you asking?"

"It's best that no word of what happened here on Balesin ever gets out."

"You can't cover up murder."

"You misunderstand me. It's the collateral damage I'm talking about." He gestured at Mount Nomenuk. "Besides, there's no surviving evidence to prove that anything of importance happened up there."

"What about the plane that blew up?"

"What plane? My men have been over the site with fine-tooth combs. They found nothing at all."

"Even after an explosion, there have to be pieces left. I'm sure I'll be able to find them with a metal detector. I won't need much to prove it was a Lockheed Electra."

Farrington shook his head. "You're mistaken. It was nothing but an old B-25. It probably wandered off course and crashed. It was nothing but war salvage, a wreck."

"Plane wrecks are my line of work. And if it was just a B-25 as you say, why was it here? This island was bypassed by our forces during the war and never actually invaded."

Farrington shrugged. "Proof, Ms. Scott. Where's your proof?"

"I'll find it."

"I'm afraid not. As of now Balesin is off-limits to outsiders. The Reverend Innis and Mr. Parker have already been flown off the island."

"What about Mr. Parker's store?" she asked.

"Mr. Parker has decided to retire from his many activities," Farrington replied. "Besides, we wouldn't want any more tragic incidents to taint this island's unique culture."

Elliot stepped in. "Just hold it. Ohmura destroyed whatever evidence there was. He came with you, he was your man. Why would he bother if all there was up there was an old war relic?"

"He wasn't my man, but only our consultant on Pacific cultures."

"Crap," Nick told him. "Since when do consultants carry guns?"

"Maybe the man was deranged. How do I know? Perhaps the heat got to him."

"That plane was rigged to explode when Ohmura got there," she said. "Somebody was there before us."

Farrington pointed to himself. "Don't look at me. While you were hiking up that mountain getting yourself injured, I was with Chief Jeban."

"I've told you that Buettner killed Ohmura, and I told you why. He wanted that plane for himself and the fame that went with it."

"What are you suggesting, that we charge Lily with murder?" He stroked his chin. "That's certainly a possibility since, according to your own statement, she was the one who pushed the button."

"She saved my life, you bastard."

"Ambassador, please. Now, let's get down to cases. If you and your father go along with me, I'm sure we can lay all the blame on Buettner. He was a psycho after all."

Nick glared. "You really are a bastard."

He spread his hands innocently. "I'm a Good Samaritan, here to offer you a free sea voyage back to Guam."

Nick spun on her heels and walked away, trying to calm herself. Farrington knew more than he was saying. That much was obvious. She suspected that the Lockheed Electra had come as no surprise to him. Or the B-25 either, for that matter. But there was nothing she could do about it. Worse yet, she couldn't prove a damn thing. Only Lily was witness to what happened, and she was nowhere to be seen. None of the villagers were either. No islander had come near them since the explosion on their sacred mountain.

"It's time to go aboard," Farrington called to her.

She turned back to see him supervising Navy personnel who were loading body bags onto the helicopter. She counted them. There were six, one too many. Dear

God, she thought. Maybe he hadn't conceded anything in Lily's case. Maybe she'd been more seriously injured than Nick thought.

"Come on, Nick," Elliot said, taking her arm. "We don't have any choice."

But when they reached the chopper, Nick dug in her heels. "I want to know who else died before I'm setting foot in there."

"There are no more nor no less bodies than there should be," Farrington answered. "Nothing for you to be concerned about. Just a little housekeeping for an old friend of mine in Tokyo."

Nick didn't like the sound of that. Or was Farrington merely being flippant? She said, "You call extra bodies housekeeping?"

"Some things are best left alone, Ms. Scott. When people don't follow orders, the consequences could be—how shall I say it?—unfortunate."

"Are you threatening me?"

"Make that *us*," Elliot said.

"You know," Farrington said, his smile showing all the warmth of a pit viper, "it's a long boat ride to Guam."

A chill climbed Nick's spine. Elliot took her hand and squeezed, but the chill wouldn't go away.

Farrington continued. "Think of it this way. Your government wants you to be careful. The best way to do that is to make certain that no one spreads lies that can't be proved. Think of how it would look to your fellow scientists if you claimed to have found pieces of a famous Electra, without so much as a scrap to show for it." Farrington snickered. "Next you'll be claiming it was Amelia Earhart's."

He leaned close, staring into her eyes, ignoring Elliot. "I can see what you're thinking, Ms. Scott. That one day you'll come back here to find your proof. Sorry. I'm afraid everything has been policed up, as our friends in the Navy would say. After all, it would be a crime to leave litter in a paradise like this, wouldn't it?"

Nick gritted her teeth, trembling with rage. Or maybe it was plain fear, because looking at Farrington she knew he would do anything necessary to keep her silent.

Elliot must have sensed that too, because he tightened his grip on her hand, squeezing hard enough to make her wince. "You don't have to worry, Mr. Farrington. She would never publish anything without evidence to back it up."

"Well, then, that is good news." Farrington rubbed his hands together in satisfaction. "Now why don't we board our bird and head for the ship. Hot showers and food are waiting."

Elliot, his grip still a clear warning, kissed Nick on the cheek and climbed into the chopper. She was about to follow when Lily appeared, supported by Josephine.

"We couldn't let you go without saying goodbye," Lily said.

Nick glanced at Farrington, who shrugged. "Just make it quick."

Lily pushed Josephine forward. "My niece has a going-away gift for you."

Shyly, the young girl handed Nick a small wooden box.

"Thank you," Nick told her. The girl scampered off immediately. "You too, Lily. Thank you for saving my life."

Lily smiled sadly. "This morning Henry went to join

his ancestors. The loss of John Frum's plane was too much for him."

"I'm so sorry," Nick said, but Lily held up her hand as if to block any more discussion.

"I've kept my promise," Lily continued. "No more secrets. I have given you John Frum." Lily hugged her.

As soon as Nick took her seat inside the chopper, the rotor blades thundered to life. A moment later they were heading out to sea. Farrington was riding up front with the pilot, while she and her father were sitting opposite one another in the cargo bay. On the floor between them, body bags had been laid out side by side. Their placement, Nick suspected, was another of Farrington's not so subtle warnings.

Sighing, she leaned back against the bulkhead and opened the box. Inside, on a bed of cotton, nestled a badly corroded oblong metal tab. Its shape identified it as an American dog tag. She rubbed it between her fingers. Because of the heavy oxidation no name or serial number was discernible.

Lily's words echoed in her head: *I give you John Frum.*

She searched in her pocket and took out a second small box, the one given to her the first night. A fragment of clothing or shoe, she thought. But whose, someone from the B-25 or the lady that was married to the tycoon George Palmer Putnam, *Mis'ta'putam*? He, indeed, would have brought great wealth to the island.

If she could identify a flier from the B-25 that had landed on Balesin, she might eventually discover the plane's mission. And that might give her the proof she needed to publish.

Smiling, she replaced the dog tag in its box and closed the lid. She tucked both boxes safely in her pocket. Technology had progressed tremendously over the last fifty years, and with a little bit of luck the dog tag would clean up nicely. She sighed and felt sorry for Lily. She was an intelligent woman, and in another culture she would not have believed so fervently in a man who didn't exist.

49

April 18, 1942
The Island of Balesin

Things hadn't turned out the way Johns had expected. The jungle had been silent and that was always a bad sign. He'd almost ordered the pilot to take off immediately, but then an unarmed man who was clearly a native had stepped into the clearing. Johns had left the plane and gone forward to meet him. He knew it was dangerous, but that was his job. Get the broad and get her off the island.

The native spoke good English and said his name was Thomas Yali. He'd been sent to tell them to wait. The woman was coming but she would be late. She'd sent him on ahead to tell them not to leave. It would only be a few minutes.

Women, he'd thought. Even on this godforsaken island in the middle of nowhere, they couldn't keep their promises. You'd think that after five years she'd be panting to get off this rock.

He should have been more suspicious, but the islander had had a pint-sized kid in tow. Who would have thought that any man would bring his own son to an ambush?

He offered the man a smoke, which was accepted eagerly. The kid looked at him with hungry eyes and Johns offered him some gum. The kid pulled a silver-wrapped stick from the pack and didn't seem to know what to do with it. Johns laughed and bent down to show him how to unwrap it and the bullet whizzed past where he'd been standing.

He heard the engines of the plane cough to life and his first thought was that the bastards were leaving him behind. His second was that he hoped they'd make it, but the mortar round put an end to any coherent thoughts after that. He'd plunged into the jungle and didn't look back.

He'd been trained to survive in the jungle, but he couldn't do much about the piece of shrapnel that had pierced his lung. When he started coughing pink froth he knew he was a goner. What a joke. It was probably a piece of metal from the plane. Well, the plane took me here, and it was going to take me away. He wondered if he was getting delirious.

The kid found him about an hour later, propped up against a tree. Shit, he thought. If the kid can find me, the Japs won't be far behind. The kid just kept staring at him, with large dark eyes.

"Beat it," he managed to croak out.

The kid held something out to him in his grubby hand. It was the package of gum.

Johns wished he had the strength to wring the kid's scrawny neck. He motioned the child to come closer.

"Henry," the child said, pointing to himself. "Henry sorry." He proffered the small package again.

Johns closed his eyes. He felt so tired. When he

opened them again, the child was still there. It was getting difficult to breathe and he guessed that he was drowning in his own blood. He felt something in his hand and realized that the child had placed the gum in his hand. He shook his head, slowly withdrew a stick, and unwrapped it. "Come," he said.

The child took the unwrapped stick and placed it in his mouth. A look of wonder passed over his face.

"Kid . . . Henry," Johns managed to breathe, "I'm Johns." He clasped his chest. "Johns from . . ." There was no more breath. He thought he felt the small child's hand in his and some corner of his brain cried out in wonderment.

ABOUT THE AUTHOR

VAL DAVIS studied anthropology and archaeology at the University of California at
Berkeley and now lives in Northern California.

Val Davis

Nicolette Scott Mysteries

Track of the Scorpion

Flight of the Serpent

On Sale Now

Track of the Scorpion	___57728-x	$5.50/$7.50
Flight of the Serpent	___57803-0	$5.50/$7.50

- -

Ask for this book at your local bookstore or use this page to order.

Please send me the book I have checked above. I am enclosing $_____(add $2.50 to cover postage and handling). Send check or money order, no cash or C.O.D.'s please.

Name _____

Address _____

City/State/Zip _____

Send order to: Bantam Books, Dept. MC 33 , 2451 S. Wolf Rd., Des Plaines, IL 600
Allow four to six weeks for delivery.
Prices and availability subject to change without notice.   MC 33 1